Hesitantly, she pushed the door open and peered inside the room. "Sandra?"

The first thing she saw was the telephone. When she'd been there before, it had been on the desk next to the computer, but now it was on the floor with the receiver off the hook, which explained the busy signal. But it didn't explain where Sandra was. It didn't make sense—like one of Cooper's picture puzzles, it felt as if some of the pieces had been confused somehow.

The only thing Tilda could imagine was that the older woman must have had a stroke or a heart attack, and had been trying to reach the phone when she succumbed. So she stepped inside, and wasn't even surprised to see Sandra lying on the floor, facedown, on the other side of the couch.

She picked up the phone from the floor and called 911. In a calm, collected voice, she explained that an older woman had fallen ill and that she needed an ambulance. It was only when the operator asked for details about the patient's condition that Tilda actually looked at Sandra. And saw the blood. Too much blood . . .

Berkley Prime Crime titles by Toni L. P. Kelner

CURSE OF THE KISSING COUSINS
WHO KILLED THE PINUP QUEEN?

Who Killed THE Pinup Queen?

TONI L. P. KELNER

BERKLEY PRIME CRIME, NEW YORK

THE BERKLEY PUBLISHING GROUP
Published by the Penguin Group
Penguin Group (USA) Inc.
375 Hudson Street, New York, New York 10014, USA
Penguin Group (Canada), 90 Eglinton Avenue East, Suite 700, Toronto, Ontario M4P 2Y3, Canada
(a division of Pearson Penguin Canada Inc.)
Penguin Books Ltd., 80 Strand, London WC2R 0RL, England
Penguin Group Ireland, 25 St. Stephen's Green, Dublin 2, Ireland (a division of Penguin Books Ltd.)
Penguin Group (Australia), 250 Camberwell Road, Camberwell, Victoria 3124, Australia
(a division of Pearson Australia Group Pty. Ltd.)
Penguin Books India Pvt. Ltd., 11 Community Centre, Panchsheel Park, New Delhi—110 017, India
Penguin Group (NZ), 67 Apollo Drive, Rosedale, North Shore 0632, New Zealand
(a division of Pearson New Zealand Ltd.)
Penguin Books (South Africa) (Pty.) Ltd., 24 Sturdee Avenue, Rosebank, Johannesburg 2196,
South Africa

Penguin Books Ltd., Registered Offices: 80 Strand, London WC2R 0RL, England

WHO KILLED THE PINUP QUEEN?

A Berkley Prime Crime Book / published by arrangement with the author

PRINTING HISTORY
Berkley Prime Crime mass-market edition / January 2010

Copyright © 2010 by Toni L. P. Kelner.
Cover illustration by Kimberly Schamber.
Cover design by Annette Fiore Defex.
Interior text design by Kristin del Rosario.

ISBN: 978-0-425-23205-7

BERKLEY® PRIME CRIME
Berkley Prime Crime Books are published by The Berkley Publishing Group,
a division of Penguin Group (USA) Inc.,
375 Hudson Street, New York, New York 10014.
BERKLEY® PRIME CRIME and the PRIME CRIME logo are trademarks of Penguin Group (USA) Inc.

PRINTED IN THE UNITED STATES OF AMERICA

10   9   8   7   6   5   4   3   2   1

Acknowledgments

I want to thank:

My husband, Stephen P. Kelner, Jr., who is always there.

My daughter Maggie, for giving me a dandy plot idea, and my daughter Valerie, for making me laugh.

My beta readers and forever friends, Charlaine Harris and Dana Cameron.

My agent, Joan Brandt, who continues to put up with me.

Sandra Sechrest, who donated actual money to charity so I would name a character for her.

Harley Jane Kozak and Lee Goldberg, who saved me from some of my misconceptions about show business.

Catherine Maiorisi, for providing the perfect answer to a plot complication.

The marvelously knowledgeable and helpful folks on the Mystery Writers of America listserv. No matter what question I come up with, somebody knows the answer.

Pat Houchin of Stickler Involved People. Though the research foundation mentioned in this book isn't real, the disorder is. When my daughter Valerie and I were diagnosed with Stickler Syndrome, SIP provided the knowledge and support we needed. Visit www.sticklers.org if you want to know more.

Chapter 1

nightmare *n* 1) Any oppressive terrifying dream. 2) Any threatening, haunting thought or experience.
  —*THE NEW AMERICAN WEBSTER HANDY COLLEGE DICTIONARY*

TILDA woke to the sound of her roommate pounding on her bedroom door.

She stumbled to the door and opened it. "I'm awake, I'm awake."

"You woke me up again!" Colleen said accusingly.

"Damn it!" Tilda said, wiping the sleep from her eyes. "Sorry."

Colleen looked nearly as tired as Tilda felt. "Tilda, you've got to do something. This is the fourth time in a week!"

Tilda didn't bother to tell her that it was actually the sixth. Fortunately for Colleen, Tilda had been sleeping over at a friend's the first time the nightmares hit and she'd suffered quietly one of the other nights.

"It's not that I'm not sympathetic," Colleen continued, though she looked anything but. "It's just that I have to be up in the morning. At least tomorrow is Sunday, but I was late for work twice last week. This can't keep happening."

"I know," Tilda said.

"Are you sure you don't want to talk about it? I'd be happy to listen—I'll make us some coffee."

Tilda might have been tempted had she not had a sense

that Colleen was more interested in the gory details of what Tilda was dreaming about than she was in helping her work through the issues. "No, that's all right. I know you need your sleep."

"You need to talk to *someone*. If not me, then maybe a professional."

"I'll talk to my sister. She's a psychologist." June was a researcher, not a clinician, and currently a full-time mother, but Tilda saw no reason to get technical.

"Whatever." Colleen yawned. "I'm going back to bed."

"You do that. I don't think I'll bother you again tonight."

In fact, Tilda thought as she closed the door, she was sure she wasn't going to have any more nightmares—she wasn't going to try to sleep. Instead she went to her desk, hoping to get some work done, but when her brain proved to be too fuzzy for that, she watched a DVD of *Power Pet* cartoons. Anything was better than waking up screaming again.

While Power Pup defeated the Evil Dalmatian of Doom yet again, Tilda kept wondering why it was her subconscious wasn't satisfied with dredging up memories of the real event. Wasn't finding an old woman who'd been bludgeoned to death gruesome enough? Why did her sleeping brain have to add the dead woman rising to chase her through snowy Boston streets, and why did the corpse have that obscene mockery of a come-hither smile on her face? Why did Tilda end up screaming, when in reality she'd barely been able to speak?

More importantly, how much longer were the nightmares going to last?

Chapter 2

Episode 1: Welcome to Cowtown
Arabella Newman arrives in Cowtown and opens the Cowtown Saloon and Hotel to fanfare from the cowboys and condemnation from the more respectable folk in town. When she slaps down a lascivious bully and then invites people whose homes were damaged by a stampede to stay at the hotel for free, she's welcomed as part of the community.
—*COWTOWN COMPANION* BY RUBEN TIMMONS

SIX DAYS EARLIER

"WHAT differences do you see between these pictures?" Cooper asked.

Tilda glanced at them. "One is on the right side, and the other is on the left."

"Very droll. There are ten differences. Find them."

"I hate these things."

"Did I ask?"

She sighed, and took a closer look. At first, the photos of the Merlotte's Bar and Grill set from the TV show *True Blood* looked identical. Then she started spotting variations.

"There's only three beers on that table in this one, but four in the other," she said.

"That's one."

"That waitress is missing the Merlotte's logo on her shirt."

"Two."

"The framed photo of the guy in the beard and the pretty redhead is lopsided."

"Three."

Tilda looked for a minute, but didn't spot any more. "Do I have to find all ten?"

"Have you got something better to do?"

She looked down at her Jack Skellington watch. Her meeting with Jillian had been scheduled for ten minutes earlier, but the editor in chief was in a previous meeting that was clearly more important than being on time for Tilda. Of course, she knew Tilda would wait—no free-lancer could afford to play diva. "Fine." She looked again. "That guy's hat is missing."

"Good. Don't stop now."

But after several minutes, she couldn't find anything else. "I give up, Cooper. I told you I hate these things."

"You forgot to mention that you suck at them."

"Why would I hate a puzzle that I'm good at? So what did I miss?"

"The nail polish on the short-order cook is a different color, the beer sign is turned off, one of the chairs is missing a leg, that menu disappeared, and the Dos Equis beer tap is missing an Equis."

"That's only nine."

He grinned. "I made that waitress's boobs bigger."

"The inventors of Photoshop must be so proud to have enabled you to reach this pinnacle of achievement. Why are you doing this anyway?"

"For the next issue. We've scrapped the personality quizzes in favor of 'Spot the Difference' puzzles."

Doesn't *People* do one of these every issue?"

"Yes, and *People* sells more copies than we do, so some genius in corporate decided that if we had a puzzle like theirs, we'd sell just as many copies."

"Brilliant strategy."

"That's corporate. It's just as well—I was running out of inspiration for the psychology quizzes anyway. Doing these is fun."

"If you say so." Tilda realized Cooper was still staring at the mismatched pictures. "Are you planning to add another difference?"

"No, ten is plenty. Just admiring that short-order cook. Do you think the actor is really—"

"Nope, he just plays gay on the show. I interviewed the guy who plays the werewolf, and he gave me the straight dope. So to speak."

"Damn."

"What difference does it make? You're married, remember?"

"Jean-Paul doesn't mind my looking."

"Well, you can still look, can't you?" Tilda had to admit that Cooper and the actor from *True Blood* would have made an attractive couple. Both men were black and well built, though Cooper's skin was lighter and his look was more handsome than sultry.

The two of them went on to discuss the charms of the other male characters on the show until the door to the conference room opened, and Nicole stepped out into the hall.

A phony smile was pasted on her face, and it took a moment for Tilda to guess what the painfully thin redhead's smile foretold. At first, she thought it meant Nicole was about to stick it to somebody, but upon reflection, she decided it was her I'm-so-pissed-I-want-to-scream smile. It was a tough call, since the latter expression often led to the former.

"Tilda," Nicole said, "I'm so glad you could finally make it. We've been waiting for you."

Tilda didn't bother to rise to the bait—anything that had Nicole pissed off was likely to be to her advantage. "Later, Cooper," she said, and followed the other woman into the conference room.

A quartet of people was arranged around the long oval table, but the only one Tilda recognized at first was Jillian, the relentlessly stylish editor in chief of *Entertain Me!*, the magazine that provided a sizable percentage of the story assignments that kept Tilda in pizza and Dr Pepper. Beside her was a pair of cowboys, an uncommon sight in Boston. The men were in their late sixties and looked enough alike in the face to be brothers, despite very different builds. Both were wearing suits with Western trim, and string ties with chunks of turquoise in the middle. Two hats that Tilda could only assume were Stetsons were on the table in front of them.

"This is Tilda Harper, the writer I was telling you about," Jillian said. "Tilda, Tucker and Hoyt Ambrose." Hands were offered and shaken. Tucker was the big, beefy one, with thick gray hair and a wide grin for Nicole when she sat down across from him. Hoyt was shorter and more trim, and was close to losing the battle against baldness.

"And this is—" Jillian started to say as she gestured toward the other person in the room, an older lady in a rose-colored suit that set off her crown of white hair to perfection.

"Arabella Newman!" Tilda said, suddenly recognizing her.

The woman smiled. "Cynthia Barth, actually, but I don't mind being remembered as Arabella."

"Didn't I tell you she was the perfect writer for this?" Jillian said to the room at large. "Tilda, have a seat."

She sat down next to Jillian, embarrassed to have called the actress by the name of the character she'd played on TV, but since the woman was obviously delighted, it was probably the best thing she could have done.

"As I was saying earlier, Tilda is our specialist in classic television," Jillian said, "so of course she's familiar with your show."

"*Cowtown* was a favorite of mine," Tilda said. "And if

I remember correctly, that would make you two gentlemen the Cowboy Kings."

"That's right, ma'am," Hoyt said with a shy grin. "*Cowtown* was one of our favorites, too."

That was no surprise, since it had been the longest-lasting and most successful of their Westerns, having run eight seasons. The Ambrose brothers had produced half a dozen cowboy shows, and a fair number of B-movie Westerns as well. She wasn't sure if they'd crowned themselves the Cowboy Kings or if it had come from some creative press agent, but the title had stuck both because of their work and because of what they were. Cowboys—real ones at least—were just as rare in Hollywood as they were in Boston. She mentally raised her age estimates for the brothers. *Cowtown* had been made in the mid-1950s, when Westerns ruled television, so the brothers had to be in their seventies.

Tucker said, "If you know *Cowtown*, you're going to get a real kick out of what we're cooking up now. My brother and I, and Miss Barth here, have gone into partnership to build a resort based on the show. We've got us a piece of land in the western part of the state."

"In Massachusetts?" Tilda asked. She'd have thought an attraction like that would be more appropriate for a more temperate area, not a state with such uncertain weather. There was still snow on the ground from the last storm, with more predicted for later in the day.

"Most of it will be inside," Miss Barth explained. "A hotel and spa, restaurants, shows, a nightclub, shops. We're hoping to add a casino—"

"Now Miss Barth, it's early days to be talking about that," Hoyt put in hurriedly.

Tilda knew that the governor was pushing for more gambling in the state, though he hadn't been particularly successful so far.

Tucker went on. "There's going to be plenty of things for

people to do during the summer, too: horseback trails, trick riding shows, maybe a Western-themed petting zoo—"

"Don't forget your golf course," Hoyt put in.

"And a golf course," Tucker agreed. "My brother doesn't think a golf course is right for *Cowtown*, but I keep telling him that the people in Cowtown didn't have hot tubs and massage tables, either, but we're putting those in."

Hoyt just rolled his eyes.

"We're still working out some of the details," Miss Barth said diplomatically.

Tilda nodded, wondering if she should suggest a compromise position of a Western-themed miniature golf place instead.

Tucker said, "Now we know people don't exactly associate Massachusetts with cowboys, but Hoyt's been doing some market research, and we figure people around here like playing cowboy just as much as anybody."

"Maybe more, since they don't know what it's like to actually have to muck out a stable!" Hoyt put in.

Tucker grinned. "Anyways, if we build something around here, we're going to have both the Boston area and New York City to draw people from, plus the whole rest of New England. We're expecting big things."

"I don't think you need to sell Tilda," Jillian pointed out.

Hoyt smiled apologetically. "It's hard to stop a salesman from selling, but I'll try to rein myself in. In order to get people excited about the resort, we've been talking to *Entertain Me!* about doing some articles about the show and our fans. Jillian here tells us you're just the person to write them."

That explained Nicole's irritation. She hated anybody other than herself getting a byline, and was particularly unhappy when the byline was Tilda's.

"Don't forget the roundup!" Tucker put in.

"Hold on to your horses. I was getting to that," Hoyt

said. "You know, most of our regular cast members have passed away—"

"God rest their souls," Miss Barth said with just the right amount of feeling.

"But when the show was running, we featured a whole lot of guest stars. We want to track down some of these folks for interviews, maybe scout the territory to see if they'd be willing to make personal appearances at the resort. What do you say? Are you interested?"

"I'm very interested," Tilda said. Then she remembered the first rule of being a freelancer: Never sound *too* interested. "Of course, we'll have to talk schedules. I'm working on some other projects." Since the second rule was to never turn down an assignment, she added, "But I'm I sure I can wrangle them all."

"Now you're talking!" Tucker said.

While Jillian looked on approvingly, Tilda and the Ambrose brothers put together a list of actors she was to track down, along with a few ideas about where to start the search. With each name, Tilda got more and more excited. Not only did the length of the list guarantee her a nice paycheck, but each actor was a potential source for future stories. After an hour or so of discussion and the ritual exchange of e-mail addresses and phone numbers for both landlines and mobiles, the Ambrose brothers and Miss Barth moseyed out.

Jillian kept her pleased-editor expression on until they were gone, then switched back to her usual look of intense focus and demanded, "What other projects? The last thing we bought from you was that comic book movie piece the month before last."

Nicole smiled at that, probably reveling in the memory of two entire months without having to send Tilda a check.

"I do have other clients," Tilda reminded Jillian, though not as many as she wanted. Whether economists called it a downturn, a recession, or just tough times, it boiled down to magazines being less willing to use a stringer when they had staff members who were anxious enough about keeping their jobs that they didn't dare turn down extra work. She suspected that Nicole had increased her efforts to make sure Tilda got as little work as possible from *Entertain Me!*, despite an agreement they'd made a few months earlier.

"Just make sure that *this* is your priority from now on," Jillian said. "I'm going to tell you something that better not be repeated outside this room. The Ambrose brothers and Miss Barth may be the figureheads for the resort, but there are other investors, including major silent partners. I'm not going to name names, but you'd find one of them on a door in our corporate offices."

"Oh? Oh." Tilda had been so sold on the project that she hadn't stopped to think that promoting a future resort was hardly the kind of story *Entertain Me!* was known for. "Consider it prioritized. What about payment?"

"Usual rates and usual expenses from us, plus the Ambrose brothers will pay a bonus for every candidate you provide for personal appearances."

"Sounds good." The word *bonus* was not one she often encountered in her line of work. "Of course, with this many people to find, I'm going to want to invoice you along the way, not just at the end of the assignment. Say a week at a time?"

Jillian considered it, and Tilda tried to look blasé. Finally the editor said, "Deal. Nicole will handle the paperwork." She started out of the room.

Nicole must have thought Jillian was already gone because she snarled, "You may as well be on the payroll!"

Jillian turned back, looking thoughtful. "That's a good point."

"So we go back to end-of-project invoicing?" Nicole said eagerly.

But before Tilda could gather her thoughts for a

counterargument, Jillian said, "Or maybe we should bring Tilda on full time. Nostalgia isn't going away, not while the Baby Boomers are still trying to hang on to their lost youth. Maybe it's time to make 'where are they now?' stories a regular feature."

"Are you serious?" Tilda asked.

"Are you interested?"

Tilda had lost track of which freelancer's rule she was supposed to apply, which left her with honesty. "I never thought about it."

"Think about it. We'll see how this project goes, and afterward we'll talk." Jillian strode out, no doubt already planning something else.

With the boss gone, Nicole didn't even bother to hide her horror. "Oh. My. God."

Tilda grinned at her. "Wouldn't it be great? You and me seeing each other every day! Gossiping in the break room, shopping on our lunch hours, exchanging presents at the company Christmas party . . ."

"Fuck that!" Nicole snapped, and stomped out.

Tilda waited, knowing that Cooper would be along in a minute. It was, in fact, only forty-five seconds.

"What in the world did you say to Nicole?"

"It wasn't me," Tilda said. "Jillian said it."

"Dirt, please?"

"She just offered me a job."

Chapter 3

"WOULDN'T it be great, Tilda?" Cooper said. "We'd see each other every day! We could gossip and shop during lunch, and—"

"You're scaring me, Cooper. That's almost exactly what I told Nicole."

"No wonder she looked like she was about to spew. Talk about having your worst nightmare come true!"

"Being somebody else's nightmare has always been a dream of mine."

They were walking up the sidewalk on Newbury Street, stepping over the piles of dirty snow left over from the previous week's nor'easter. Knowing that she had to come to town to see Jillian, Tilda had scheduled an interview for that evening, and when Cooper heard who she was going to see, he volunteered to act as her photographer, just so he could come along. Normally he'd have been working late on a Monday—he had to get the copy for the next week's issue finished by quitting time Tuesday—but he'd arranged to come in early the next day to make sure he made his deadline.

"Why don't we grab a cab?" Cooper asked the second time he nearly slipped on frozen slush.

"Because we need the exercise," Tilda said. "If you don't want to go—"

"Oh, no you don't!" Cooper said. "Not after I missed the other interview you did with her—the one you didn't even tell me about!"

"Why would I take a gay man to see a former pinup queen? Jean-Paul might not mind you looking at other men, but women?"

"Sandra Sechrest is different," Cooper said reverently. "She's a classic. It'll be like meeting Bettie Page!"

"That reminds me. Speaking of Bettie Page, don't."

"Come again?"

"Don't mention Bettie Page. It's a sore spot."

"Got it." By then, they'd reached Massachusetts Avenue, and were heading toward the neighborhood where Sechrest lived. The sidewalk was clearer, but the January wind was considerably stronger. "Not that I'm complaining, but why are you interviewing her again? In fact, why did you interview her in the first place? I thought Jillian turned the story idea down."

"You guys keep forgetting that I do sell to other markets. The full interview was for a magazine for senior citizens with attitude, and shorter versions went to a men's magazine that targets older men, a women's studies journal, a nostalgia magazine, and a newsletter for amateur photographers."

"Nothing for the children's market?"

She ignored him. He knew as well as she did that the only way to stay afloat as a freelance entertainment reporter was to rewrite the same article for as many markets as possible. The number of pieces she'd sold about Sandra wasn't even close to her record. "When I first interviewed Sandra,

I told her how other former celebrities have been using the Internet to take advantage of their former fame, and back in November she and her niece put up a site to sell autographed pictures, T-shirts, and so forth. She's doing really well with it, and today I'm talking to her about running a Web-based business so I can write a how-to piece."

"Is there a market for that?"

"Yes, but not a high-paying one, which is why I don't want to take a cab. The fare would eat up most of my profits."

"Just wait!" Cooper said with gleeful anticipation. "You won't have to worry about rewriting every story umpteen times, or scrimping on expenses for very much longer. You'll just have to write one story per topic. And you'll have an expense account. Company plastic!"

"Geez, Cooper, can we hold off on counting chickens? Jillian hasn't exactly made a formal offer, and I don't know that I'll take it if she does."

"Jillian wouldn't have said anything if she wasn't serious! And why wouldn't you take the job? No more scrounging for assignments, no more sending out query letters to every magazine in the known universe, no more pitching a dozen stories to get one lousy assignment."

"It's not that bad!"

"Oh yeah? Then why is it we're not taking a cab?"

There was no real answer to that, so Tilda didn't bother to devise one as they continued their trudge.

"We've got to go shopping," Cooper said suddenly.

"Why?"

"You know how Jillian is about the clothes we wear in the office. If you can't be high fashion, you at least need to be stylish."

"Thanks for the self-esteem."

"Let me rephrase that. You have amazing style, but it's not exactly working-in-an-office style."

Tilda glanced at her reflection in the plate-glass window

they were passing. She was currently wearing lace-up black Doc Marten boots and a thigh-length black parka, along with a red knit hat with rhinestone skulls to cover her black, curly hair with a matching scarf around her throat. The outfit concealed by her winter gear—a well-worn pair of black jeans and a dark purple tunic-length sweater—wasn't exactly corporate wear either. And that was what she'd worn to a business meeting.

"You may have a point," she conceded.

"Now if you put aside a bit of each paycheck to spend on clothes—"

"Cheep, cheep, Cooper."

"No, don't buy cheap—buy classic."

"I meant that you're counting unhatched chicks again. Can we change the subject?"

"Sorry. I'm just so excited for you."

Tilda was leaning toward excited, too, but she wasn't sure if she was as excited as she should be. Sure, a steady paycheck and actual benefits had definite appeal. Then again, setting her own hours and picking her own stories was nothing to sneeze at, either, let alone spending most of her time in a Nicole-free environment. She was just as glad she didn't have to make a decision right away.

Finally they arrived at their destination, an elderly but well-maintained building in the South End. They stepped into the paneled entryway, and a few seconds after pushing the buzzer, a young woman already bundled up for outside came to the door to let them in.

"Hi, Tilda," she said.

"How's it going, Lil? Lil, this is my friend Cooper Christianson. He's my photographer." Actually, Cooper was no better with a camera than she was, and it was her camera anyway, but Tilda felt the excuse sounded more professional than, "He's planning to dine out on the story of having met a real-life pinup queen for the next six months."

"Pleased to meet you, Cooper. Aunt Sandra's waiting

for you in her place. I hate to rush off, but I want to get back home before the snow starts."

"You're in Bedford, right?"

Lil nodded. "I don't think my street has been decently plowed since the last snow, so I figured I better head home now or I'll never make it."

"Good luck," Tilda said, as the younger woman braced herself to step into the cold air.

As she and Cooper walked down the hallway toward Sandra Sechrest's apartment, Tilda said, "Lil has been handling the Web design and whatever coding Sandra needs. She does a good job, too."

The former pinup queen herself was waiting in the doorway. In her heyday, Sandra Sechrest had been known as Sandy Sea Chest and had specialized in nautical themes: skimpy sailor dresses, mermaid costumes, and revealing pirate outfits. These days, she usually wore some variation of her current ensemble: a mauve velour jogging suit that nobody would ever wear to jog in.

"Tilda! Good to see you!" Though the sea chest for which she'd been famous was no longer so generously filled as it had been when she'd been a photographer's model, her hair was the same color of red that had contrasted so nicely with the copious amount of fair skin she'd displayed in countless magazine spreads. Only her hands, badly twisted with arthritis, betrayed her true age.

"Sandra, this is my friend Cooper Christianson. He's a longtime admirer of your work."

"Work, she calls it. For years it was dirty pictures, but now I've got a body of work." Sandra winked at Cooper. "It's a shame I don't have the body for the work anymore! Come on in, kids."

Like many older Boston dwellings, Sandra's condo included oddities that revealed that it had started out life as part of a larger home but had subsequently been chopped up into bite-sized living spaces. Sometimes the

unusual shapes that resulted were awkward, but fortunately for Sandra, her long, narrow stretch of rooms was
just eccentric enough to be charming, especially with the
clean-lined wooden furniture that kept it from looking
cluttered, and a scattering of mirrors which provided the
illusion of space.

"Have a seat," she said, and settled herself on the couch
while Tilda and Cooper divested themselves of their coats,
scarves, hats, and other cold-weather accessories.

"How's business?" Tilda asked as she sat next to Sandra, and pulled a pad out of the black leather satchel she
used as both purse and briefcase.

"Booming," Sandra said with a big smile. "And I'm not
just saying that for the article. We had to reorder T-shirts
three times to meet the Christmas rush, and once more
since then. Plus we're selling eight-by-tens as fast as I can
sign them." She looked at her hands ruefully. "Which isn't
as fast as I'd like it to be. But I can't complain. We're doing
great, and this is in a bad economy!"

"That's awesome," Tilda said, and they got down to the
formal part of the interview. Her previous conversations
with Sandra had been focused on the modeling itself, with
a good dollop of gossip about sex to sweeten the pot. This
story was about the nuts and bolts of running a Web business: getting eyeballs to the site and keeping them coming,
taking advantage of search engines and eBay shops, and
the use of PayPal. Of course, the fact that the product being
sold was sex wouldn't hurt this piece, either.

Meanwhile, Cooper took shots of Sandra, the miniature
brass and teak sea chest on her coffee table, and even the
computer and scanner that Lil used to keep Sandra's website up and running. Tilda would rather have had Lil there as
well, but knew from earlier meetings that the Web designer
was camera shy, which was ironic, given her aunt's claim
to fame. As for Sandra, the camera loved her as much as
it ever had, and she had a knack for being able to keep the

conversation going while still managing to present her best angles to Cooper's lens.

They were discussing the online community that had developed around her site's bulletin board when Sandra said, "You wouldn't believe the people who've come out of the woodwork since I started the site. I've gotten e-mail from models and photographers I hadn't heard from in decades."

"Really?" Tilda said, eager to add more names to her database. Of course, it might not be worth the effort if she was going to take the job with *Entertain Me!*. Since Jillian had already turned down her pitch about pinup queens, she wouldn't be able to try another for a while. Then she firmly reminded herself that nothing was definite yet. "Anybody I might have heard of?"

"A few," Sandra said. "I hoped some of them might want to join in on the business—more people means more attention on the Web, you know. But one found Jesus, and the others went into different lines of work, so they don't want to make a big deal over their pictures." She shrugged. "I've still got feelers out."

"Let me know if you find anybody who'd be interested in talking to me."

"Will do. Now the models may have gotten shy, but not the photographers. I've had three invitations to dinner from guys in the camera clubs I used to pose for, plus a marriage proposal. And that's not the best part. Cooper, would you mind getting that envelope from the desk?"

He got up long enough to grab a plump cardboard photo mailer and handed it to her.

She tapped it. "You know what I've got here?"

"More pictures?" Tilda asked.

"Got it in one. There was this one set of pictures I did where I was dressed as a pirate who'd captured some sweet young thing. I tied her up and made her walk the plank and so forth. These days, they'd probably have crotch shots and tongues and all that. We settled for spanking."

"I remember that pictorial—you and Virginia Pure," Cooper said. "It was great spanking."

Sandra smiled indulgently. "Well, this is a batch of pictures from that same shoot."

"Really? I thought that photographer died," Tilda said.

"Yes and no. Red Connors put the shoot together, and he did pass away years back, God bless him. But this was a special case. The pirate ship setup was pretty elaborate for those days, and Red had to rent props and equipment on top of paying the two of us girls. He was nervous he wasn't going to be able to sell the pictures for enough money to make it all back, so he invited some guys from the camera clubs to come in and shoot, too, as long as they didn't get in his way. They paid me and the other girl extra, and paid him, too, so he could be sure of making a profit."

Tilda saw that Cooper looked confused, and thought she had better give him a little background. "Back then, there were a lot of camera clubs for amateur photographers. They'd hire models and then all show up to take pictures of them."

Sandra nodded. "The pros didn't always let the amateurs in on their sessions—they didn't want the competition—but like I said, Red was anxious about the dollars. He made the guys in the club promise to keep the pictures for their own use and not sell them, and as far as I know, they all kept their word." She tapped the envelope again. "This guy did, anyway. It turns out that he lives just up the road in Medford. He got in touch with me through the site, and asked if I wanted the pictures, and of course I said I did. They've never been printed anywhere before, and I'm going to debut them on my site."

"Wow!" Cooper said.

She gave him a coquettish smile. It was honestly coquettish, too, not the parody that was the best most women Tilda's age could muster. "Would you like to take a look?"

"You mean it?"

"Sure, why not? They'll be on the Web next week anyway." She opened the envelope and pulled out a stack of photos, and while Tilda and she looked on, Cooper put the camera aside so he could reverently lift each photo.

Tilda was fascinated by one that showed Sandra and the other model in street clothes. Both were wearing neat suits with high heel pumps, gloves, and cunning hats.

Sandra saw what she was looking at, and shook her head. "He must have taken that one when we first got there. Can you believe how we used to dress, just to take our clothes off? And those were everyday outfits!"

"You looked great," Tilda said, "but I bet what you're wearing now is a lot more comfortable."

Meanwhile, Cooper was going for the skin. "These are amazing," he said. "I can really see where you and the other model loosened up later in the session."

Sandra giggled. "Yeah, we did, didn't we?" She pulled one photo out of the stack. "The guys gave us a little extra for this pose."

"I'll bet they did! Whatever they paid, it was worth it."

"Cooper!" Sandra said in mock shock. "I see that ring on your finger—what would your wife say?"

"Husband, actually," he said. "And Jean-Paul wouldn't mind—he knows your pictures helped prove that I'm gay."

"Come again?"

"The fact is, my whole family knew by the time I hit high school, but one uncle had it in his head that he could 'cure' me. One day he showed up and said he wanted to take me out for lunch, but on the way home from the restaurant, he pulled out one of his prized girlie magazines and told me to look at it alone that night. That's the one that had the pirate spread."

"It was one of my more popular ones," Sandra said modestly.

"It opened my eyes, I can tell you that. If anything would have set me straight, those pictures would have. But though I tried to . . . appreciate them, nothing happened. Uncle Mac asked about it the next day, and when I told him, he just patted me on the shoulder and said that if those pictures wouldn't do it for me, no woman ever would."

"Cooper, that is the sweetest thing I ever heard," Sandra said.

Tilda wasn't sure if *sweet* was the right word for it, but it did explain why Cooper had been so interested in coming along. Before Sandra and Cooper got the urge to share any more Hallmark moments, she asked, "What happened to the other model? I've done a fair amount of research on pinup queens, and I don't remember seeing many pictures of her. I'm guessing Virginia Pure wasn't her real name."

"Wasn't that the dumbest thing?" Sandra said. "Her real name was Esther something. Esther Marie . . . Esther Marie Martin, that's it. What a name to hang on her! She had the cutest Southern accent you ever heard, and used to guzzle iced tea with so much sugar in it you'd think it was syrup. She was from some little bitty town in Virginia, which is what gave her the idea for the name—I don't think she even made the connection between Virginia and virgin, even though she probably was one. Esther was one of those sweet young things who came to New York to be a star on Broadway, but she wasn't tough enough or lucky enough. She kind of fell into modeling, but she never did learn to like it. Some people are comfortable in their skin, and some aren't—poor Virginia didn't think she was pretty enough because she wasn't as big busted as I was."

"Not many women are," Tilda said, resisting the impulse to check out her own rack.

"Big breasts aren't everything, not even in that line of work," Sandra said. "Red was really pleased with that shoot, and wanted Virginia and me to do more together, but that day was the last time I saw her. She started feeling sick near the end of the session, and I don't know if it was because she was really coming down with something or if the modeling had finally gotten to her. Next thing I knew, she'd left New York to go back home, and I never heard from her again. Broke a few hearts, too."

"I thought it was 'look, don't touch' with the camera club members?"

"It was supposed to be," Sandra said with a little smile. "Most of the guys were too shy to even speak to us outside of shoots. But not all."

"And?"

"And . . . And I could use a tonic. How about you two?"

Tilda admitted defeat, and both she and Cooper accepted the offer.

Sandra went into the tiny kitchen to fetch Cokes and a bowl of pretzels, and once they were all settled again, she said, "So, Cooper, do you know who Bettie Page was?"

He looked at Tilda, but she had no way of giving him a hint of how to respond, so he cautiously said, "I think I've heard the name."

Sandra rolled her eyes. "Everybody has heard of her, but nobody knows that I taught her everything she knew about posing."

"Really?"

"You bet! It was me who taught her to walk in high heels, too. Do you ever do drag?"

Tilda leaned in, curious about that herself, since she'd never dared ask.

But Cooper said, "Just for Halloween, and I stay away from heels."

"Well, there's a real art to wearing them gracefully. You know what I'm talking about, don't you, Tilda?"

"Practice, practice, practice," she said. "And never wear heels in the snow."

Sandra laughed. "That's a good place to start." She took a swallow of Coke and said, "Is there anything else you need for your article?"

As hints went, Sandra's was remarkably polite, so Tilda took a quick look at her notes. "I think I've got it. If I do seem to be missing something, I'll give you a call."

"Hate to rush you two off, but I've got company coming and I want to make myself beautiful."

"Don't waste your time," Cooper said. "You're already there."

Sandra beamed. "Cooper, if you were straight and maybe twenty years older, I'd just keep you and cancel my date."

There was a flurry as Tilda gathered up notes and pens, she and Cooper suited up for the winter weather, and Sandra walked them to the building's front door. The predicted snow had arrived, and as Tilda stepped unwillingly into the quarter-inch that had already fallen, she looked back and saw Sandra waving at them cheerfully.

Chapter 4

The cowboy is the ultimate American archetype. Literally and figuratively negotiating the boundaries between nature and humankind, lawlessness and civilization, he rides the range of our imagination, adding nuance to our definitions of good and evil with every story, every serial, every song. Embodying both the rugged individual and the citizen capable of constructing and maintaining a community, the cowboy—and cowgirl—reflects the essential American desire to be both a leader and team player, with the qualities of toughness, fairness, resourcefulness, and self-sacrifice.

—*AMERICANS IMAGINED: IDENTITY AND ARCHETYPE FROM ROY ROGERS TO BATMAN* BY LORINDA B. R. GOODWIN, PhD

IN between amiable cursing at the snow, Cooper mentioned that Jean-Paul was working late, so they decided to stop at California Pizza Kitchen for dinner, partially for the food and partially for the amusement of being able to look out the wall of windows and watch people trudge through the snow while they ate in flake-free warmth. While waiting for their order, Cooper said, "In all the excitement about your newly employed status—"

"My *possibly* employed status," Tilda said.

"Negative thoughts give you wrinkles. I saw that on the Web."

"Then it must be true."

"As I was saying, in the excitement about which I shall not go into detail, I forgot to ask what the big meeting was about. I'm assuming Jillian didn't bring in all those other people just to offer you a job."

"No, the *tentative* job offer was an afterthought. The meeting was about a nice, fat assignment. Do you remember the show *Cowtown*?"

"It rings a very vague bell."

"Way before our time. It was set in a Western town with the usual crew of kindly doctor, cranky shopkeeper, virtuous farmer, aristocratic rancher, and saloon gal with a heart of gold. But those were only the backdrop. Since the town was along a regular cattle trail, there were always cowboys coming through, bringing their stories of adventure to trade for free drinks with the golden-hearted saloon gal. It was almost an anthology series—lots of guest stars, and generous use of stock footage of stampedes, Indian attacks, and so forth."

"Sounds eminently forgettable."

"Some of the episodes were decent, but it varied a lot with the guest stars and the guest writers. If you like Westerns, that is."

"And you don't?" he asked.

"Are you serious? Did it never strike you how bogus the whole cowboy mythos is? John Wayne and Matt Dillon? The Cartwright brides on *Bonanza* dying off like bimbos in a slasher flick? The way Indians are portrayed is horrible, and women don't come off much better. Then there were the spaghetti Westerns, where suddenly everything was grubby and the women got raped instead of being menaced in some nonspecific way. That's how the world sees the United States, as a bunch of cowboys." Tilda noticed that Cooper had one eyebrow raised. "What?"

"How old were you when you had your cowboy birthday party?"

She sighed. "When I turned eight."

"Did you have a cowboy hat?"

"A cowgirl hat, thank you very much. Red, to match the vest."

"Boots?"

"Just for dress-up. They were no good for actually playing cowboys and Indians."

"I bet you used to watch Rex Trailer on TV."

"Please. *Boomtown* had gone off the air long before I was interested in cowboys."

"And yet you recognized Rex Trailer's name."

"He *is* a Boston celebrity. I've seen him at parades, once or twice."

"What's his horse's name?"

"Goldrush," she said, defeated. "Okay, I had a secret addiction to Westerns."

"Had?"

"Correction. I *have* a secret addiction to Westerns, which is why I recognized Cynthia Barth, the actress who used to play Arabella Newman, the saloon gal on *Cowtown*. And I forgot to tell you the best part of the show. At the end of every episode, Arabella would do a voiceover with the episode's moral. Stuff like, 'A real man never harms a woman—any man that does is nothing but a snake.' And the end was always, 'That's the Cowtown Code.' "

"You have got to be kidding me!"

"Cowboy's honor," she said. "A true cowboy never lies. That's the Cowtown Code."

"Stop it!"

The pizza arrived before Tilda could quote more, and while they ate, she explained the plan for a *Cowtown* resort.

"With the economy the way it is, it seems like the worst time imaginable to build a tourist trap," Cooper said. "Is there a market for something like that?"

"Hard to say. There used to be an attraction based on *Bonanza* outside of Lake Tahoe and it did pretty well. It only closed because the owners wanted to sell the land. Nostalgia is big, and cowboys are always big. I don't know if this will fly or not, but the Ambrose brothers seem pretty gung ho on the idea, and I'm just happy to get the work."

"Something to tide you over until you start at *Entertain Me!* full time," Cooper said.

"Changing the subject now," Tilda insisted, and they moved on to talk forthcoming movies for the rest of the meal. When they left the restaurant, the plan was for Tilda to hit the subway while Cooper hoofed it toward his apartment, but before they separated Tilda said, "Wait. I need my camera back."

"I thought you had it."

After several minutes of searching, it was obvious that neither of them had it.

"Shit!" Tilda said.

"Sorry, kiddo. I must have left it in Sandra's apartment."

Tilda pulled her cell phone out to dial Sandra's number, but the line was busy. "At least she's home. I hope she doesn't go anywhere before I can get back there." She looked out the window into the snow, and sighed. "Once more into the breach, dear friend."

"I'll walk with you."

"That's okay. No reason for you to go that far out of your way and then still have to get home."

"But it's my fault for leaving the camera."

"So you can buy me dinner next time."

"Are you sure?"

In response, she shoved him in the direction he needed to go and said, "Good night, Cooper!" before heading outside into the muck.

The temperature had dropped while they'd been eating dinner, and the snow was falling even more heavily. Tilda's commentary as she trudged would have been wildly unsuitable for *Cowtown.* She was tempted to grab a cab, even if it put her in the hole for the story, but naturally there were none in sight, so there was no choice but to walk. She tried to call Sandra again along the way, but the line stayed busy.

Finally she made it back to Sandra's building, and was about to ring the bell when a delivery man on his way out paused to hold the door for her. After stamping her feet to shake the accumulated snow off of her Doc Martens, she went to Sandra's door and knocked.

There was no response.

Surely Sandra hadn't gone out since she tried to call last. Besides, hadn't she said that she was expecting company?

Tilda knocked again, harder, and when there was no answer, pulled out her cell phone to dial Sandra's number yet again. It was still busy, so presumably the woman was inside, but Tilda didn't hear sounds of conversation.

Now she pounded on the door, but there was still no reply, and when she checked the doorknob, she found that it was unlocked. Hesitantly, she pushed the door open and peered inside the room. "Sandra?"

The first thing she saw was the telephone. When she'd been there before, it had been on the desk next to the computer. Now it was on the floor with the receiver off the hook, which explained the busy signal. But it didn't explain where Sandra was. It didn't make sense—like one of Cooper's picture puzzles, it felt as if some of the pieces had been confused somehow.

The only thing Tilda could imagine was that the older woman had had a stroke or a heart attack, and had been trying to reach the phone when she succumbed. So Tilda stepped inside, and wasn't even surprised to see Sandra lying on the floor, facedown, on the other side of the couch.

She later wondered why she didn't panic, but somehow the shock gave her the illusion of complete control. Since she knew she couldn't handle anything more serious than a paper cut herself, obviously professional help was needed. She still had her cell phone in her hand. Then she remembered that the police would be able to track the call more easily if she used Sandra's landline, so she picked it up from the floor to call 911. In a calm, collected voice, she explained that an older woman had fallen ill and needed an ambulance. It was only when the operator asked for details about the patient's condition that Tilda actually looked at Sandra. And saw the blood. Too much blood.

It had run down the woman's velour top to soak into the rug, and there were spatters across the couch and on the mirror. The back of Sandra's head was . . . misshapen.

Tilda's mind stopped working, and she dropped the phone and started panting in an effort to keep from screaming. She couldn't bring herself to move Sandra, or step over her, so she stepped around the couch to where she could see her face, to try to see if there was any chance that the woman was still alive. Sandra's open, unblinking eyes gave her the answer she'd already known to be true.

Seconds later, she recognized the tiny noises she was hearing as coming from the phone, and went back to tell the operator that she needed the police, too.

Chapter 5

Empowering? Some women's studies PhD candidate asked me about that once. I told her there's nothing empowering about girlie pictures. I must have posed for thousands of them—if girlie pictures were empowering, I'd be running the whole damned country.
—SANDRA SECHREST, QUOTED IN "QUEEN OF THE PINUPS" BY TILDA HARPER, *NOT DEAD YET* MAGAZINE

"I can't believe somebody murdered that poor woman," Cooper breathed some hours later.

The police had come quickly and questioned Tilda at Sandra's apartment before taking her to the police station to go through it all once again for a tall, dark-haired man who introduced himself as Detective Salvatore. Naturally the cops were interested in the company Sandra had mentioned, but Tilda didn't know anything other than what the older woman had said, though she'd assumed Sandra was expecting a man, since she said she wanted to make herself beautiful. Tilda gave them Lil's name, suggesting that Sandra might have told her niece more details, but that was all she could offer.

Next they asked if she was willing to let them take her clothes and boots for analysis, which was the first time she'd realized that she'd gotten so much of Sandra's blood on her. It was all she could do to keep from ripping off everything she was wearing.

A combination of modesty and the realization that it

was too cold to go around undressed saved her, and she asked if she could call a friend to bring her something else to put on first. Her sister June was all the way out in Beverly, way too far away to come out on a snowy night. There was her roommate, but Tilda hadn't known Colleen long enough to impose on her. So it had to be Cooper. As it turned out, the police had already intended to talk to him for verification of her description of their interview with Sandra. With snow still falling heavily, Detective Salvatore offered to send a squad car to pick him up.

Cooper brought her a whole set of outerwear—sweatpants, sweatshirt, socks, a worn but serviceable pair of Ugg boots, and a coat he rarely wore. It didn't fit perfectly, but it was warm and blood-free. A policewoman took Tilda to the bathroom to change, then carried away her things. The cops did let her keep her bag, but asked permission to examine the contents, which she allowed. She even let them check the list of calls in and out on her cell phone, and photocopy her notes from the interview with Sandra.

In retrospect, she wondered if she should have stood up for her rights, whatever they might have been, but it didn't occur to her at the time. Anybody who had watched as many TV cop shows as Tilda had knew that the person to find the body was always a suspect. If letting the police have what they wanted would convince them that she hadn't killed Sandra, then what did it matter?

Tilda had thought she'd be able to leave after the bag search, but Detective Salvatore went through the day's events with her one more time. Then she had to wait while Cooper had his turn. An eternity later, Salvatore told her that they could leave. His manner had eased, which she hoped meant that he didn't suspect her, and he gave her his card and asked her to call if she thought of anything that might help him. Then he got another squad car, or maybe the same one, to take them both to Cooper's apartment.

She couldn't have faced the prospect of going home to her place in Malden—she needed a lot more comforting than she could expect her roommate to provide. When they got back to Cooper's, Jean-Paul was waiting for them, and had them both on the couch, wrapped in quilts, supplied with hot chocolate in nothing flat. He'd laced the hot chocolate with something warming, too.

"Was it robbery?" Jean-Paul wanted to know.

"The cops don't think so," Tilda answered. "The computer was still there, and the TV. Aren't those the first things thieves take?"

Cooper shrugged. "Maybe they were after jewelry or cash."

Tilda shook her head. "I heard one of the cops say that the bedroom looked undisturbed, and Sandra's purse was on the table by the front door, with money and credit cards in it."

"Then why would anybody kill that sweet lady?" Cooper asked again. "She was so nice."

"And it was so mean, Cooper. It couldn't have been that hard to kill Sandra—you saw her. She was old. She could barely use her hands. But he hit her over and over again. You remember that miniature sea chest on her coffee table? That's what he used. The cops found it all covered in—" Tilda shuddered.

"That's enough talking," Cooper said, and Jean-Paul brought her a refill on the hot chocolate with even more of the secret ingredient. "You need to get some sleep."

"I don't think I can," Tilda said.

"All right, then I'll sit here and keep you company."

"You don't have to do that."

"Shut up." He sent Jean-Paul off to bed, refilled his own mug of hot chocolate, and rejoined her on the couch. "If you won't sleep, we can play Monopoly, or we can read my new batch of comic books, or we can watch TV."

Tilda picked TV, and they watched *Labyrinth* to

admire David Bowie's goblin king wardrobe and *Hop-scotch* to revel in Walter Matthau's hijinks before she finally dozed off.

Cooper was smart enough to stay with her, so when she had the inevitable nightmare about a pinup queen with her head bashed in, he was there to soothe her back to sleep.

Chapter 6

Episode 35: Be It Ever So Humble
Newcomer Clay Hollister runs into trouble when he tries to build a cabin. Every night, somebody destroys the work he'd put in during the day. Finally he hides to wait and watch, and catches an Indian boy in the act. When Clay confronts him, the boy explains that his family has used that spot to burn their dead for as long as anybody can remember, but that he didn't think a white man would understand. Clay agrees to build elsewhere because, as the voiceover says, "Just as every man must face life his own way, every man must face death his own way, and a cowboy respects that. That's the Cowtown Code."

—*COWTOWN COMPANION* BY RUBEN TIMMONS

THOUGH morning seemed to take forever to arrive, Tilda felt as if she hadn't slept at all. After they all chowed down on corn muffins from Dunkin' Donuts, both men offered to stay with her, but she knew Jean-Paul had a meeting and Cooper was on deadline, so she shooed them away. She did agree to get more rest, but after an hour of dozing on the couch, decided that what she really wanted was to go home. Leaving Cooper and Jean-Paul a thank-you note for all their help, she climbed back into the previous night's borrowed clothes.

By the time she got to the Kenmore Square T station, the rush-hour crowd was thinning, but there were still plenty of subway trolleys running, so it didn't take long for her to get back to Malden. Even then, she nearly fell asleep on the train. From the Malden Center station, it was only a five-minute walk to the double-decker on Russell Street she'd moved into a couple of months earlier. The landlady, a consultant of some sort who spent more time on the road than at home, lived in the larger apartment upstairs, while Tilda and Colleen shared the first floor.

Normally Tilda would have taken a moment to admire the original woodwork that had sold her on the place, from the built-in china cabinet to the generous moldings around every door and window, but that morning, she could have been walking around a prefab mobile home for all the notice she took. She didn't even bother to check for mail, phone messages, or e-mail before crawling into bed.

She woke whimpering three hours later.

After that, sleep lost its appeal, so she took a long, hot shower so she would at least look better. Then she grabbed her copy of the *Boston Globe* from the front porch, warmed up some leftover pizza in the microwave, and ate as she read the paper's coverage on Sandra's murder. Though she hadn't really expected the police to have made an arrest yet, she couldn't help but be disappointed when the article contained nothing more promising than the usual polite code language for "we haven't got a clue so leave us alone and let us get to work." Sandra's niece, Lil, apparently the only family Sandra had nearby, was described as being heartbroken and shocked by her great-aunt's murder, and Tilda herself was mentioned only as "a friend of the deceased" who found the body.

She didn't expect her anonymity to last, and there was a chance that enterprising reporters already had her name, which meant that she needed to be prepared for an onslaught of calls. More urgently, it meant that she needed to call her sister before she heard about it from some other source.

She picked up her phone to dial the number. "June? Tilda."

"Hi, Tilda. What's up?"

"Well . . ."

"Are you okay?"

"I'm fine, but—"

"Is it your father? Is it Mom?"

"June, take a breath! Everybody you know is fine, as far as I know."

"Then what's wrong?"

Tilda didn't bother to ask how she'd realized there was something wrong. June could always tell. Instead she explained how she'd come to find Sandra's body, finishing with, "I don't know if I'm going to be mentioned by name anywhere or not, but I thought you'd want to know."

"Of course I want to know," June said, then added an affectionate, "Idiot!"

"Moron."

"Dingbat."

"Housewife!"

June laughed. "That's a new one. You win this time."

Tilda suspected her sister was letting her off easy for a change, but gracefully accepted victory by saying, "I always win, and I always will."

"Seriously, Tilda, are you okay?"

"I'll be fine."

"You're not in any danger, are you?"

That was the first time Tilda had considered that angle, but she said, "No, of course not. I didn't see anything, and I don't know anything—I've already told the cops that. There's no reason anybody would come after me."

"Because murderers are always reasonable people."

"Fair enough, but I don't know how the killer would even know who I am. I'd only spoken with Sandra three times in person and twice on the phone, so it's not like we were close. And if it was a serial killer, I don't exactly match Sandra's demographic."

"You be careful anyway."

"Always."

"Yeah, right." They moved on to a discussion about whether or not Tilda should tell their mother or Tilda's father, but concluded that it could wait until her weekly duty calls. Calling in midweek would imply more urgency than Tilda wanted them to feel. They finished up with the usual status report on June's kids, complaints about Tilda's roommate, and curses about the weather.

Now that Tilda had dealt with her family obligations, she couldn't help wondering about Sandra's family. What was the appropriate way to express condolences to the relatives of a person who'd been murdered? After a moment, she decided that the reaction should be no different from that for any death. Of course, there was the complication that she'd been the one to find the body. Would that make her wishes more or less welcome? She weighed the idea of a card or e-mail, but finally decided she was wimping out, and looked up Lil's phone number.

An unfamiliar voice answered the phone, and guardedly said, "Lil Sechrest's residence."

"Hi, this is Tilda Harper. I'm a friend—" She paused, because she wasn't really a friend. "I just called to express my condolences over the loss of Lil's aunt." That matched the formula her mother had taught her.

"I'm sorry, what name did you say?"

"Tilda Harper."

Tilda heard the other person speaking to somebody else, and a second later, Lil came to the phone. "Hi, Tilda. How are you holding up?"

"Aren't I supposed to ask you that?"

"I guess neither of us is doing too well."

"I'm so sorry about your aunt, Lil." Then she departed from her mother's script. "She was cool as hell."

"She was, wasn't she? I just can't believe she's gone, especially like this." She paused. "The police told me you found her."

"Yeah, I did." Tilda explained the whys and wherefores of her going back to the condo, and as delicately as she could, what she'd found. "I wish I knew more to tell the cops. Have they got any ideas?"

"They're not telling me a lot," Lil said. "I think I'm a suspect."

"Yeah, I guess you are." Tilda heard a sharp intake of breath. "Shit! That's not what I meant. It's just that everybody knows that cops always look at the family, whether or not it makes any sense." When Lil didn't respond, she added, "They were pretty interested in me, too, because I was the one to find her."

"It's crazy, isn't it? They actually asked me about her will and—" She stopped. "Tilda, are you talking to me as a friend, or as a reporter?"

"Jesus Christ, Lil, of course I'm not going to report on this! I mean, it's not what I do anyway, and—God, I'm screwing this up so badly. Okay, even the worst muckraking, scandal-hunting, bottom-feeding reporters follow one rule. If you ask me to keep this off the record, I will."

"Tilda, can we keep this off the record?"

"Absolutely."

"Thank you. I'm sorry to be so suspicious, but I've already had a lot of calls from reporters."

"It's okay. I don't blame you. They haven't come after me, but I'm halfway expecting it."

"Won't it be strange, being on the other end of an interview?"

"Maybe I'll grade their techniques—I can even hold up scorecards."

Lil snickered, and Tilda bet it was the first time she'd done that all day, so maybe calling her had been the right thing to do.

"Lil, I know you've got things to take care of, but I was hoping you'd let me know when the funeral is. I'd like to be there."

"That's really nice of you. The police haven't released the body yet, but as soon as we get things settled, I'll let you know."

"I'd appreciate that. Is there anything I can do?"

"I don't think so. The family has been gathering around. It's getting crowded around here, to tell you the truth. But thanks for asking."

Tilda felt better when she hung up, despite the awkward spots. How awful for Lil to have to suspect Tilda's motives, and for her to be suspected by the police in turn. Admittedly, there was statistical evidence for why the cops looked at relatives first, and certainly Lil was strong enough to have killed her elderly aunt. From what Lil had said, she was mentioned in Sandra's will, and she must not have an alibi or the police wouldn't still suspect her.

Tilda shivered, as if she could shake the thoughts out of her head, but she was stuck with two of them. One, she was ecstatic that she didn't write crime stories, and two, she no longer felt so good about the phone call.

Chapter 7

Episode 59: The World's Best Tracker

Hunters, Texas Rangers, and Indian scouts converge on Cowtown to compete for the title of World's Best Tracker. Then a young boy trying to emulate them goes missing, and with all those experts, it's his mother who finds him. The judges give her the prize as the voiceover says, "The best tool any tracker can ever have is love."

—*COWTOWN COMPANION* BY RUBEN TIMMONS

TILDA figured that since she'd spoken to June and given Lil a condolence call, she was free to get to work. It was only when she got to her computer that she remembered that she had one last obligation. She needed to break the news to the group that had led her to Sandra in the first place.

While idly surfing the Web, Tilda had come across a site about former pinup queens. Joe, the guy who'd started the site, had begun by searching for Bettie Page, a popular quest for many years. Though Page had been a huge celebrity in the 1950s, when she left the public eye in 1957, she did so thoroughly. New celebrities took her place, but enough of her pictures remained that people remembered her. Somehow she became a cult figure in the 1980s, and the speculation began. Why had she disappeared in the midst of her popularity? Had she been assassinated, kidnapped, enslaved, imprisoned, undergone a sex-change operation? No possibility was too outlandish.

Of course, Page eventually resurfaced, and it turned out

her celebrated disappearance was an intentional exit due to a combination of reasons: new laws making her photos illegal, her concern that at age thirty-four she was getting too old, and a newfound devotion to religion. Her actual death in 2008 had only given birth to a new set of conspiracy theories about the circumstances of her death and whether or not she was really dead.

Joe still regretted that somebody else had found Betty before he could, and since he'd developed an intense interest in all pinup models, he decided to track down as many as he could. A community of pinup fans had formed around his site, and they'd given Tilda the clues it took to find Sandra.

She owed it to the fans there to tell them about the woman's death, so as soon as she'd booted up her computer, she logged onto the bulletin board for Joe's Lost Pinups, and checked to see if the news had hit.

There was the usual brand of postings, most of which Tilda skipped. Page-Boy had a new idea for where Bettie Page was hiding, Bettie-Fan wanted comments on her new short story about a sexual encounter between Page and all three of the Cartwright boys from *Bonanza*, Pinned-Up was panting for somebody to argue with about the underlying feminism of fetish photos, and Joe had posted his weekly update to the list of ongoing pinup searches. Plus Di was chiding somebody for using a harsh tone in a post, which was totally inappropriate for a group of loving friends, while Deb detailed her latest medical issues. Tilda didn't know why, but every online community she'd ever observed had one member who adopted the role of peacekeeper and at least one who had serious health issues and needed lots of emotional support from the group. Since the former often took it upon him or herself to tend to the latter, Tilda usually ignored them both.

There was nothing about Sandra, so Tilda quickly composed a message.

TILDA: I have bad news. Sandra Sechrest, A.K.A.
Sandy Sea Chest, was found murdered in her Boston
apartment last night. The police have no suspects at
this time.

She added the link to the online version of the *Boston
Globe* article and posted it along with her message, then
went on to check her e-mail. Though there was nothing
urgent, it took her half an hour to read through and deal
with the accumulation. Then she couldn't resist doing a
little Web surfing to see if there'd been any news about
Sandra's case, hoping that maybe an arrest had been made.
No such luck.

While she'd been hunting for info, a wave of messages
had come through on the Lost Pinups site, and she found
the group abuzz with the news. Unsurprisingly, there were
already warring theories about the murderer. The most
popular contender was a serial killer going after former pinups, which also explained why the group had been having
so much trouble finding the women—the killer had struck
first. Next in line were vague conspiracy theories involving
either the mob or the radical Right. Joe himself figured the
killing was a normal, random crime—a phrase that made
Tilda wince—but suggested that the police ought to look at
this "friend" who'd found Sandra's body. Tilda wasn't sure
whether or not she should tell them she was the friend or
not, but finally decided not to. She didn't want to have to
answer a lot of questions. In fact, she didn't want to think
about the woman, at least not for a while.

Tilda figured the only way to get her mind off the murder was to get to work. Unfortunately, the first thing on her
agenda was to write up the interview with Sandra and send
it to the editor who was waiting. But even if she'd been up to
writing, the police still had her camera. Eventually, she was
going to need to call about getting it back, but she couldn't
bring herself to do it yet. It just sounded too callous.

Besides, she didn't think the editor would want the story anymore. It was a how-to journal for Web entrepreneurs, not a true crime magazine. She called the editor to explain the situation and asked if he wanted her to interview another formerly famous actor who was using the Web to sell memorabilia, possibly Mike Teevee from *Willy Wonka and the Chocolate Factory*, but wasn't surprised when he said he'd pass. He did offer a kill fee, a phrase that made Tilda wince, and she accepted it gratefully.

With that off her docket, she was free to contemplate a subject guaranteed to provide plenty of distraction: tracking down guest stars from *Cowtown*. The Ambrose brothers wanted ten interviews and had given her the names of ten actors they were particularly interested in locating, people who'd been in more than one episode or whose episodes had been particularly well received. It was exactly the kind of challenge Tilda liked.

Her first step was to create a spreadsheet to keep track of basic information about each of the ten actors. Then she hit the Internet Movie Database, her favorite site for information about movies and TV shows. Though Tilda had quite a list of contacts for current actors and more recently forgotten stars from the 1970s and 1980s, the further back a show went, the harder it was to find people involved.

According to IMDb, two of the guest stars were already dead, but she wrote a note to herself to check out obituary sites for verification. Though the movie site was usually accurate, occasionally mistakes were made. Besides, the circumstances of the actors' deaths might make for interesting stories, too.

That left eight, and since she already had permission to find replacements, she flipped through her copy of *Cowtown Companion* to pick two other guest stars. She found one who'd gone on to work in a soap opera, which would draw crossover interest with soap fans. Since she was currently playing the matriarch on *A Life Worth Living*, it would be easy to find her.

For the other, Tilda chose a character actor who'd worked steadily for years without ever making it big. She'd found that actors like him knew everybody, and since they weren't dependent on any one show for their bread and butter, didn't mind dishing the dirt. To add to his appeal, Tilda had interviewed the guy once before because of a red-shirt appearance on *Star Trek*, which is to say that he'd been cast as a security officer and then killed six minutes into the episode. So she already had enough of a rapport to ensure a good interview.

With her list back up to ten, she was ready to start hunting.

Had *Cowtown* been a more recent show, she might have been able to track down actors via the paper trail of residuals paid for reruns. But it had been produced before anybody anticipated the long life a TV show might have, which meant that residual payments had stopped after the sixth broadcast of each episode. So even if she'd been able to access studio records, those records would have been so out-of-date as to be nearly useless.

Tilda was going to have to get creative. She knew that the secret to finding anybody in the entertainment industry was connections. Actors rarely stayed with one show for long—the average show didn't even make it through the first season and even the most successful shows only lasted a few years. Even if an actor was with a series for an entire run, that would still be only a slice of a career, so actors ended up working with a whole lot of other actors, plus behind-the-scenes people like producers, directors, agents, casting consultants, makeup artists, script writers, lighting people, and people with titles she didn't completely understand. That meant her next job was to find convergences between her targets and people she already knew.

Next she looked to see if any of her other targets were still working regularly. Those would be the easiest to find, either via their agents, casting directors, or the networks for the shows on which they worked. That gave her strong links for a couple more. Then came the painstaking process of reading the credits for each of the remaining actors, trying for more connections with people she knew or people she knew how to find.

By five thirty, she had a pretty good idea of how to locate most of the ten.

She might have worked a little longer had the doorbell not rung. She was hoping it was the UPS delivery man with her latest eBay splurge, but it was Cooper.

Chapter 8

A pard sticks till hell freezes over, then goes as far as he can
on the ice.

—*PARDS* BY TEXAS BIX BENDER

"DUDE! What brings you out to the wilds of Malden?" she
asked, knowing that he regarded anything farther from
Boston than Cambridge as untamed wilderness. Malden
was two whole towns beyond Cambridge.

"Jean-Paul had another gig tonight, so I've come to res-
cue you from the terrors of leftover takeout pizza."

Tilda checked the front of her shirt for pizza crust
crumbs, but she was clear. "In other words, you came to
make sure I was okay."

"Which I could do a whole lot better from inside your
apartment."

She stepped back to let him in, and they went into the
living room. It was small, saved from being cramped by
having a large archway that opened onto the dining room.
In one of the compromises of living with a roommate, the
couch, lamps, and TV were Tilda's, while the easy chair,
coffee table, and end table were Colleen's. Unsurprisingly,
the styles didn't mesh even a little bit.

Cooper said, "I hope you respect the fact that I manfully
resisted the impulse to check on you today, thinking that
you'd be catching up on your sleep. But when I got home
there was no Tilda, just an uninformative note."

"Sorry, I should have called. I just got restless and decided to head back here. Then I got working on my *Cowtown* research."

"So how are you doing?"

"I'm fine. Been working hard on the *Cowtown* story."

"Did you get any sleep today?"

"I napped a little this morning. Woke up ready to get going on my—"

"Yes, on the *Cowtown* story. Are there a lot of research facilities on Denial River?"

She sighed. "Okay, I'm freaked out, Cooper, and yes, I had more bad dreams. But sitting around being freaked out isn't going to make the problem go away."

"Do you want to talk about it?"

She hesitated, not sure if conversation would help or make it worse. The decision was made for her, at least temporarily, when she heard the front door open and a voice called out, "Tilda, are you home?"

A second later, Colleen stuck her head into the room. When Tilda had first met the wide-eyed brunette, she'd had high hopes for their rooming together. Colleen was younger than Tilda, and they had almost no interests in common other than a desire for affordable housing and similar standards of cleanliness. Tilda had expected this to lead to a cordial but distant relationship in which each went her own way, with as few encounters as possible.

Unfortunately, Colleen found Tilda's life both exotic and fascinating, and wasn't shy about asking questions about her work, her friends, and pretty much everything else. Tilda, on the other hand, had limited interest in Colleen's life, and even less in talking about her own.

After having gone through far too many roommates, Tilda was seriously starting to contemplate becoming a hermit. The problem was making enough money to be able to afford a roommate-free hermitage. Of course, she knew what Cooper would say, that once she went to work for

Entertain Me!, her regular salary would help her save up enough for a place of her own, maybe even a condo. He had a point, too, or he would have if she ever actually told him what she was thinking.

"Hi! You must be a friend of Tilda's," Colleen said brightly.

Tilda wanted to say, "Why no, we've never met. I just let a stranger come in and hang with me," but that would not have been conducive to congenial roommate relations. So what she actually said was, "Colleen, this is my friend Cooper. Cooper, this is my roommate Colleen."

They exchanged hellos. Then Colleen asked, "Where were you last night?"

Tilda tried not to wince, because it really wasn't any of Colleen's business. "Did somebody call? You can always give people my cell phone number if they're bugging you."

"No, it's not that. I was just worried."

"You're welcome to call my cell phone, too," Tilda said. Then, because Colleen looked hurt, she added, "I was out later than I expected, so I crashed at Cooper's place."

"Really?" Colleen said meaningfully. "Are you two, you know . . ."

"No," Tilda said. "How was work?"

"Oh my gosh, you would not believe it!" Colleen launched into a convoluted and seemingly endless anecdote involving coffee, a package that had been left in the snow, and a stray cat.

Though Tilda didn't bother to pay enough attention to determine the connection between the three elements, Cooper really was trying to follow along, but even his eyes glazed over after a few minutes. So she made a show of looking at her watch. "Oh, shit, look at the time. We've got to run! Cooper, I'll be ready to go in a minute." She bustled down the hall to the bedroom, ran a brush through her hair, and grabbed her bag.

When she got back, Cooper was already in his coat and edging toward the door as Colleen came to what Tilda could only hope was the climax of her story. While Tilda tried to get into her outdoor gear as swiftly as possible, Colleen chirped, "Where are you guys going?"

"Dinner," Tilda said, which was a safe bet. "We'd love to take you with us, but it's business. Bye!"

They were out the door fast enough that Tilda thought it was reasonable to pretend she hadn't heard Colleen asking, "When will you be back?"

"Oh. My. God," Cooper said. "Is she always like that?"

Tilda nodded sadly.

They discussed dinner options while they brushed off the accumulation of snow that had fallen on Tilda's car since the last time she'd driven it, and decided that fajitas at the Border Café in Saugus were just what they needed, particularly if preceded by margaritas.

The restaurant was boisterous enough that Tilda didn't even consider talking about Sandra. Instead they stuck to safe topics like movies and cowboy stars and which was the cutest Border Café waiter.

Tilda was willing to continue avoiding the dead elephant in the room even after they'd left the restaurant and were driving back toward Malden, but as they were passing Johnnie's Foodmaster, Cooper said, "Can we pull over there?"

"You need some groceries?" Tilda asked as she parked the car.

"No, but you need to talk. I know you didn't want to spill your guts where your current roommate from Hell could hear, and you didn't want to talk in the middle of the restaurant, but now it's time."

Tilda took a deep breath, meaning to tell him that she was fine, but the breath caught in her throat and before she knew it she was half sobbing as she described the scene and how awful it was and that it just didn't seem real and did he know that people peed on themselves when they died and other total inanities that probably every person who'd ever found a dead body before had thought.

Cooper mostly kept quiet as he listened, only putting in enough comments so she'd know he was there, and pulled tissues from his pocket as needed.

"I cannot believe this is happening again," she finally said.

"Excuse me?"

"Me getting people killed."

"Excuse me!?"

"Sandra had a nice life before I interviewed her. Then I tracked her down and showed up at her door to ask her about her modeling, and I put her in a magazine. If that weren't enough, I told her how much money she could make selling her pictures on the Web, something she'd never even thought of before, and suddenly she was a cottage industry."

"Boy, she must have hated you for it, too, making all that money."

"No, she liked me. That's what makes it so awful. She liked me, she did as I suggested, and she ended up dead. And it's not like this is the first time."

"Back up!"

"You know what I'm talking about, Cooper. Holly Kendricks from *Kissing Cousins*. And it was just luck that the others didn't die, too."

"We've been through this, Tilda. It wasn't your fault then, and it isn't your fault now."

"No? After I put enough information in the article that anybody with half a brain could find Sandra? Half a brain. That's about what she had left."

"Stop it! Number one, you didn't kill her, and number two, you didn't lead anybody to her. You cannot be responsible for some psycho finding her, if that's what it was. Maybe her death had nothing to do with the Website or the article. We won't know for sure until the cops find the killer."

"If they ever do. They don't solve all cases, you know."

"I'm sensing another *Murder, She Wrote* moment. Didn't we go through this before? You're not a detective, and all that?"

"It worked out last time, didn't it?"

"So if you cross Boylston Street once with your eyes closed and survive, it's okay to do it again?"

"I know, you're right. I just—I just don't want to have bad dreams again."

Normally Tilda and Cooper weren't hugging friends, but this once, she didn't mind when he put his arm around her. It made it that much easier for her to pretend that she wasn't crying, and for him to pretend he hadn't noticed.

After that, he tried to talk her into coming back to Boston with him, but she wanted to sleep in her own bed. If she woke up again, she'd much rather disturb Colleen than Cooper and Jean-Paul. So she drove him to the Malden Center T stop before going back home herself.

Luck was with her. When she opened the door, Colleen was on the phone, so she got away with grabbing a glass of Dr Pepper before retreating into her bedroom.

She was exhausted, but made a quick e-mail check. It was a good thing, too. The Ambrose brothers wanted her to come to a meeting the next morning, something about a promotional event for the *Cowtown* project. After a look in her closet to make sure she had a semiprofessional-looking outfit, she crossed her fingers and got into bed. Then she remembered something she'd seen in the closet and got back out to get it. It had been a while since she'd slept with her stuffed cat, Pyewacket, but this seemed like the perfect time to resume the habit.

Maybe it helped. She managed a full five hours of sleep before she woke with Colleen shaking her, telling her she'd been screaming.

Chapter 9

Episode 48: A Tisket, A Tasket, Arabella's Basket

In order to raise money to build a schoolhouse, the single ladies of Cowtown fill picnic baskets with their finest goodies to auction them off. Each winner gets the company of the lady who prepared his basket, but since nobody knows whose basket is whose, the cowboys in town go crazy trying to figure out which one is Arabella's.

—*COWTOWN COMPANION* BY RUBEN TIMMONS

FORTUNATELY, Colleen was sleepy enough that she didn't push for details about Tilda's nightmare before stumbling back to her own bed. As for Tilda, she found that forty-five minutes of playing Bejeweled on her computer was enough to hypnotize her back to sleep, and she made it through the rest of the night. It wasn't enough sleep, but it was more than she'd had the night before. With the judicious application of makeup, she looked reasonably good as she stepped into the Ambrose brothers' suite at the Boston Park Plaza Hotel.

Tucker greeted her with a hearty handshake before taking her parka to hang in the suite's coat closet, which Tilda noted wistfully was roomier than the largest one in her apartment. When she came into the living room—which was as big as all the rooms in Tilda's apartment put together—she saw Hoyt, Miss Barth, and a very attractive man she didn't know.

Miss Barth nodded graciously and Hoyt shook her hand

as if he was afraid to hurt a woman's dainty fingers. Then he took her over to the stranger, who had sandy blond hair, green eyes to die for, and a suit that should have been retired at least five years before.

"Tilda," Hoyt said, "I want you to meet Dr. Quentin Beaudine. He's with the Stickler Syndrome Research Foundation. We're sponsoring their annual fund-raiser this year, and I just know it's going to raise barrels of money. Quentin, this here is Tilda Harper, who's going to write about the shindig for *Entertain Me!*"

That was the first Tilda had heard about the assignment, but she certainly wasn't going to turn it down. The doorbell rang again, and Hoyt left Tilda and Dr. Beaudine looking a bit stunned.

"I have no idea what's going on," Tilda said conversationally. "How about you?"

"I'm not sure," he admitted. "My boss usually handles fund-raising, but he's out of town, so I got drafted—I'm just a researcher."

That explained the suit. "Researching Stickler Syndrome, I take it."

He nodded.

"Then I'm two for two. I don't know what that is, either."

He smiled, and Tilda was delighted to see that he had dimples. She'd had a fondness for dimples ever since the third grade, when she'd harbored a secret passion for a sixth-grade love god named Stevie Thatch.

"It's a genetic condition caused by mutation in the collagen system."

"That sounds bad."

"It can be. It can affect the eyes, ears, joints, bones, and often causes cleft palates."

"I'm surprised I haven't heard of it before."

"It's such a concatenation of symptoms that it's not always diagnosed, and not everybody who has it is affected strongly. A big part of the research is trying to determine if it really is one syndrome, or several. Also, it's not fatal—fatal diseases tend to get more attention, and therefore more research dollars."

"Is it disfiguring? Everybody loves a good disfiguring disease."

"No luck there, either. Sticky kids are as cute as buttons."

"Sticky? Do they leave sticky notes for each other?"

"I suppose they should."

"In fact, that's what you should use for your signature piece. Instead of pink ribbons, you could get your supporters to wear sticky notes on their tuxes and gowns at the Oscars."

He smiled even wider, and Tilda admired his dimples once again. She would have kept talking, hoping to maintain that smile, but she saw Jillian arrive with Nicole in tow, and Shannon following Nicole. Technically, the buxom blond staff editor was the same rank as Nicole, but somehow Shannon ended up with the scut work every time. Which explained why she was carrying a heavy tote bag.

Tucker said, "I think that's everybody now, so if y'all will get settled, we'll get this show on the road."

The dining room table, like everything else in the suite, was enormous and highly polished. Tilda maneuvered a seat next to Quentin, just in case those dimples made another appearance, and saw that Nicole grabbed the chair on the other side of him. Some women were so competitive, Tilda thought disdainfully, secure in the knowledge that she'd seen him first.

Tucker called the meeting to order, and explained what they were there for. Tilda was pretty sure they all knew that already, but she listened politely and even took notes. She continued to listen as the question of venues for the fund-raiser was discussed, though she quit taking notes when Nicole went into rapturous details about Boston's swankiest restaurants and clubs, each more ludicrously expensive than the last. Finally, she'd had as much as she could stand.

She waited until Nicole took a breath in the middle of waxing poetic about the appetizers at Le Snob Appeal, and said, "Can I make a suggestion?"

Nicole glared at her, but Tucker said, "You bet."

"What about going with someplace more thematic?"

"I don't follow you."

"*Cowtown* was a Western family show, and the *Cowtown* resort is aimed at families, too, right?"

Miss Barth nodded.

"Then how about the Hillside Steakhouse in Saugus?"

Nicole rolled her eyes. "With that giant neon cactus? You have got to be kidding."

Tilda ignored her, instead focusing on Jillian, Miss Barth, and the Ambrose brothers. "What Nicole is talking about is their sign, which is a fifty-foot cactus—it's a local landmark. The place is so big it's broken into dining rooms, and each dining room has a different Western motif: Kansas City, Sioux City, Dodge City. Any one of those rooms would be big enough for a benefit, and they've got function rooms, too. Now the food is plain—steak, baked potatoes or fries, tossed salads—but it's good, and the prices are reasonable. So you wouldn't be spending all of your profits on the party—it would go to the foundation. Best of all, it wouldn't look like every other benefit for every other foundation."

Jillian nodded, probably attracted by the cheapness, and Miss Barth said, "It sounds perfect, like a modern-day Cowtown Saloon."

Nicole looked disgusted, but since she could see the wind was blowing against her, she kept quiet.

"What do you think, Quentin?" Hoyt asked.

"I like it," Quentin said. "It's much more appropriate for our foundation, which isn't a big-bucks operation."

Tucker said, "Tilda, I think you've got something there. Nothing highfalutin', just good food and good times."

Quentin grinned. "And I won't have to rent a tux this year."

"I think you'd look wonderful in a tux," Nicole purred.

"But maybe even better in a cowboy hat," Tilda said. "We could ask people to wear Western clothing."

"Terrific photo ops with that," Jillian pointed out. "The *Boston Globe* has got to be tired of running pictures of men in suits and women wearing little black dresses."

Miss Barth actually clapped her hands. "This is starting to sound like such fun!"

Hoyt started scribbling figures. "We'll make some money on ticket sales, but we'll want to give people a chance to give more, so I want some speakers to get them fired up. Quentin, you can speak for the foundation, right? Slide show, pull on the heartstrings, that kind of thing."

"My boss is much better at that," Quentin said, looking alarmed, "but I'll give it a shot."

"Nothing long and drawn-out," Tucker said. "Just enough to convince people to pony up the money." He chuckled. "Pony up! We can use that."

Hoyt rolled his eyes. "How about some special guests, too, to attract people? Miss Barth, of course."

She nodded modestly.

"Maybe Rex Trailer," Tilda said hopefully. To the out-of-towners, she explained, "He's our most famous local cowboy. He used to host a kids' show, but he's still quite popular."

"Sounds like our kind of cowpoke," Tucker said. "Tilda, see if we can get a couple of the guest stars you're tracking to come, too. We can give them a few cue cards about Sticker's Syndrome—"

"Stickler's Syndrome," Quentin corrected him.

"—and let them pass the hat. A ten-gallon hat, of course. That ought to get us a few dollars."

"How about a silent auction?" Tilda said. "We could see if any of the guest stars have any memorabilia to donate, or get them to sign copies of the *Cowtown* companion book that came out a few years ago. Or we can print out a bunch of stills for them to autograph. Maybe set up photo ops with the stars. Stuff like that would get the *Cowtown* fans enthused."

"Now you're talking!" Hoyt said.

After that, the discussion got more into details than Tilda cared about, and she started wishing she'd had more sleep the night before. It would be awfully embarrassing if she dozed off in the middle of the meeting. There was a bit of controversy about the date, which spiced things up a bit. The foundation had already scheduled their annual fund-raiser, and though Quentin got his boss on the phone to agree to switching venues so that the *Cowtown* crew could get involved, he couldn't change the date. Since that date was less than two weeks away, there was some concern that arrangements couldn't be made. After a certain amount of dithering, Jillian announced that it could be done and would be done. Very few people argued with Jillian when she used that tone.

Then it was back to persnickety details like open bar versus cash bar, and Tilda had to work hard to look interested as she wondered if long, boring meetings were a regular part of the full-time *Entertain Me!* experience.

Finally enough of the decisions had been made to parcel out the rest, and Tilda tuned back in enough to get her own assignments, which were to continue her guest-star roundup, see if anybody was willing to attend the fund-raiser, and let the *Cowtown* fan community know about the event.

The meeting broke up into smaller conversations after that, and Tilda was happy to stand and stretch. She noticed Quentin looked a little stunned.

"Is this not what you were expecting?" she asked him.

"All my boss told me to do was to sit in on the meeting, but now I feel as if I've been sucked into some sort of tornado."

"Don't worry. I think it's going to raise a lot of money, and Tucker may even learn the actual name of the syndrome before it's all said and done."

He smiled, though not quite enough for dimples. "Don't get me wrong, it's great that you people are willing to go to so much trouble. But wouldn't it be easier to just send out a letter and ask for money? Do we need all this?"

"Quentin, are you familiar with the concept of positive reinforcement as a teaching tool?"

"Of course," he said, sounding impressed.

She saw no reason to tell him she'd heard about it from her sister during an overly detailed discussion of potty training. "People need to be taught to give to charity—it doesn't come naturally. Picture this. I'm sitting in my living room, paying bills, which is tedious and reminds me of how little I make. Mixed in with those bills are charity solicitations, but I deal with them last, after the bills that have to be paid. Except by the time I get to them, I've added up how little I've got left in checking, and I can't possibly give to all of them. Even if I do write a check or two, I'm doing it out of guilt, and I'm hoping none of the checks bounce before my next paycheck arrives. In other words, giving to charity that way is no fun.

"Now picture me at a party where I get to meet my favorite TV star of all time. I shake his hand, and my friend takes our picture as he tells me what a fine thing I'm doing by helping out. The room is filled with people working for the charity, so you've got that whole group dynamic happening. *That's* fun. And the next time I get something in the mail from that charity, I'm going to see that picture of myself and Mr. Beefcake and remember how much fun it is to give to charity. See? Positive reinforcement, with a bit of Pavlovian conditioning thrown in."

He still looked doubtful. "Does it have to be fun? Doesn't anybody give from the goodness of their heart?"

"Can't it be good and fun?"

"I guess."

"Well, in case you think this effort is entirely altruistic on anybody's part, I'll remind you that both *Entertain Me!* and the *Cowtown* resort are going to get plenty of publicity, too. But I honestly think your foundation will benefit."

"I think so, too." He smiled again, and this time the dimples were present and accounted for. "I like the way you look at things." He checked his watch. "I've got to get going, but maybe you and I could get together sometime. I mean, in a social way."

"That sounds like just what the doctor ordered." They exchanged phone numbers, and he left to say his good-byes to the Ambrose brothers.

Jillian was giving Nicole instructions, but when she saw Tilda was alone, waved her over.

"Good participation, Tilda. You added value to the meeting."

"Thank you. I really appreciate being—"

But Jillian, having given her own version of positive reinforcement, was moving on. "So what's this about the dead stripper you found?"

"You mean Sandra Sechrest? She was a pinup model, not a stripper."

"Whatever. Why did I have to read about it in the *Globe* when you were there on the scene?"

"Cooper was there—"

"Cooper is a copyeditor, not a reporter, and he's not the one who found the body."

Tilda could have said that the police had asked her not to discuss the case or that she'd been too upset, but the fact was, she just hadn't thought about it. "Since you didn't want the story on Sandra I pitched before, I didn't think you'd be interested."

"That's not your decision. She was local, and we had the inside story. You should have given me the details and let me decide. If you want to come on full time, you need to be with us full time. You got that?"

"Got it," she said, gritting her teeth.

"Good."

"Do you want me to write something up? I can get it to you by—"

"No, Nicole is handling it." Nicole smirked as Jillian went on. "I want you to give her what she needs to finish."

What Tilda wanted was to remind Jillian that she wasn't her employee yet, but that would be one way to guarantee that she never was. So she just nodded, not trusting herself to speak.

Jillian nodded back, and left the two of them, one still smirking and the other one still gritting her teeth.

"When do you want to talk?" Tilda asked.

Nicole made a show of checking her iPhone. "How about four?"

Tilda looked at her watch. It wasn't even eleven. "Can we make it sooner? Otherwise I've either got to make the trek to Malden and back, or kill time here in Boston."

"Sorry," Nicole said unconvincingly. "If you hadn't sat on the story, I wouldn't be squeezing it in, but that's my only available slot."

"Fine. I'll meet you at the office."

Nicole continued to smirk as she scanned the room. "Now I think I'll snag that hunky doctor for a little private examination."

"Sorry," Tilda said in exactly the same tone Nicole had used with her. "He already left."

Tilda made the rounds to say good-bye to everyone except Nicole, then headed downstairs to the lobby to find a quiet corner where she could make a phone call.

"Cooper? Tilda. I just got out of the *Cowtown* meeting, and thanks to Nicole, I'm stuck in town until four. Are you free for lunch?"

"Of all the people in the world you could have chosen to kill time with, you called me. I'm speechless."

"As if. But if you're busy, I'll go eat by myself. It's a

shame, too, because I wanted to tell you about the hunk I met at the meeting."

"You bitch! Charley's at eleven thirty."

Lunchtime conversation consisted of five minutes about the meeting, since Cooper would get the official word back at the office; ten minutes of kvetching about Nicole, because it was traditional; and talking about Quentin Beaudine. No detail was too small for Cooper's vicarious pleasure.

"Your own Dr. McDreamy, only with lighter hair," Cooper said with a happy sigh when he'd squeezed out every last bit of information she had about the man. "And it's about time you got back on the horse."

"That's a particularly crude way of putting it."

"What? No, not that. Not that a large dose of 'that' wouldn't do you a lot of good. I meant that you need to be dating again, and not moping over that bodyguard."

"I have not been moping over Nick." It was true that she hadn't been pleased when Nick Tolomeo, her most recent boyfriend, got a job accompanying Orlando Bloom during a three-month shoot in Prague, and even less so when she found out that it might turn into a six-month gig. Even if the set hadn't been declared a no-press zone because of the director's desire to keep the script a secret, she and Nick had been too early in their relationship for him to ask her to come along. They had been keeping in touch via e-mail, and he'd even shipped her a set of nested dolls and a gorgeous hand-painted Easter egg, but it was hard to know if they'd still have a viable connection by the time he got back. "You know we aren't exclusive. I just haven't met anybody worth dating."

"Until now?"

"Until now," she confirmed. "Quentin is definitely worth dating."

"My little girl dating a doctor," Cooper cooed. "I never thought I'd live to see this day."

"Keep it up, and you won't live to see the end of the day."

With lunch over, Cooper had to get back to *Entertain Me!*, but Tilda was feeling at loose ends.

Cooper said, "Why don't you come back to the office and work there until time for your meeting? The freelancer desk is open." Since the magazine used quite a few free-lance writers, they maintained a work area for them in case it was needed.

"I've got phone calls to make."

"Use the conference room."

"Are you sure nobody is using it?"

"Tilda, you've made phone calls at that desk a dozen times, and you've used the conference room before, too. What's the problem?"

"It's different now. Jillian talking to me as if I was already under her thumb threw me, not to mention Nicole bossing me around."

"Sweetie, Jillian talks to everybody on the planet as if they're under her thumb, just like Nicole tries to boss everybody around. Nothing's changed."

Tilda weighed the unexpected awkwardness of working at the office versus the even greater awkwardness of trying to work at some random Wi-Fi zone versus the annoyance of wasting an hour making the trip to Malden and back. She concluded that Cooper was right.

Chapter 10

Workin' behind a plow, all you see is a mule's hind end. Workin' from the back of a horse, you can see across the country as far as your eye is good.
—*DON'T SQUAT WITH YER SPURS ON!* BY TEXAS BIX BENDER

IT took Tilda a while to put her finger on why the *Entertain Me!* office looked different that day. It was the same experience she had had when she moved to Malden. She'd been in the area plenty of times while dating a guy who lived there, and had become fairly familiar with the town. But once she made the decision to move there, suddenly the place looked strange. There was a shift in perspective between visiting a place and moving in.

For the first time, she was wondering what it would be like to come to work at *Entertain Me!* every day. It definitely wasn't the work environment she was used to.

The main office was a long, narrow room. Since Jillian was eternally feuding with managing editor Bryce, their desks were at opposite ends, facing each other. This maintained maximum distance between them and provided the opportunity to spy on one another.

One of the long walls between them was lined with windows that overlooked Newbury Street. That made it bright and cheery when the weather outside cooperated, and when it didn't, there were vertical blinds to conceal the gloom.

The other wall was covered with framed covers of some of the more successful issues of *Entertain Me!*

The middle of the room was filled with two rows of four desks each. Staff editors Nicole and Shannon sat nearest to Jillian. Then came Cooper's desk. The one next to him belonged to the rarely seen ad manager, who was usually out selling the ads that kept the magazine afloat. Then came desks for the just as rarely seen production editor and art director, who spent the majority of their time on the floor below in production. Of the two desks remaining, one was a catchall for stacks of magazines, press kits that nobody cared about, and unwanted swag from unpopular movies and TV shows. The other was the freelancer desk.

Tilda supposed it wasn't a bad place to work, really, but for the time being, she was glad to have a bit more privacy. Nobody was scheduled for the conference room for the rest of the afternoon, so she could use it to make phone calls in peace.

The first call was to check in with Detective Salvatore. Since she was going to have to talk to Nicole, she wanted to know the latest about Sandra's murder. Unfortunately, there was nothing he was willing to tell her, but at least he didn't need her to come in for more questions. Reluctantly, she asked about her belongings, apologizing for even thinking of them in the midst of a murder investigation, and got a mixed response. She could come by the station to pick up her camera, now that Lil had verified that it hadn't belonged to Sandra, but he wanted to hang on to her clothes for a little longer. Tilda decided that a shopping trip was definitely called for. She couldn't keep wearing Cooper's old coat and boots for the rest of the winter.

After she hung up, she tackled her assignments from the meeting. First she wrote up a brief announcement about the upcoming fund-raising event, keeping it vague while details were worked out, but making sure it was enticing. Then she sent it to the freelancer who maintained the

Entertain Me! Website and posted it herself on half a dozen Websites and blogs for TV Western fans. Given the way the Web worked, the news would be cross-posted to a ludicrous number of related sites before the day was out. Some of the posts might even be accurate.

Next was the job of getting more celebrities to attend to draw attention. Though she would have loved an excuse to talk to Rex Trailer, Jillian had said she had a connection for approaching him herself, so Tilda would have to content herself with getting in touch with some of the more easily found *Cowtown* guest stars instead. She went through her list, and picked the working soap opera actress to try first. Her show was filmed in New York, so she might be willing to make a quick trip to Boston.

Tilda had had some dealings with the publicist from *A Life Worth Living*, and it didn't take long for her to get Louise Silberblatt on the phone.

"Ms. Silberblatt?"

"Call me Louise," the woman said, her voice sounding just as sultry as it had when she'd played a voluptuous half-breed named Anna Silver Leaf on a *Cowtown* two-parter.

"Hi, I'm Tilda Harper, from *Entertain Me!*, and I'd like to discuss a couple of projects with you. First off, we're going to be interviewing some of the more illustrious guest stars from the show *Cowtown*, and of course your name came up."

"That's lovely, but I was only on the show for two episodes. I never even worked with the major cast members—I was only in flashback scenes, so we weren't on the same set."

"I realize that, but those episodes are consistently listed as two of the favorites by *Cowtown* fans."

"Really?"

"Absolutely. Would you be willing to set up a time to talk to me? And of course, I'll put in a plug for your long-running role on *A Life Worth Living*."

"Long-running, and underused," she said with a laugh. "But yes, I'd be happy to talk to you."

"Wonderful. The other projects are related. I don't know if you've heard, but there's a plan to build a *Cowtown*-themed resort in western Massachusetts."

"A Wild West town in New England? Don't tell me— the Ambrose brothers are behind it. The Cowboy Kings ride again!"

"That's it exactly. They want to know if you'd be interested in making promotional appearances once the resort is complete."

"Possibly, but anything like that would have to be cleared through the network."

Soap opera contracts could be restrictive, and few actors wanted to risk upsetting the source of their regular paychecks, particularly not an older, underused actress.

"I'll tell the Ambrose brothers, and let them take it from there. One other thing. As an early promotion, the *Cowtown* resort is sponsoring a fund-raising event for the Stickler Syndrome Foundation here in Boston. I'm afraid it's short notice, but they'd love it if you could come."

"Again, I'll have to clear it with the network. What's the date?"

Tilda told her.

"You weren't kidding about the short notice. Let me get back to you about that, Tilda. I'm tentatively planning a trip to Boston in the next week or so anyway."

"Maybe I could interview you then."

"That might work, though I may not be in the best mood for an interview. I'll be coming to town for a funeral."

"I'm so sorry," Tilda said awkwardly.

"Thank you. A very old friend of mine passed away. Unfortunately, I don't know when the funeral will be. There are some complications with the arrangements."

Tilda's story spider-sense started tingling. A funeral at an undetermined time, in Boston. Two such funerals would be a statistical anomaly. "Was your friend Sandra Sechrest?"

There was a long pause. "How on earth did you know that?"

"One of those odd coincidences. I interviewed Sandra a few months ago, and then again on the day she died."

"Oh?" the actress said, her friendly voice suddenly frosty. "Miss Harper, are you telling me the truth?"

"I beg your pardon?"

"Do you *really* want to interview me about *Cowtown*? Or did you have something else in mind?"

"What else would I have in mind? I mean, I'd be happy to talk to you about some of your other work, but—"

"What other work?"

Tilda desperately checked her notes to see if she'd listed any of the actress's other appearances. "Your stage work, your roles in early live TV?"

"What about my modeling?" she asked, still sounding suspicious.

Tilda had a split second to decide between slinging bullshit and telling the truth—she decided on truth, which at least had the advantage of being unexpected. "I apologize for my inadequate research, but I didn't realize you'd done any modeling. I'd be very happy to learn more."

"Oh, no, that was a long time ago," Louise said, her voice friendly again. "Nobody would be interested in a bunch of clothing ads, and for a local department store at that."

"Whatever you think," Tilda said, glad to have saved the interview even if she wasn't sure how it had nearly slipped away from her. They arranged to talk again later that week, when both Sandra's funeral arrangements and plans for the fund-raiser were more definite, and Tilda hung up, relieved but confused.

She drummed her fingers, trying to figure out what had just happened. As soon as Tilda mentioned Sandra, Louise had gotten suspicious and mentioned modeling. Could

Louise have been a pinup model herself? Sandra had said something about getting in touch with other models who didn't want their former career known. Could Louise Silberblatt have been one of those?

Tilda had to know more. She booted up her laptop and logged onto the office network to get to the Web. Her first stop was Louise's IMDb page, but there was nothing there about pinup work. Next she looked at Louise's personal Website, and while there was no mention of modeling, there were dates from New York stage work Louise had done early in her career. The years just happened to match the years when Sandra had done her modeling, which had also been in New York. That wasn't conclusive, of course.

Her next stop was Joe's Lost Pinups site. The bulletin board was still filled with posts about Sandra's murder, but as far as she could tell, no real information had been added. She did, however, pause at one exchange. Page-Boy was still sold on the idea of a serial killer with a taste for old pinups, and somebody named Pinup_King wrote in claiming that Page-Boy was correct, and that Pinup_King himself was the killer. He then went on to describe in nauseating detail how he'd killed several of the pinups Joe had on his list of missing models.

She didn't know about those other women, but Pinup_King's account of Sandra's death definitely didn't match what Tilda herself had seen, so she was fairly sure that he was just a sicko troll. Still, it wouldn't hurt to let Detective Salvatore check him out. The card he'd given her had included his e-mail address so she copied the descriptions of the murders, added the URL for the Website, and sent it to him. If nothing else, having the police question him might make Pinup_King think twice before airing his sick fantasies.

With that done, she checked Joe's most recent list of missing pinups. He was currently on the lookout for information about nearly fifty pinups, and each name was linked to a page of information about the missing woman, including a selection of pictures. Tilda looked through the names, hoping for an obvious clue like someone named Louise, but of course, that would have been too easy. All she could do was work her way down the list. So much for the glamour of entertainment reporting.

An hour later, she had five strong possibilities, women whose ages and appearance matched well enough for a closer look. Unfortunately, the screen on her laptop wasn't huge or of the best quality—buying a replacement was high on her wish list. Making a comparison would be a lot easier with hard copy, so she sent a current headshot of Louise and the best pictures of her five possibilities to the office printer.

Once she had the photos in hand, she carefully examined the first three, but it was obvious that none of those women could have aged into Louise Silberblatt without the aid of CGI technology. But the fourth . . . Tilda spent a solid minute looking at the picture of dignified Louise made up as the brunette matriarch of the Pearson family on *A Life Worth Living* side by side with the photo of a platinum-haired vixen with an impish smile holding her hands over her presumably bare breasts. Then Tilda smiled, her expression not unlike the vixen's. She was sure. At one time, Louise Silberblatt had been known as Fanny Divine.

Tilda basked in the glow of discovery for a moment—finding this kind of factoid was the best part of her job. Of course, she wasn't actually planning to use the information, though it would have violated no journalistic ethics to do so. Louise hadn't told her about it, let alone asked her to keep it off the record. But from her behavior on the phone, she clearly didn't want the story made public, and Tilda had no reason to go against the woman's wishes. Then she remembered Jillian's reaction at that morning's meeting, and knew she would expect Tilda to bring the information to her attention.

She drummed her fingers on the table again, trying to decide if she owed it to the magazine. A long moment later, she decided that she didn't. She was still a freelancer, which meant that the information had been found on her time, using her own resources. Okay, she had used the printer, but surely a dollar's worth of *Entertain Me!* supplies didn't compare with Louise's peace of mind.

Of course, she didn't know what she'd do if a similar situation came out once she was officially on the payroll, but she could wrestle with her conscience when the time came.

Tilda was about to tuck the pictures away in her bag when another thought occurred to her. What if Louise had another reason for wanting her connection with Sandra hidden? Or rather, what if her desire to keep her former career hidden was so strong that she'd go to great lengths to keep it secret? Was it important enough to her to want to kill?

Tilda shook her head as if contradicting someone. There was no way that old woman could have bludgeoned some-body to death. But she looked at Louise's head shot again. She was in good enough health to work full time, and in better physical shape than Sandra had been. How hard would it have been to crush her skull with the weapon that had been right there on the coffee table? One blow would have been enough to stun Sandra, and once she was down on the floor the rest would have been easy. The murder hadn't required a strong arm nearly so much as a strong stomach.

This was a little tougher to work out than journalistic ethics, or giving up an Internet troll. Now Tilda had to decide whether or not she needed to give Detective Salvatore another suspect to investigate.

Chapter 11

You could tell the girls who were shy about the size of their bosoms by the way they posed. Look at Bettie Page and Virginia Pure. They're always arching their backs, pushing out what they've got. I never had that problem. They didn't call me Sandy Sea *Chest* for nothing.

—SANDRA SECHREST, QUOTED IN "QUEEN OF THE PINUPS" BY TILDA HARPER, *NOT DEAD YET* MAGAZINE

BEFORE Tilda could make up her mind, Nicole appeared at the doorway. "I'm waiting."

Tilda glanced at her watch. It was twenty minutes after four, which explained Nicole's irritation. She suspected the other woman had been purposely delaying their interview, just to make a point, and had been expecting Tilda to get riled over the wait. Instead, she'd been so distracted she hadn't even noticed.

"Do you want to talk in here or at your desk?" Tilda asked.

"At my desk, of course," she snapped, and stood tapping her foot as Tilda packed away her laptop.

The pictures she'd printed were still on the table, and Nicole grabbed them. "You're looking at porno? Can you say 'inappropriate for the workplace'? Can you say 'sexual harassment suit'?"

Tilda snatched them back, and pushed them into her satchel. "Those are classic pinup photos, and are considerably less revealing than the photos of Madonna and Britney that *Entertain Me!* published in the last issue."

Nicole's eyes narrowed. "Did you print those here? I saw you getting something from the printer."

Tilda rolled her eyes. "You caught me. I printed six pictures—I must be punished. Beat me, hurt me, make me write bad checks."

Nicole sniffed. "I bet most of your checks are bad."

"Oh, snap!" Tilda held up the head shot of Louise. "This happens to be one of my interviewees for the *Cowtown* series."

"What about the porno?"

Tilda wasn't about to explain the connection to Louise. "I got bored waiting for our appointment, so I printed out some whacking material. Would you like copies?"

Nicole was momentarily speechless, so Tilda took the opportunity to walk past her and into the main room, where she demurely seated herself at the guest chair by Nicole's desk. A moment later, Nicole stomped over and threw herself down into her own chair.

"Let's get this over with," she snarled. "Tell me what happened with the dead stripper."

Tilda was sorely tempted to make Nicole drag it out of her, monosyllable by monosyllable, but with Jillian in the room, she decided to play nice. So she told Nicole everything from her interview with Sandra, to going back to retrieve her camera, to finding the body, to her dealings with the police. To her credit, Nicole kept it businesslike, asking only a few questions as they went along. It was only when Tilda was finished that she asked, "Did you get your camera back?"

"Not yet, but Detective Salvatore says I can come by the station any time to pick it up."

"Do you have pictures of the old woman on it?"

She nodded. "Cooper took a bunch while I was talking to her."

"What about when you went back?"

"What do you mean?"

"Didn't you take any pictures of the body?"

Still trying to keep it civil, Tilda swallowed several responses before saying, "Even if I'd thought of it, which I did not, I knew better than to touch anything in the apartment. It was a crime scene. Besides, the police would have wiped them off the memory card anyway."

"Doesn't your phone take pictures?"

That was it. "Are you shitting me? No, I did not take a fucking photograph of a dead woman!" She realized her voice was louder than it should have been, and that the other people in the office were looking at her. Nicole was smirking, and Tilda wanted to smack herself for playing into her hands. Nicole was obviously willing to do a lot to keep Tilda from getting a full-time job at *Entertain Me!*, and Tilda would be damned if she'd let her get away with it. She took a deep breath and in a normal tone of voice said, "Any other questions?"

Nicole looked at her notes, and Tilda hoped she was disappointed that Tilda hadn't continued her rampage. "I need some background on the stripper."

"Pinup model."

"Whatever. Give me what you've got on her."

"Of course. I'll be happy to send you my interview. Would you prefer it electronically or as hard copy?"

"Both. Send me your notes, too."

"I'm so very sorry, but I no longer have any notes. Hard disk problems." That part was a lie, of course, but there was no way Nicole could prove it, so she was going to have to eat it. Besides, she didn't need Tilda's notes—the article itself would give her more than enough background.

"What about pictures?"

"I'll be happy to include those, too." She gave Nicole her best Prozac-addict smile. "Is there anything else?"

"I'll let you know."

"Then I'll get that material for you right now."

"Use the freelancer desk this time."

"Certainly. Am I allowed to use the printer?"

Nicole just gave her a look.

Tilda, her plastic smile still in place, took her stuff to the open desk and unpacked her laptop once again in order to send Nicole everything she'd asked for, and then sent it to the printer, too. She was waiting for the printout when an instant message appeared on her screen.

Cooper: WTF?

Tilda: I hate her.

Cooper: Don't let her get to you.

Tilda: I hate her.

Cooper: She just wants to keep you from getting the job.

Tilda: I hate her.

Cooper: I'm sensing hostility.

Deciding to send a different kind of instant message, Tilda made sure that Cooper and nobody else was looking, then stuck her tongue out at him.

When the printer finished, Tilda retrieved the pages, carefully collated them, and paper clipped them together before placing then on Nicole's desk. "Here you go!" she said perkily.

Nicole just glanced at them, then looked back at her computer screen. "We're done."

"Okay. Bye now!" Tilda continued to grin like an idiot as she packed her things back away, relaxing only when her cell phone let loose with the theme from *The Addams Family*.

The caller's number was unfamiliar, but she answered it in case it was business-related. "Tilda Harper."

"Hi, this is Quentin Beaudine from this morning."

Raising her voice, she said, "Hi, Quentin! How nice to hear from you." She had to restrain herself from laughing when she saw Nicole's back stiffen.

"I was wondering if maybe you'd like to go to dinner this week."

"I'd love to go to dinner."

"Are you free tomorrow?"

"Tomorrow is perfect." They negotiated details, and she ended it with, "I'll be looking forward to seeing you again."

As she put the phone away, Cooper asked unnecessarily, "Was that the doctor you met today?" to make sure Nicole had gotten it.

Tilda's answering smile was entirely sincere.

Chapter 12

Cowtown not having a sheriff was an accident. We had a man in mind for the part, but he found himself another job right before we started shooting. So we wrote him out of the first script, meaning to cast the sheriff later. Then we got to thinking that it made sense for a town like that to be missing a regular lawman. That meant that the Cowtown Code was the law, and that made for some mighty good stories.

—HOYT AMBROSE, QUOTED IN *COWTOWN COMPANION*
BY RUBEN TIMMONS

TILDA wasn't looking forward to her next stop, a visit to the police station to get her camera back, but it was almost a nonevent. She explained to the officer at the front desk why she was there, he made a phone call, and after a ten-minute wait, another uniformed officer brought the camera out to her. There was no opportunity to tell Detective Salvatore about Louise Silberblatt, and she still wasn't sure if she wanted to or not.

Surely it couldn't hurt to check on Louise's alibi first. How hard could it be to find out if she'd been on set at *A Life Worth Living* the day Sandra was killed? Of course, a show filmed that day wouldn't be on air for another couple of weeks, going by normal industry standards, but maybe she could casually ask the people in makeup or costume. Backstage people always knew what was going on. She knew that if she discussed the idea with either June or Cooper, they'd chide her about playing Nancy Drew, but they'd never been murder suspects. Tilda was pretty sure she was in the clear, or the police would have questioned her further, but she hadn't enjoyed being suspected. It made her feel as if she was walking on eggshells, that anything she did or didn't do would make her look somehow guilty, no matter how innocent she was. She wasn't willing to put Louise through that unless she had more to go on than the facts that she'd known Sandra and had worked in the same job half a century ago.

Colleen was waiting for her when she got home, obviously dying to question her about something.

"Oh, good, you're back," she said. "There's a message for you on the machine. It sounds pretty important."

In other words, Colleen had already listened to it. Tilda knew she should have dumped the landline when she moved the last time. It was just that sometimes she forgot to charge her mobile. Besides, she'd had the same phone number for years, meaning that it was on her mother's and father's speed dials.

"Thanks," she said, trying to hide her exasperation, and pushed the Replay button on the answering machine.

"Miss Harper, this is Viola, the publicist from *A Life Worth Living.* I understand that you're hoping to meet with Louise Silberblatt, and I found out that Ms. Silberblatt will be in Boston later this week. Please give me a call and we'll arrange details." Tilda jotted down the number the woman read out.

"Louise Silberblatt the actress?" Colleen said. "Really?"

"That's right," Tilda said. "Sorry, but I need to return this call."

She was guessing that the police must have released Sandra's body so the funeral could be scheduled, which the publicist confirmed once she got her on the phone. They decided that Tilda would meet Louise after the funeral.

As soon as she was off the phone, Tilda checked her e-mail, and, as expected, there was a message from Lil with information about Sandra's funeral. The viewing had been set for the next night, with the funeral the morning after that. Both would be held at the Hawkins Funeral Home in Boston. Tilda considered rescheduling her date with Quentin, but decided she could skip the viewing— she'd already seen Sandra's body. After sending a response to Lil to let her know, she called a florist to arrange to have flowers delivered.

"Who died?" Colleen asked. Tilda turned to see her roommate standing outside her bedroom door.

"Eavesdropping much?"

"I wasn't eavesdropping," she said indignantly. "I just happened to be walking by and heard you say something about a funeral. Did somebody in your family die?"

There had to be a polite way to blow her off, but Tilda couldn't come up with one off the top of her head. "No, not a relative. A woman I interviewed died this week."

"That's awful. Car crash? Or was she sick?"

"She was murdered."

Colleen's eyes grew wider. "Murdered? Oh my gosh, I never knew anybody who was murdered! What happened? Was it a robbery or what?"

"The police don't know what it was. She was just this sweet old lady, and somebody killed her."

"Are you going to go to the funeral? Do you need company?"

"That's nice of you to ask," Tilda said dryly, "but the family is trying to keep it private."

"Oh, of course. The notoriety and all." A thought occurred to her. "Was it in the newspaper?"

"Yesterday's *Boston Globe* had a story—I don't know if there's been anything since. I don't think it got a lot of play." For a moment, she felt sorry for Sandra, whose death had caused so little stir. "The paper should still be in the recycling bin if you want to read it."

"I think I will. I've never been this close to a murder

before. It's kind of scary." As she went to hunt for the paper Colleen added, "I mean, why would anybody kill a sweet old lady?"

That was the sixty-four-thousand-dollar question. Why would anybody have wanted to kill Sandra?

Lil might still be a suspect, though Tilda didn't think Sandra could have had enough of an estate to be worth killing over. Then again, Sandra had confided that Lil had been out of a job for quite a while, which was why she'd been free to work on Sandra's Website. Maybe a comparatively small inheritance would look big enough if you'd been job hunting long enough. On the other hand, with Sandra no longer around to sign photos and interact with fans on her Website, sales and interest would probably dwindle, which would leave Lil out in the cold again.

If pressed, Tilda would also have to put Louise on the list of suspects, at least until she could find out differently.

Who else? Another family member? Another closeted pinup queen? The ever-popular crazed fan? A serial killer, or a totally random killer? Maybe she should go to Joe's Lost Pinups site, copy all the theories Page-Boy and the others had come up with, and put them in a spreadsheet? Or create a video blog about her suspicions and post it on YouTube? Hell, why not get "I'm a fan girl!" tattooed on her fanny divine and be done with it?

Or she could get some dinner, then get to work tracking down guest stars from *Cowtown*.

Dinner and work won the debate, and by bedtime, Tilda was feeling fairly well satisfied with herself. Mindful of the last few nights of bad dreams, she decided something soothing was called for, so she treated herself to a long, relaxing soak in the tub, with a mix disc of TV theme songs in the background. She was practically purring by the time she went to bed.

But she still dreamt about Sandra.

Chapter 13

It makes me feel wonderful that people still care for me . . .
that I have so many fans among young people, who write to
me and tell me I have been an inspiration.

—BETTIE PAGE

DESPITE her restless night, Tilda was determined to keep
her mind on business the next day, at least until time to
get ready for her dinner with Quentin. She tracked down
two *Cowtown* guest stars living in New England, and interviewed both by phone.

The first was William Sonnett, an actor who'd spent his
career acting in cowboy serials, cowboy movies, and cowboy shows on TV. There was something about his rugged
good looks that just screamed "cowboy," and he looked terrific in a ten-gallon hat and chaps. So what if he'd been born
in northern Maine, where he'd returned once he retired?

He was pleased as punch to be remembered for his role
as the cowboy who'd stolen Arabella's heart, only to die
in an Indian attack while shielding a baby with his body.
He'd had one of the longest death scenes on TV up until
that of Mr. Roarke's gal pal on *Fantasy Island*, and could
still recite it. Sonnett said he'd be happy to do promotional
work for the *Cowtown* resort once the weather improved,
but would have to pass on the fund-raiser at the Hillside.

Lucas McCain, who'd played a visiting preacher, was
in Connecticut, and was more than willing to come for

the fund-raiser and participate in promotion for the resort. Tilda said she'd let the Ambrose brothers know so they could arrange details, and wanted to go on with the interview. McCain, on the other hand, wanted to talk about hotel accommodations, per diem payments, and limos. It took the better part of an hour to convince him that she wasn't playing hardball, lowball, or even bocce ball—all she wanted to do was ask him some questions about his experiences on the set of *Cowtown*.

Unfortunately, when she finally got to the interview part, it didn't take long because he remembered almost nothing: not the storyline, his costars, or even the character he'd played. All she could do was get some biographical information and a few anecdotes about working in Hollywood in the 1950s and 1960s. She was relieved to finally get him off of the phone.

With the interviews fresh in her mind, Tilda went ahead and wrote them up. Jillian had told her to keep them short and snappy, only a couple of thousand words each. It was hard to keep the William Sonnett interview to that limit, and hard to stretch Lucas McCain's enough, but two hours later, she had them finished.

She was extremely glad that she'd been so productive when the phone rang. It was Nicole, demanding to know what her status was. It was a pleasure to tell her that she'd finished two articles already, and had an interview set for the next day. It was an even greater pleasure to tell her that she was sorry she couldn't talk longer because she had to get ready for her date with Quentin.

Chapter 14

If you're in doubt about whether to kiss somebody, give 'em the benefit of the doubt.

—*JUST ONE FOOL THING AFTER ANOTHER*
BY GLADIOLA MONTANA AND TEXAS BIX BENDER

TILDA preferred to arrange her own transportation to a first date in case the evening went poorly, and usually explained it by saying her apartment was too far off the beaten path. She was glad she'd done that for her dinner with Quentin because it meant Colleen wouldn't have a chance to interrogate him. Instead she drove her own car to Not Your Average Joe's in Burlington.

Like her decision to drive herself, the restaurant had been a conservative choice. It had plenty of variety on the menu and a good bar, and though it was a step above the average chain restaurant, it wasn't so expensive that a date might decide he was owed added value for paying for dinner. As Tilda parked and looked around to see if Quentin had arrived, she reflected that if she picked her roommates with the care she took on a first date, she'd probably make it to a second lease without having to switch.

Quentin was waiting for her in the restaurant, which was a good sign. The kiss on the cheek he gave her was another.

"You look particularly nice tonight," he said.

"Thank you," Tilda said, hoping to sound as if she always

wore black velvet slacks with a royal blue silk blouse, and just a bit of bling. "You're looking pretty spiffy yourself." She was glad to see that he wasn't in the outdated suit, but was instead wearing a nice pair of khaki slacks with a navy blue blazer over a softer blue sweater.

Quentin said, "I put our name in when I got here, so we shouldn't have to wait very long."

A few minutes later, they were seated, and began the time-honored rituals of a first date. First came the discussion of the menu. The drink choice provided the opportunity to see if Quentin was a drinker, a wine snob, a teetotaler, or in recovery. He ordered a beer, which was certainly in the zone, while Tilda went for a margarita. Next came an appetizer, which they agreed on with comparative ease. Finally the main course, and Tilda noticed that he avoided dishes with garlic. That could mean he didn't like garlic or it could mean he was trying to keep his breath pleasant for later activities. She did the same, and it wasn't because she didn't like garlic.

With that hurdle passed, they moved on to getting-to-know-you questions: educational backgrounds, favorite TV shows, sports affiliations, political leanings, and delicate references to marital status. Quentin was, of course, a doctor, but though he had a Ph.D. as well as an MD, he didn't sneer at Tilda's lowly BA. They both enjoyed *Mythbusters!*, *Battlestar Galactica*, and *The Daily Show*, and though Quentin hadn't watched *True Blood*, he said it sounded good. As loyal metro-Bostonians, they rooted for the Sox and the Patriots, but it wasn't a serious addiction for either. Both voted to the Left, and neither had been married.

By the time their food arrived, they'd moved past the preliminaries and were actually having a conversation.

It was, in short, a promising beginning.

Midway through the meal, Tilda said, "Did you always intend to go into research rather than practice medicine?"

"At first, I was just planning to be a doctor of some description. My family is big into doctors—by big, I mean that I've got uncles and cousins working in hospitals all up and down the East Coast. I think we've got seven in New York City alone. Then my grandmother died of cancer when I was thirteen, even though she had the best medical care available. That's when I realized that care wasn't enough—there has to be better science behind it. So I decided on research. I started out in genetics, looking for cancer warning signs, but got sidetracked into Stickler Syndrome. It needs investigation, but isn't the political minefield that cancer research can be, so I can concentrate on the work."

Another man might have milked the pathos, or played up the nobility, but Quentin kept it refreshingly matter-of-fact.

"How about you?" he asked. "Was journalism your first choice?"

"Thank you for calling it journalism," she said with a grin, "but I usually just go with 'entertainment reporting.' Anyway, my first ambition was actually to be a cowgirl."

"Is that right?"

She nodded. "I took it very seriously. I read up on the types of cows and Indian tribes, and taught myself to successfully lasso my sister, as long as she was sitting still. Somehow I missed out on the fact that the cowboy business wasn't exactly a growth industry."

"How old were you?"

"Seven."

He nodded sagely. "What made you reconsider?"

"It was what my family likes to refer to as 'the horse incident.' The day after my eighth birthday party—we had a cowgirl theme, of course—my parents took me for my first horseback riding lesson. The horse and I did not get along, and the horse expressed her dislike by removing me from her back, repeatedly. But I was determined. The first four times, I got right back up in the saddle, the way a true cowgirl is supposed to. The fifth time, that damned horse threw me onto a pile of fresh dung."

He tried not to laugh, but Tilda couldn't blame him for failing.

She continued. "After that, I weighed other options, but hadn't come to a definite conclusion before starting college. I was majoring in communications, but I was pretty vague about what I was going to do with it. You can imagine how that thrilled my parents. To make them happy, and to try to make up my own mind, I signed up for every internship that fell in the right area: public information office, alumni magazine, college paper, corporate newsletter, radio program. By the time I graduated, I had stacks of clippings, but still wasn't sure what to do with them or myself, and the job market was tight. But I'd made an awful lot of contacts with all those internships, so while I was sending out resumes, I started taking freelance jobs. I'd always liked TV and movie trivia, so it's no surprise that I liked the entertainment work the best, especially the where-are-they-now stuff. Before I knew it, I was making a living as a freelancer. So I tore up my resume and never looked back. The irony is that Jillian at *Entertain Me!* has tentatively offered me a full-time job."

"Congratulations! Shall we drink to it?"

"Thank you," Tilda said, raising her glass to clink against his. "Maybe I'll be able to stay on this particular horse."

"And out of the dung!"

They both decided against dessert, and once the check was paid it was time for the next first-date hurdle: what to do next. Since it was a weeknight and they both had to work the next day, it was too late to go to a movie, and a little early in the relationship for your-place-or-mine, so they decided to wander through Borders bookstore, which was in the same shopping center as the restaurant. Tilda noted that while Quentin had zero interest in graphic novels, science fiction, and urban fantasy, at least he didn't turn up his nose at them. And if his interest in political biography and history books didn't ring her chimes, neither was it a warning bell. They sat in the store's coffee bar to discuss books for a while, but then called it a night. Quentin promised to call her, and after his good-night kiss, Tilda was sure he meant it. She was very glad they'd skipped the garlic.

Chapter 15

I like being a pinup girl, there's nothing wrong with it.
——Jayne Mansfield

NOT only was Tilda's date with Quentin a pleasure, she only had one bad dream that night, and it was quiet enough that she didn't wake Colleen. She got back to sleep easily, slept through the rest of the night, and woke up rested and refreshed. She was also eager to continue rounding up *Cowtown* guest stars, but unfortunately, she had Sandra's funeral to attend at ten. She recycled the black velvet pants from the previous night, and added a dark red sweater and a black blazer. By rights, she should have carried a nice pocketbook instead of her usual leather satchel, but she would never have been able to fit her pad, pen, laptop, and camera into her good bag. So she went with the satchel, adding a good-but-roomy bag to her mental shopping list. As she once again shrugged into Cooper's hand-me-down parka, she dropped her friend a quick e-mail to ask if he was available to do some shopping that afternoon. Then it was time to hit the subway to get to the funeral.

Sandra's funeral was sparsely attended, and Tilda wondered if it was because Sandra had been murdered or in spite of it. Given her distant relationship with Sandra, she took a seat near the back of the chapel, which gave her a chance to watch people as they arrived.

Most of the mourners were strangers, of course, but she

did see Lil, and assumed the people with her were family members. One woman looked quite a bit like Sandra had when younger, albeit more thoroughly clothed.

When Louise Silberblatt came in, dressed impeccably in a black Chanel suit, she actually had to politely put off a couple of women who recognized her as Gwendolyn Pearson from *A Life Worth Living*. Tilda didn't introduce herself then, deciding it would be more appropriate to wait until they met for their interview.

Tilda also saw Detective Salvatore sitting with a woman, presumably another cop, she thought she remembered seeing at Sandra's apartment the night of the murder. She didn't know if it was cop instinct or just coincidence that he turned toward her just as she was looking in his direction, and she hurriedly looked the other way. Damn it, why did she feel so guilty around him? She hadn't killed Sandra, and she didn't know who had. Then she glanced back over at Louise, and remembered one piece of information she could be passing on to him. Maybe that was the source of her guilt. She hoped his cop instincts weren't good enough for him to figure out that she might know something.

The service started, and Tilda was relieved to have something else to occupy her mind, even if it was a relentlessly standard funeral. A pastor read appropriate Bible verses about loss and rebirth in a better place, one family member read a lengthy eulogy from a crumpled piece of paper, a friend gave a short one from memory, and the organist played what were probably two of Sandra's favorite songs. She was sure it was reasonably comforting, but such a vanilla service didn't match the woman she'd known, albeit briefly. Then again, would people really want a wildly original and flamboyant funeral?

Tilda knew from Lil's e-mail that the body was to be cremated, so there would be no burial service. The family formed a receiving line in the hall just outside the chapel, and Tilda went to pay her respects. Lil seemed pleased that she'd come, but when she introduced her to the other relatives, Tilda could see them stiffen as it registered that she was the one who'd found Sandra's body. If there was a protocol for such a situation, she'd never heard it, so she repeated some of the phrases her mother used at funerals. "I'm very sorry for your loss. She was such a genuine person." Lil, seeming to miss the awkward undertones, invited her to join the family at a nearby restaurant, but Tilda pled a previous engagement and ducked into the ladies' room to hide. She'd have left the funeral home entirely if she hadn't arranged to meet Louise outside, and when somebody started to come in, she fled into a stall to take care of the obvious physical need.

She peered through the cracks around the edges of the stall's metal door, and though she couldn't see the woman's face, she could tell that it wasn't one of Sandra's family members, which was a relief. A moment later the door opened again, and this time Tilda recognized Louise, but didn't think it would be entirely professional for her to call out to the woman while sitting on a toilet.

Still she couldn't resist spying on her through those cracks.

The two women nodded at each other, then inspected themselves in the mirror and pulled out compacts and other equipment to effect repairs. Tilda could see Louise's face clearly, and noticed when the actress started to study the other woman.

"Excuse me," Louise said. "Have we met?"

"I don't think so," the other woman replied.

The funny thing was that though Tilda couldn't see her, the woman's voice sounded familiar.

Louise shook her head slowly, as if trying to remember. "You remind me of someone."

The other woman hurriedly finished with her hair, and started stuffing things into her bag.

Then Louise snapped her fingers. "Glory! Morning Glory!"

The other woman froze. "I don't know what you're talking about."

"Glory, don't you remember me? I'm—"

"My name isn't Glory." The woman reached for the door, and despite her best efforts, Tilda couldn't see her face. All she could do was sit and fume that the woman hadn't hung around long enough for Louise to finish her sentence.

For a moment Louise stared after the woman she had called Glory. Then she went back to work on her makeup. After what seemed an inordinate length of time, but what was probably standard preparation for an actress about to be interviewed, she finished and left. Tilda gave her a few minutes before coming out of the stall, checked her own face, and decided it was ok as it was.

The funeral home had emptied of mourners by the time she came out, which was fine with Tilda. Louise was looking the other way, so she maneuvered around to look as if she were coming from any direction other than the bathroom, and approached her.

"Ms. Silberblatt? I'm Tilda Harper."

"Tilda, lovely to meet you. I was afraid I'd missed you."

"I had to take a call," she said to explain her absence. "Are you ready to go?"

"Yes, let's." As they stepped outside, Louise said, "At my age, I'm becoming uncomfortably familiar with funerals, but I don't enjoy them."

"It's not my favorite thing to do either," Tilda admitted. She saw an empty cab coming, threw up her hand to hail it, then stepped out of range of the splash as it pulled up in the middle of an icy puddle. She and Louise had already arranged to conduct the interview at the Colonnade Hotel where Louise was staying, and during the cab ride they limited their conversation to the inevitable discussion of Boston weather. Louise's suite was smaller than the Ambrose brothers' at the Park Plaza, but the baby grand piano gave it a homey touch.

After they unwrapped themselves from their winter wear and Louise offered a drink from the minibar, which Tilda gladly accepted, they settled on the couch.

"So, Tilda, how did you say you knew Sandra?" Louise asked carefully.

"I'd interviewed her. Did you know she used to be a pinup model?"

"Oh yes," Louise said with a tolerant smile. "I was in New York doing stage work back then, and some friends of mine worked with her and introduced us. It wasn't unusual for actresses to use modeling as a stepping stone."

"I understand Bettie Page tried to do that."

"Bettie wasn't much of an actress," she said, waving a hand dismissively. Then, as if afraid she'd revealed too much, she added, "I ran into her at a couple of auditions."

"Really?" Tilda said. "How about Sandra?"

"No, Sandra was no actress, either, but at least she knew it. She actually seemed to enjoy the modeling."

"She certainly spoke of it fondly." Since it was pretty obvious that Louise wasn't going to break down and confess her pinup past, Tilda moved on to Louise's stint on *Cowtown*. It turned into an interesting interview.

The two-part episode on which she'd appeared had been early on in the show's run, meaning that the Ambrose brothers were still feeling their way, and it was Louise's first television role, which meant that she wasn't familiar with the differences between working onstage and working on camera. Plus the horses used for the shoot hadn't been properly trained, which made for some unintentionally exciting moments. It must have been frightening at the time, but the way Louise told it had Tilda in stitches.

"No wonder you looked so convincingly scared during the runaway stagecoach scene."

Louise laughed. "I was petrified. I assure you that I wasn't that good an actress!"

From that, they moved on to Louise's work at *A Life Worth Living*, and once again she lamented the lack of screen time. "I've been with the show forever, and they'll never let me go completely, but all the big stories are about the young ones." She sighed. "Some weeks I get no work at all, and when I do, it's not exactly challenging. Like earlier this week."

"Oh?"

"We've been shooting Tanya and Tony's wedding, and you probably know what that's like. Endless days, extras, costume problems, continuity issues, musicians. And of course Tanya's daughter Arianna had to be flower girl, which complicated it further, because we had to work around the restrictions for child actors. I had to be on set twelve hours a day, but only had half a page of lines all week long. The rest of the time I was looking proud and pleased, or teary, or gently amused by Arianna's antics." In rapid succession, she demonstrated the three expressions.

Tilda couldn't help but laugh again. Maybe Bettie Page couldn't act, but Louise sure could.

"Thank goodness we wrapped up the nuptials yesterday." Louise checked her watch, and politely asked, "Was there anything else you wanted to ask?"

Tilda looked back over her notes. "Just one other thing. You said *Cowtown* was your first TV role. Can you tell me how that happened?"

"What do you mean?" Louise responded a trifle stiffly.

"Did you have an agent, or did the Ambrose brothers see you onstage or—"

The woman's eyes narrowed. "You know, don't you?"

"I beg your pardon?"

"You know about the modeling."

Tilda thought about lying, but since she wasn't even as good an actress as Bettie Page, decided against it. "I suspected. Were you Fanny Divine?"

Louise shuddered. "That awful name. Though I suppose it did its job, since nobody but you has ever made the connection."

"Sandra had told me that she'd been in touch with some of the other pinup models she knew, but that they were trying to stay under the radar."

"Actually, Sandra and I had been in touch since long before the Website venture. We've exchanged Christmas cards for years, and had visited one another a few times. But I never thought she'd tell anybody."

"Oh, she didn't give you away," Tilda said, "even when I asked about other models. It's just that I was curious after the way you reacted when I asked you about Sandra, so I checked out pinup models until I found your picture. But don't worry. I'm not going to use this in the article or even tell anybody if you don't want me to. It's completely off the record."

"Do you mean that?"

"Absolutely." After all, she didn't have an assignment— she was only being nosy, so she made a show of putting away her pad and pen.

Louise let out a deep breath. "Thank you."

"But what does the pinup stuff have to do with you working on *Cowtown*?"

She smiled ruefully. "That's how I got the job. Tucker said that he'd seen the pinup photos, and then recognized me when my agent sent in my head shot, but he was discreet about it. I think he was hoping I would be grateful enough to show my appreciation. Physically, I mean."

"How sleazy is that?"

"It wasn't that bad, actually. He hired me even after I made it plain that I wasn't going to sleep with him. And I can't really blame him for thinking I would be willing, given those pictures." She shuddered again. "Have you seen them?"

"A few, but honestly, I find them pretty mild by today's standards."

"I suppose, but I hated doing that kind of work."

"Then why did you do it?"

"Money, of course. I wanted to be an actress, but I had to have enough to live on and pay for acting classes while still having time for auditions. I'd pose for a few hours a week, and get as much as I would in a forty-hour-a-week desk job. But as soon as I got my first decent acting role, I quit modeling for good."

"Nobody ever connected Louise Silberblatt with Fanny Divine?"

"Never, and I worked hard to keep it that way. When I was Fanny, I wore a wig, and I knew all kinds of makeup tricks to make myself look different. It was just another kind of acting, really. I pretended to be the kind of woman who would allow men to take those kind of pictures."

"Amazing. Did you know there are Websites dedicated to trying to find you guys?"

"For God's sake, why?"

"People love a mystery—they're still coming up with theories about Bettie Page."

"Bettie's dead!"

"Some people want to believe she's still out there."

"But why would anybody care about Fanny Divine? I wasn't famous, not like Bettie or even Sandy. I never made any films, or posed for magazines, just for the camera clubs. I only recently realized that any of those pictures were still around, let alone online. Nobody in my day ever dreamed of anything like the Web."

"I suppose not. Would it be that bad if the story came out?"

"Tilda, my career would have been ruined if anybody in the industry had known about those pictures. Nobody would have taken me seriously as an actress. Other soap actresses complain that they aren't respected, but they have no idea what a former pinup had to endure. Look at Bettie. Did you see that movie about her? *The Notorious Bettie*

Page. That's what they called her. She could have been another Meryl Streep, and they would only have remembered her cheesecake and bondage photos."

"I can understand your keeping things quiet then, but now? Those pictures may have been shocking at the time, but they're less revealing than what plenty of teenage girls post on MySpace—now they're even sending nude pictures of themselves via their phones. In fact . . ." Tilda thought for a minute, then for a minute more. "Okay, I know people must give you lame plot ideas all the time, but I'm going to run this past you anyway. You've heard of sexting, right?"

"Of course."

"And you know that girls are starting to realize there are repercussions if those photos make it onto the Internet, which they always do."

"I could have told them that. The dirtier a photo is, the more likely it is to stay around."

"Exactly. You could have told them that. So why couldn't your character?"

"What do you mean?"

"Suggest a sexting plot to your writers, along with a nice storyline for you. It would make a terrific contrast—their secrets on the Web and your character's hidden past. And they wouldn't have to mock up your photos—they could use your real pinup work. Revealing the fact that you actually did that kind of work would make terrific publicity for the show and for you."

Louise was speechless for a moment, and when she did speak, all she said was, "Oh, my!" But her eyes were gleaming at the prospect.

"Just a thought," Tilda said, "but if you ever decide you want to come out of the darkroom, so to speak, I sure would appreciate it if you'd let me know."

"I certainly will," Louise said. "Thank you, Tilda."

Tilda didn't know if anything would come of the notion, but if it did happen, she'd get one hell of a story. And even better, she knew for sure that Louise hadn't killed Sandra. She knew enough about soap opera wedding shoots to know that there was no way Louise could have snuck away long enough to get to Boston and back, even if she'd felt that strongly about keeping her past in the past.

Chapter 16

I never kept up with the fashions. I believed in wearing what
I thought looked good on me.

—BETTIE PAGE

TILDA didn't even try to guess what the windchill was
when she stepped out of the Colonnade and onto Hun-
tington Avenue, but she knew it was obscenely cold. She
stayed on the street just long enough to cross over and go
into the Prudential Center Mall. Then she called Cooper
to see if he'd gotten her message about shopping, and if
he was willing to get lunch first. He had and he was, and
they arranged to meet at the mall food court. Though they
usually preferred eating at California Pizza Kitchen, given
what had happened the last time they ate there, neither of
them was eager to repeat the experience. Besides, Tilda
reasoned, a quick bite at the food court would give them
more time to look at clothes.

An hour and a half later, she wished they'd dined so
leisurely that there would have been no time at all for the
stores. It wasn't that Cooper wasn't an excellent companion
for shopping. He had a gift for putting together outfits, and
thanks to a side gig editing copy for a fashion magazine,
knew what was in style, what was coming in, and what was
going out. Plus he seemed to be able to sniff out bargains.
But this time, he was a bit overwhelming. Apparently he'd

been saving up advice ever since hearing that she might be taking a position at *Entertain Me!*

"This is exactly what you need for daily office wear," he proclaimed, holding up a wool suit at Saks.

"The skirt is too short."

"You look good in short skirts."

She checked the price tag. "Shit, Cooper, do you know how many stories I'd have to sell to buy this?"

"One, it's an investment. Two, you're not going to buy it now. You're going to come on a sale day and get it for 20 percent off."

At Ann Taylor, he put a blouse and pants together. "This would be stunning on you."

"Should I try them on?" she said.

"Not until the clearance sale next week. Take a picture with your phone, and don't forget."

"Can I buy *anything* today?"

He considered the matter. "January . . . Boots will be on sale."

"I can get a pair of Doc Martens at Newbury Comics."

"Please tell me you're kidding."

The boots she let him talk her into buying at Lord and Taylor were nearly as comfortable as the boots the police still had, and considerably less militant. Plus they were at such a deep discount that she would probably still be able to afford new Doc Martens, even if Cooper wouldn't let her wear them to the office.

They agreed to wait on a handbag until Cooper had a sense for the spring styles, because neither of them were loving the winter stuff, but they had no luck at all with coats. Since it was the dead of winter, naturally most of the stores were showing spring jackets and cruise wear.

Finally Cooper admitted defeat, albeit temporarily. "I've got to get back to the office," he said, "but I'm going to call my connection at Marshalls. There was a coat there last week that would be perfect, but there's no reason to go all the way down there if it's already gone."

"You have a connection at Marshalls?"

"It's a discount store within walking distance of the office—of course I have a connection. Where are you heading?"

"Home?"

"Why don't you come back with me until I get a chance to call Marshalls?"

"Sure, why not?" Since she had her laptop with her, she could write up the interview with Louise while it was fresh in her mind. It turned out to be a good choice. When they arrived back at *Entertain Me!* headquarters, Nicole snapped, "Tilda, don't you ever check your e-mail?"

"They've got this amazing new device for sending messages," Tilda retorted. "It's called a telephone." She pulled hers out. "Now if you'd called my phone, I would have a message and would therefore be able to find out what you want." She pretended to check. "But lo and behold, there are no messages."

Nicole gave her what was doubtless intended to be a withering look. "I understand that you can't afford an iPhone, but can't you at least scratch up enough to pay for a low-end BlackBerry? I mean, get with the program!"

That hit a nerve, since Tilda had been trying to scratch up enough to pay for an iPhone, not that she was going to admit that to Nicole. "You may not realize it, but an iPhone is also a type of telephone. All you have to do is—"

"Whatever," Nicole said, waving it aside. "The Ambrose brothers are coming to meet with Jillian this afternoon, and they want to see what you've done so far."

"I thought my deadline was—"

"Did I ask about your deadline? They want to make sure they like what you're doing before any time is wasted, if that's okay with you."

Tilda looked for Jillian, but unfortunately her chair was empty. Nicole might be jerking her chain, but it was barely possible that Jillian really wanted the articles right away. "No problem. I've got two interviews written up already, and I can do a quick draft of a third right now."

"I suppose that will have to do, if that's all you've got."

She stepped away before Tilda could come up with a snappy comeback, which was just as well, since Tilda was out of snappy comebacks.

Cooper whispered, "Don't let her get to you."

"How do you stand working with her every day?" Tilda wanted to know.

"By not letting her get to me!"

It didn't take long for Tilda to get herself situated so she could print up the interviews with William Sonnett and Lucas McCain. Then she went to work on the story about Louise Silberblatt, consulting her notes and online databases as needed. She was halfway through a rough draft when Cooper sent her an IM.

Cooper: My connection has the coat put aside! Sneak out with me to get it.

Tilda: Can't. Have to finish article. Nicole is watching.

She looked up, and sure enough, Nicole was giving her the evil eye. Tilda gave her a wide but slightly crazed smile, which convinced the redhead to transfer her attention elsewhere.

Cooper: My connection goes off duty in an hour, and will be off all weekend. Must buy from her to get the discount.

Tilda: Have to do without.

Cooper: Hell, no! Give me your credit card and I'll go get it.

Tilda: Your connection lets you forge signatures?

Cooper: Yes.

Tilda: Can I meet her?

Cooper: No.

Tilda decided that she needed to get a connection of her own, but until she found one, she'd have to rely on Cooper's.

Tilda: I'll hide the card in a paper airplane and fly it to you.

Cooper: Smart ass. Just get it out.

She slipped the card out of her wallet and held it in her lap while continuing to work, waiting to see what Cooper had planned.

A few minutes later, he stood and stretched. "I better get going if I'm going to make it to the dentist's office."

"I don't remember you saying anything about a dentist appointment," Nicole said.

"Didn't Jillian tell you? The note I gave her must be on her desk somewhere." Of course, he knew Nicole wouldn't dare touch anything on Jillian's desk. The one time she had, Jillian had nearly fired her.

Nicole looked suspicious, but since Cooper was caught up with his work, there really wasn't anything she could complain about. When he walked by Tilda's desk on his way to the door, he managed to knock some of her papers onto the floor, and as he helped her pick them up, he somehow ended up with her credit card in his pocket. After making sure Nicole wasn't watching, he gave Tilda a wink and left.

With Cooper gone, Tilda could concentrate on finishing the interview with Louise. A couple of drafts later, she was ready to print it out. Despite Nicole's riding her, Jillian and the Ambrose brothers hadn't shown up yet, and she wasn't sure if they would need to see her or not. Knowing what the answer would be if she asked Nicole, she didn't bother. Instead she checked e-mail, and when she found responses from more *Cowtown* guest stars, sent off notes suggesting times over the next couple of days when they could conduct phone interviews.

That done, she really didn't have anything to do but wait for Cooper to let her know about the amazing wonder coat, but she didn't want to look as if she was killing time, even though that's what she was doing. Her first time killer was to print out a batch of photos of the guest stars she'd interviewed or had scheduled to interview. This time she was smug that she had a legitimate reason to use the *Entertain Me!* printer, which was two generations newer than hers at home. But once she had slid those into one of the cardboard photo mailers the magazine kept handy she was out of ideas.

Not surprisingly, she started thinking about Sandra's murder again, and of course, the funeral. That led to speculation about the woman Louise had encountered in the bathroom, the one who'd denied knowing the actress. What had Louise called her? Morning Glory, which sounded like another nom du pinup.

She hit the Web to visit Joe's Lost Pinups site one more time. There was no Morning Glory on the list of missing pinup queens, but when Tilda searched the site more thoroughly, she found Glory's name on a list of dead models. Somebody had e-mailed Joe the previous year to let him know. Had Louise been mistaken? That would certainly explain why the woman in the bathroom had denied being Glory.

Tilda was curious enough to do a little more hunting, and found a few photos of Morning Glory that had been posted online. Glory had been blond with big brown eyes that gave her an innocent look despite her decidedly less-than-innocent poses and outfits. Tilda was about to shut down the screen when suddenly Nicole appeared next to her.

"Are you looking at that shit again?" she asked in a voice that was just short of yelling. "Didn't we discuss this?"

"Yes we did," Tilda said, "which is why you should remember that it's research."

"Research? Do you think I don't know porno when I see it?"

Naturally, Jillian, the Ambrose brothers, and Cynthia Barth picked that very moment to walk into the office, and of course, Tilda's laptop was angled perfectly for the foursome to get a glimpse of what was displayed.

Jillian looked annoyed, and the Ambrose brothers looked surprised, but Miss Barth's expression was the scary one. Her mouth was a perfect *O*, and her eyes were wide with shock. Her brown eyes. Her big brown eyes.

Tilda twisted around to look at the woman on her screen, then turned back to stare at Miss Barth. Now she knew why the voice of the woman in the funeral home bathroom had sounded familiar. Morning Glory was Cynthia Barth.

Chapter 17

The girls willing to work nude could also get regular work from amateur photo clubs and art schools, and maybe a day's work from one of the photographers who sold his work to calendar companies. The decision, however, even to appear nude once on a calendar, meant the end to a serious career on Broadway or in films.

—*BETTIE PAGE RULES!* BY JIM SILKE

AFTERWARD, Tilda could have kicked herself for being so damned obvious. Miss Barth's eyes darted from her computer screen to her face, and of course the woman realized right away what Tilda had discovered. Knowing it was too little, too late, Tilda closed the file with the photo that had revealed so much more than freckled skin.

Nicole must have been satisfied with the effect she'd had because she went back to her own desk, but Tilda could see her smirking. She'd probably known Jillian and the others were on their way in before she put on her "shocked and disgusted" act, which was no doubt part of her campaign to keep Tilda from getting hired.

Tilda opened a word processing file, and pretended to refer to her notepad as she typed random sentences. When she heard Jillian and the others going into the conference room, she tried to decide if it would be possible for her to get out of the office unseen. She was going to give them ten minutes to get thoroughly involved in whatever it was they were doing, then sneak out as best she could.

Unfortunately, at the ninth minute Jillian stepped back out long enough to say, "Nicole, Tilda, can you join us?"

"Sure," Tilda said, and picked up her pad, a pen, and the interviews she'd printed, oddly relieved. Jillian might intend to chase her out of *Entertain Me!*, but she was far too much of a professional to do so in front of company. Nicole pushed by to get into the conference room ahead of her.

The Ambrose brothers smiled as Tilda came in, but Miss Barth was looking pointedly elsewhere. Again, Tilda was relieved. The last thing she wanted was the older woman glaring at her while she was trying to keep her mind on business.

"Tilda, what's your status on guests for the fund-raiser?" Jillian asked. "Rex Trailer can't make it, so we need celebrity wattage."

"Lucas McCain is willing, if you want him," she said, "but apparently he's forgotten even being on the show."

"Lucas always did hit the firewater a bit too much," Tucker said. "Never knew anybody else who could act so well when blind drunk."

"He's also pretty demanding when it comes to perks and per diem. I explained it was for charity, but . . ." She shrugged. "Here's a draft of the interview with him, if that will help you decide." She handed it to Jillian, who skimmed it and passed it to Hoyt. "William Sonnett doesn't travel in the winter," she said, "and Louise Silberblatt is going to check, but she thinks she has a previous commitment." She thought she saw Miss Barth flinch at that last name, but ignored it, and gave Jillian the other interviews. "I've got feelers out for a few more, but it is short notice, and we're talking about old people."

"Ahem," Jillian said, but Tucker just laughed.

"She's right. We are pretty damned old. Pardon my French, Miss Barth. Keep at it, little lady. There must be a couple of geezers willing to make the trip."

"Will do."

Jillian handed the other two interviews to Hoyt and said, "These look good. Have you got pictures to go with them?"

"Do you want 'then' or 'now'?"

"Get both, and we'll play with layout."

Tilda nodded. She was used to having to produce at least twice as much material as Jillian ever used.

"One other thing," Hoyt said. "Have you and Miss Barth set up a time to talk?"

Both Tilda and Miss Barth froze, but Tilda thawed out first. "Not yet. Miss Barth, why don't you check your schedule for availability, and we'll go from there?"

The woman nodded, still not looking directly at her.

"Keep us up-to-date on status," Jillian said, and Tilda was happy to take the hint and get the hell out of Dodge.

It only took her a minute to pack up her things. The packet of photos was so big she ended up shoving it into an outside pocket of her satchel, hoping it wouldn't fall out. Then she suited up and headed for the elevator. When she hit the ground floor, she called Cooper on her cell.

"I got it!" he said triumphantly when he answered. "You are going to love it, love it, love it."

"How much do I love it? In dollars?"

He named a figure that really wasn't that bad.

"Excellent. But what's taking you so long?"

"I had to accessorize, didn't I? You aren't going to wear that skull hat with this coat."

"How much do I love the accessories?"

"Trust me. All bargains. Just wait until you see everything."

"I'm ready now. Where are you?"

"Hustling down Boylston. You?"

"Just leaving the office."

"Grab me some coffee along the way, would you? I'm half-frozen, and my hands are full with your new acquisitions."

"I don't know if I can afford it after all those acquisitions."

"My connection gave me a large discount, so make it a large. Ciao!"

At least carrying the coffee would keep her hands warm, Tilda admitted as she stopped at the nearest Dunkin' Donuts. Unfortunately, others must have had the same idea, because the line was long and slow, but eventually she got Cooper's coffee and a hot chocolate for herself and started up Gloucester Street toward Boylston.

Despite the frigid temperatures, the sidewalk was crowded with the usual assortment of shoppers, businesspeople who were so busy they had to yell at their phones as they walked, and even a few hardy tourists. Tilda stopped at the crosswalk at Boylston Street, and was waiting for the signal to change when she felt a sharp shove and suddenly she was off-balance, falling headlong into the street.

Chapter 18

Heroing is one of the shortest-lived professions there is.
—WILL ROGERS

TILDA knew it couldn't have taken more than a few seconds for her to fall, but she could distinctly remember cursing at each stage: as she lost her footing, as both cups went flying through the air, as her right knee hit the pavement, and then as the rest of her body tumbled and slid into the street.

There were screams, and the agonizing sound of screeching tires that stopped inches from her body. Or so Tilda imagined—as soon as she stopped falling she threw her arms over her head and shut her eyes tight, as if that could protect her from a speeding SUV.

It was only when she heard Cooper's voice that she dared to look up, and saw that she was surrounded by concerned bystanders. The SUV had managed to stop two whole yards away from her, and the driver was as pale as Tilda suspected she was herself. The cups she'd been carrying were squashed flat.

"Tilda! Are you okay?" Cooper knelt beside her on the street, and started patting her clothes as if checking for blood and protruding bones. "Where does it hurt?"

Tilda started to stir, despite some woman who said, "Don't move, honey. You just lie still."

"I think I'm okay," Tilda said. She rolled over to a sitting position, and bent her elbows successfully. "Help me up."

"Are you sure?" Cooper said, but he did so, helped by several other people who supported her as she stood, and then he brushed off the snow and dirt from the street.

She stood gingerly. Everything seemed to be working, though her right knee hurt a bit when she took a wobbly step.

The driver of the SUV was asking, "Are you okay?"

"I'm fine," Tilda said, more confident that she was telling the truth. "Just a bruise or two."

"I'm so sorry—I didn't see you in the street."

"It's not your fault. I slipped and fell," Tilda said, not ready to accuse anybody for what was likely an accident. "Are you okay?"

The woman gave a shaky grin. "Yeah, thanks. Are you sure you don't need an ambulance?"

Tilda shook her head. "Just bruised my dignity." The woman insisted on giving Tilda her business card, just in case she needed medical care later. It was only when Tilda went to stick the card in her satchel that she realized she was no longer holding it. "Cooper, do you see my bag?"

"Here," he said, handing it to her. "Somebody picked it up for you. Come on, let's get out of the street." As they stepped back onto the sidewalk, the bystanders dispersed and traffic started flowing again.

Cooper said, "I don't know about you, but I need a drink."

Tilda looked at the cups in the street. "I spilled your coffee."

"Screw that. I mean a *drink*. Come on." He led the way down to the closest bar, which turned out to be the Pour House, and got her inside and seated at a table in minutes. Cooper ordered a beer, but when Tilda did the same, he objected.

"You shouldn't drink if you have a concussion."

"I can't get a concussion on my knee."

"I guess not," he relented, "but I'm getting some cheese sticks, too. You shouldn't drink on an empty stomach, especially not after that."

After the waitress went to get their order, Tilda caught Cooper staring at her eyes and realized what he was checking for.

"Are my pupils the same size?"

"I think so." Then, almost accusingly, he said, "Jesus, Tilda, you scared the hell out of me!"

"I am so sorry, but it's not like I asked to get pushed into the street."

"Are you shitting me? I thought you just slipped. Somebody pushed you?"

She thought about it, then nodded. "Yeah, I think somebody did."

"On purpose?"

"No, of course not. You saw how crowded it was."

"What an asshole! Not you, but the asshole who pushed you and then didn't even stick around to see if you were okay."

"Maybe he did," Tilda said. "There were a bunch of people helping me up—maybe he just didn't want to admit it."

"It's a good thing he didn't," Cooper said. "I'd have had a few words for him."

Tilda grinned. "You're a good friend, Cooper."

"Damned right I am! You think I'd go coat shopping for just anybody?"

"Hell, I forgot all about the coat! Gimmie!"

"Are your hands clean?" he asked, holding on to the bag. "Are your pants dry? I don't want you getting stains on it if you don't like it—they won't take it back if it's stained."

Tilda dutifully went to the bathroom to wash up and brush her clothes as free of contaminants as she could.

Then she came back to the table and displayed her clean hands. "I'm clear."

With the air of a magician about to produce the finest rabbit in history, Cooper stood up, reached into the bag, and pulled out the coolest coat Tilda had ever seen. It was black wool, nearly as soft as cashmere, double-breasted with a vaguely military feel, like something a British officer would have worn in World War II. Tilda took it from him, and slid her arms into it.

"How does it look?" she asked anxiously.

"It fits like a dream, it's stylish as hell, and it still has the Tilda edge we know and love."

"Cooper, if you and Jean-Paul ever decide to have children, I will bear them for you."

"When you see the rest, you're going to want to throw in free babysitting."

The waitress arrived with their beers and cheese sticks, and Tilda realized that she'd actually stepped back to make sure nothing got spilled on her. Then Cooper pulled out a pair of deep purple gloves, a purple paisley silk scarf, and an honest-to-God black fedora.

"Okay, babysitting, too."

"I'll drink to that," Cooper said.

Tilda took the coat off, and laid it carefully over the back of an empty chair. Only when it was safely out of range, did she reach for her beer and grab a cheese stick.

"Am I good?" Cooper said.

"You're the best. I don't care if I have to pay on that credit card for the rest of my life. Speaking of which . . ." She held out her hand.

"Damn, so much for my nefarious plan," he said, reaching into his pocket for the card. "You're probably too close to the limit for me to be able to go to Vegas on it anyway."

"I wasn't, but I probably am now."

"The receipts are in the bag, and you know I never overpay."

It was only when Tilda reached into her satchel to get her wallet to replace the credit card that she realized something was missing. "Hey, my pictures are gone!"

"What pictures?"

"I used the good printer at the office to print out a batch of head shots of the *Cowtown* guest stars. They were in my bag." She looked through her bag more thoroughly. "Nothing else is missing."

"Are you sure they were in there?"

"Of course I'm sure. Jeez, Cooper, I only had one beer, and my pupils still match."

"Maybe they fell out on the street."

"Maybe," Tilda said doubtfully, "but I think we would have seen them."

"We'll go check after we finish." Then Cooper caught a look at the clock. "Hell, I've got to get home!"

They finished up and paid the check, and Tilda carefully put her coat back into the bag, ignoring Cooper's snicker at her caution. She didn't want to get it dirty tromping around the slushy streets.

Then they went back to where Tilda had fallen, but there was no sign of the thick photo mailer in the street or in the gutters nearby. They walked half a block in either direction, just in case it had been blown around, but there was nothing. The Dunkin' Donuts cups she'd dropped were still there, though considerably flatter for having been driven over. Tilda tried not to think about that too much.

"Shit," she said. She checked her watch, and saw it was well after six, so the office would be closed. "Now I have to reprint them. This has been one sucky day. I went to a funeral, then I had to put up with Nicole being an asshole, then some other asshole pushes me into the street, and then yet another asshole steals my pictures." Not to mention the epiphany with Cynthia Barth, but she wasn't going to discuss that on the street.

"What if it was the same asshole?" Cooper asked. "It was part of Nicole's evil plan to make sure you had a sucky day. After annoying you in her usual clothing, she disguised herself to push you into the street and steal your pictures."

"I'm sure she would have if she'd thought of it." In fact, Tilda was fairly sure she hadn't looked behind her, so even if Nicole had been wearing a black cape and top hat and twirling a mustache, she wouldn't have noticed.

After Tilda assured Cooper once again that she was fine, and that she would call him if she suddenly started showing meaningful symptoms, he started walking toward his place while she headed for the T.

From that piece of Boylston Street, she could have picked up the Green Line at either Auditorium or Copley, but then she'd have the annoyance of changing subway lines in mid-rush hour. Or she could go back through the Prudential Center and then through Copley Place and pick up the Orange Line at Back Bay Station. Deciding that it wouldn't hurt to walk off her beer and make sure she had no lasting effects from the fall, she picked Back Bay Station.

Normally Tilda enjoyed people-watching as she walked through the Pru Mall. Most of the shops were upscale, so there were a lot of people with too much money, but it was attached to the convention center, which meant tourists. Plus there were office workers and urban dwellers on their way home, and street people looking for somewhere to warm up. But this time she was too preoccupied.

She'd just passed the food court when a thought occurred to her. What if it really had been the same asshole? Not Nicole—Nicole was a bitch but had no real motive to push her into the middle of Boylston Street. She'd have pushed her down the stairs at the office instead. But what if some other person had pushed her? Miss Barth, for instance, who had apparently been horrified that Tilda had discovered her hidden past. Could she have resorted to such drastic measures to make sure Tilda didn't tell anybody?

Tilda tried to shake off the thought—the idea of that elegant lady pushing her underneath the wheels of a car was ludicrous. She wouldn't even cuss! Then again, Cotton Mather and the other guys up in Salem had been God-fearing men, too, yet still managed to hang a bunch of accused witches.

As she stepped onto the elevated walkway that connected the Prudential with Copley Place, she started wondering about the missing pictures. Why would anybody steal pictures? Sure, if she'd had baby pictures of some celebrity's offspring, they might be worth something, but not head shots of old TV actors.

The whole idea that somebody had attacked her to get a batch of pictures was crazy, but when she got to the bottom of the escalator just before the Copley Place exit door, she hesitated. Normally she would have taken the tunnel that led under the street to go the rest of the way to the T station. The poorly lit, long, lonely tunnel. There was no good reason to make her way across the slushy courtyard, in the cold, and then have to wait to cross a busy street. She continued to tell herself that as she crossed the slushy courtyard, in the cold, and waited to cross the busy street.

The rest of her way home, Tilda alternated between watching the people around her with suspicion and trying to imagine how those photos could have made her a target.

Chapter 19

Don't never interfere with something that ain't bothering you none.

—*DON'T SQUAT WITH YER SPURS ON!* BY TEXAS BIX BENDER

THE evening was not pleasant. It started out all right, with Tilda heating up a can of tomato soup as a follow-up to the cheese sticks she'd shared with Cooper, and trying to eat while watching the episode of *Buffy the Vampire Slayer* when it is revealed that Oz is a werewolf. Then Colleen came home, intent on interrogating Tilda about Sandra's funeral.

It wasn't that Tilda didn't have her own morbid streak, as demonstrated by her addiction to a show about vampires, but she had limits. Colleen, as far as she could tell, did not. When Tilda finally lost her temper and snapped at her, she got wounded puppy dog eyes and even a sniffle.

Of course, Tilda could have gone to her bedroom and barred the door, but this was her apartment and she had a right to watch her own TV in her own living room. So she ignored her moping roomie, watched *Buffy* without enjoying the banter, and forced down her soup. As moral victories went, Tilda reflected, it was pretty pathetic.

The phone rang as she was washing out her bowl. Colleen answered it and handed it to her. "It's for you. I didn't ask who it is because it's none of my business." She flounced away.

Tilda gave her back a one-fingered salute, and said, "Hello, this is Tilda."

"Hi, Tilda. This is Lil Sechrest."

"Lil, hi. How are you holding up?"

"Okay, I guess. It's still so hard to believe Aunt Sandra's gone, and I don't know what I'm going to do about her things and her condo."

"I can only imagine. I remember when my grandfather died, my mother was just drowning in paperwork. At least you've got some family in town to help you."

"Not for long. Everybody is heading off early tomorrow, so the rest is up to me. Anyway, one thing I've got to deal with is the Website, and I know this is an imposition, but I need to put up something about what happened, and I just can't get the wording right. Do you think you could—?"

"I'd be glad to take a look at what you've got. Whatever you need."

"I'll pay you."

"You will not," Tilda said firmly.

"But—"

"Look, people are supposed to bring over food when there's a death in the family, and I'm a lousy cook. Let me do this."

"Thanks. I can't even get to my computer right now—there are two cousins sleeping in my bedroom, where my desk is. But I'll be going to Aunt Sandra's place tomorrow to get things moving, and I can use hers. I haven't been able to get over there since . . ." She stopped for a second. "Anyway, I need to get to her computer to update the Website. Could I send you a draft tomorrow?"

"Absolutely." Then something occurred to her. "Lil, you're not going to Sandra's place alone, are you?"

"Well, yeah. Like I said, everybody is heading home."

"Haven't you got a friend you can take with you?"

The silence was answer enough.

"What time are you going? I'll meet you there."

"Tilda, I didn't expect you to—"

Afraid that Lil was about to get emotional, Tilda cut in. "What time?"

"About ten? I've got to drop people at the train station first."

"I'll be there." Tilda hated to lose part of a Saturday, but she just couldn't let Lil go to the scene of Sandra's murder by herself. Besides, it had to be better than spending the day with a cranky Colleen.

Chapter 20

A cowboy must help people in trouble.
—"THE COWBOY CODE" BY GENE AUTRY

BETWEEN the funeral and the possible attempt on her life, Tilda expected a whole parade of bad dreams, so she did something she shouldn't have. She took a dose of NyQuil before bedtime. It was a mistake. Sure, she slept through the night, but that only meant she couldn't escape from the nightmares as they came. Instead she'd stir just long enough to fall back into another horror movie. She was relieved when her alarm went off and pulled her fully out of sleep.

Apparently Colleen was still miffed, because she didn't even bother to complain about how noisy she must have been. Tilda took that as a bonus.

After a hot shower, a brisk walk through the bright but chilly morning to the T, and a stop at Dunkin' Donuts for milk and a chocolate chip muffin, Tilda made it to Sandra's building a few minutes ahead of Lil.

"Hope you haven't been waiting long," Lil said when she saw Tilda on the sidewalk.

"Just got here," Tilda said, noting that Lil looked as tired as she did.

Lil let them into the building with a key, stopped to get a bundle of mail out of her aunt's mailbox, and led the way to Sandra's door. Then she hesitated long enough for Tilda to wonder if perhaps she should have waited a couple of days.

"Are you up for this?"

"No, but better now than later."

Tilda patted Lil's back awkwardly, wishing that either Cooper or June were there. They were a lot better at comforting than she was.

Lil finally got the door open, and went just far enough inside for Tilda to step in beside her. Both of them stared at the spot where Sandra's body had been. Tilda had been expecting to see bloodstains, and was intensely relieved that it had all been washed off the shiny floor—even the spatters were gone.

"The police helped me get in touch with a company that specializes in this kind of cleanup," Lil explained. "I didn't think I could handle it."

"Smart," Tilda said. Lil didn't move for a long time, and Tilda again asked, "Are you *sure* you're ready?"

"It's got to be done and I'm the only one who's willing. What I said about my family having to get back home wasn't completely true. The fact is, they didn't approve of Aunt Sandra."

"Because of the photographs?"

"Because of the photographs, the Website, the attitude." She shook her head. "Mostly it was because she wasn't like them. They live in a small town in New York State, and they don't do anything to cause talk or make waves. Aunt Sandra made waves."

"That she did."

"They also aren't happy about her leaving everything to me, which is another reason they wouldn't stay to help."

Tilda nodded, but was feeling wildly uncomfortable. She was learning far more than she wanted to about Lil. Not that she wasn't nice, but she was just barely more than a stranger. Plus the fact that Lil had inherited everything made her a dandy suspect for Sandra's murder. "Well, since they bailed, what do you want me to do?"

Lil seemed to pull herself together. "First, I need to see

what orders have come in—we've had a lot of orders since word hit the Web about Aunt Sandra. Then we need to get the orders ready for shipping."

The next hour or so was taken up with the mundane task of putting together packages of T-shirts, photos Sandra had signed before her death, and books that included shots from the Sandy Sea Chest photo layouts. Conversation was limited to what was needed to get the job done.

Finally they'd taped up the last padded envelope. "I'll drop these off at the post office on Monday," Lil said.

"What next?"

"I need to update the site itself with the news about Aunt Sandra."

"Do you have a draft for me to work on?"

"Not exactly. I had some notes, but I think I left them at my place."

Tilda could tell where this was heading. "Lil, do you want me to write something for you?"

"Would you?"

"Hey, it's what I do." Tilda understood intellectually that some people had a horror of putting words to paper, or to disk, though she'd never understood why. "Mind if I use the computer?"

"No, go ahead. I've got plenty of other things to do."

It didn't take Tilda long to pound out a brief account of Sandra's death, making it informative but not overly graphic. Then she added links to the *Boston Globe* article and Sandra's obituary. Lil was working in the bedroom, and Tilda made sure to ignore the sniffling she heard. Writing was easy—comforting a mourning niece wasn't. Once she'd gone through the piece a couple of times, she called out, "Lil, do you want to put up a particular picture of Sandra?" Words might be her life, but on the Web, every picture's value was inflated to at least two thousand words.

Lil came back in, and they spent a few minutes looking at the photos on the Website, but decided that no picture that included that much skin would be appropriate, even if they added a black border.

"How about that last batch of photos?" Tilda said. "The ones the guy from the camera club just sent? Sandra showed them to me and my friend Cooper. Wasn't there one of her in regular clothes?"

"I remember that one." Lil went rummaging around the desk, and then the coffee table. "That's funny. They're not here."

"Maybe the police moved them when they were here."

But Lil shook her head. "They gave me a list of everything they took, and they didn't take any pictures." Tilda got up to help, but though the two of them searched the room thoroughly, they couldn't find the thick envelope of photos Tilda had seen the day Sandra died. Finally Lil said, "I don't know where they are, but it doesn't matter. I'd already scanned them to the hard disk." She went to the computer and started looking through file directories.

Tilda wasn't so willing to let the matter die. "Lil, maybe the killer took them."

"Why would anybody do that? Those shots weren't important."

"What do you mean?"

"I mean they weren't that good—just amateur stuff. Why would anybody care about them?"

"I don't know." But Tilda started thinking about the pictures she'd had the day before, the ones that had disappeared from her bag. Two sets of pictures, two attacks. It wasn't a comfortable pattern. "Maybe you should call the detective investigating the murder and tell him. He should know that they're missing."

"They're not missing," Lil insisted. "I've got them on disk. So what if the prints got thrown out? Maybe a cop stole them—most of them were men, and you know how men are." But she wouldn't turn to meet Tilda's eyes.

After a minute, she found the photo scan files, and

pulled up the shot that Tilda remembered of Sandra in a smart suit and hat. "How about this one?" Lil asked.

"Looks good. And I've got some shots Cooper took during that last interview, too. You're welcome to use one of them. I could e-mail them to you later. No, hang on, I think they're on the thumb drive I've got in my bag."

Tilda dug a bright red thumb drive out of her bag and switched places with Lil, but before she could insert the drive, started coughing. "Sorry," she choked out, "just thirsty. Could I have something to drink?"

"I'm sorry, I should have offered before." Lil went into the kitchen.

As soon as she was gone, Tilda started copying the scanned photos from the hard drive to her thumb drive. Worried that Lil would come back before she finished, she called out, "Do you suppose I could have some crackers or something, too? I'm starved."

"Sure, no problem."

By the time Lil came back with a glass of Coke and a bowl of pretzels, Tilda had the files copied and the thumb drive back in her bag. "That's perfect," she said, taking the snack.

"Did you find the pictures?"

"No, I'm an idiot. Wrong thumb drive. I'll e-mail them to you later."

Tilda felt a little guilty about sneaking off with the files, but since she wasn't going to publish them, she could live with the guilt. Maybe there really was nothing odd about those photos or the fact that they'd gone missing, but there was something odd about Lil not wanting to tell the police. If that wasn't enough of an excuse for her to sneak away with them, it would do until a better one came along.

While Tilda ate stale pretzels that she didn't want, Lil read the piece she'd written about Sandra.

"This is perfect," she said. "I really appreciate it."

"So will you be keeping the Website going?"

"I think so, for now at least. I've got the new pictures to put up, and the bulletin boards are still active. If orders keep coming in, I may as well fill them." She looked down at her hands. "Do you think that's bad, to take advantage of Aunt Sandra's death that way?"

Tilda figured she needed more than a halfhearted answer, so she said, "Hell no! Of course I may be the wrong one to ask—I write articles about dead celebrities all the time, and that's no different. But bottom line? Your aunt would want you to make what money you can. Why else would she leave everything to you?"

"You're right—she would," Lil said, looking pleased by the thought.

They ate pretzels in silence for a while, and Tilda wondered how much longer she should stay. Then Lil suddenly said, "I guess you're wondering why I don't have any friends around to help me. It's just that I haven't been in the area that long, and I don't make friends easily."

Tilda didn't know the proper response to that. Should she protest that it wasn't true? Point out that anybody who didn't want to be friends with Lil was missing out on something special? Neither struck her as the way to go, so she tried for a nonjudgmental grunt.

"It's probably because I'm not good at trusting people anymore," Lil said matter-of-factly. "The counselor at the rape crisis center said that was a common reaction to being a rape victim. I mean, rape survivor. She wanted me to say it that way."

Now Tilda really didn't know what to say. Not that she hadn't met other rape victims—or survivors—before. The statistic she'd always heard was one woman in four, and Tilda knew a lot more than four women. Of course, she hadn't known what to say in those instances either. Since she had to say something, she said, "God, I'm sorry, Lil. Did they put the bastard away?"

"It was his word against mine. I went out with him a

couple of times, and one night at his apartment, he drugged my drink. I woke up and I could tell that he'd—What had happened. The funny thing is, I'd have slept with him if he'd asked me. He didn't ask."

"And the police didn't believe you?"

"There was no evidence. He didn't injure me, and the drugs were out of my system before I could get tested." She shrugged. "Nobody believed me."

"Not even your family?"

"They didn't want me to make waves," she said. "That's when I moved up here. I wanted to start someplace new, and Aunt Sandra thought I'd like it in Massachusetts."

"Do you?"

"It's good," she said unconvincingly. "I just need to get a job. Aunt Sandra wanted me to see somebody, like a psychiatrist or something, but I need the job to get insurance."

"You know, I've got some friends in programming. I could give you some names to call."

"Thanks, Tilda, you've really been great. I mean, coming to the funeral, and helping with Aunt Sandra's things, and everything."

"I really liked Sandra," Tilda said. "I can't believe somebody killed her. I'm still having nightmares about finding her."

"Oh, Tilda, I'm so sorry."

Tilda shrugged. "It'll pass. I just wish we knew what happened. Have the police said anything? Do they have any clue at all?"

"Not that they've told me—I don't have a lot of confidence in the police, anyway."

Tilda wouldn't either in Lil's position, though she thought Detective Salvatore seemed pretty sharp. "I'm still wondering if it would make sense to tell the cops about those missing photos. Maybe there's a connection."

"Those pictures had nothing to do with Aunt Sandra's death," Lil said shrilly.

Tilda couldn't help but draw back a little, and Lil was instantly contrite.

"No, no, you're right. I should tell them. I'll call that detective later today. Okay?"

"Good," Tilda said. Let him decide if they were worth worrying about.

Chapter 21

Episode 10: Into Their Own Hands
Since Cowtown has never had a sheriff, the townsfolk have always taken care of their own disputes. Then a local rancher is found robbed and murdered. Finding the killer is the easy part—now they have to decide what to do with him.
—*COWTOWN COMPANION* BY RUBEN TIMMONS

AFTER they finished their snack, Lil said, "I think this is about all I can manage for one day. Being here is getting to me."

Tilda nodded. It was getting to her, too.

"The only thing is, I've still got work to do on the Website. Would you mind helping me pack the computer up and load it into my car? I'm going to have to get it out of here sooner or later, anyway, and I'll feel safer if it's not sitting in an empty apartment."

"Sure, I can do that," Tilda said. It took judicious wrapping with blankets and several trips to get the computer and all the related equipment into Lil's Mazda.

"Are you going to be able to get all this into your apartment on your own?" Tilda asked.

"I'll manage. Thanks."

Tilda was relieved. She couldn't wait to get away from the apartment and its memories, let alone her increasingly uncomfortable thoughts about Lil. So after promising to e-mail the photos from the final interview with Sandra and

the names of some friends in the computer business, Tilda
made her escape.

It was well past lunchtime, and the pretzels hadn't been
particularly satisfying, so the first order of business was
to find food, preferably with company. In fact, the idea of
congenial company was of even greater interest than the
food, but though she checked her home number as well as
her cell, there was no message from Quentin. By the usual
dating customs, calling Friday after a Thursday night first
date would have been too soon, but she'd had hopes that by
Saturday, he'd have been ready for a second date.

She hesitated before calling him. She hadn't gotten a firm
feel for whether or not he expected to make all the moves
in the beginning of the relationship, so she didn't know if
her initiating contact would please him or chase him off.
Then she dialed his number. If he was that old-fashioned,
she'd rather know sooner than later. Unfortunately, there
was no answer, and she left a noncommittal message about
wanting to say hello.

Still not in the mood to be alone, she called Cooper,
who invited her to join him and Jean-Paul for an afternoon
of calzone and videos. After making sure that she wasn't
interfering with marital quality time, which led to his shar-
ing far too much information, Tilda made her way to their
apartment.

Though she was exceedingly curious about the files
she'd liberated from Sandra's hard drive, she put it all out
of her head for a while. First off, there was the calzone,
hot and cheesy and fully deserving of her complete attention. Then she had to referee the dispute between Cooper
and Jean-Paul about which movie to watch. Both were
up for Westerns, after all the planning for the *Cowtown*
fund-raiser, but while Jean-Paul wanted something traditional, preferably involving John Ford, Cooper was interested in something postmodern, like *Pale Rider*. Tilda
broke the tie by suggesting *Little Big Man*, which had both

scope and political correctness, and a good time was had by all. And of course she couldn't bring up murder while they were watching Indians attacking settlers, soldiers attacking Indians, or the Battle of Little Big Horn. Once the movie was over, there was sinfully delicious ice cream from Toscanini's—she couldn't very well spoil that.

Of course, the real reason she was dodging the issue was that she needed a break. It had been a freakishly stressful week, and spending time with Cooper and Jean-Paul was just what she needed. Cooper was a bud, of course, and there was something sublimely relaxing about Jean-Paul. When he was working as a DJ, he filled even the biggest event venue with energy, but at home he was surprisingly quiet. It wasn't until he'd left for a wedding gig in Arlington that Tilda even thought about the pictures on her thumb drive.

"Can I use your computer to look at some stolen files?" she asked Cooper.

"Sure. Blackmail material? Secret government papers? Spoilers for the next season of *True Blood*?"

"Dirty pictures."

"Even better."

They retired to the spare bedroom he and Jean-Paul used as a combination home office and comic book storage facility, and Cooper obligingly let her load in the photo files from her thumb drive. Then she opened up all the files, and went from one to the other.

Cooper said, "Those look like the pictures Sandra showed us, the ones from the camera club member."

"They are."

"So why did you bother to steal them?"

"Curiosity. Somehow that batch of printed photos disappeared from Sandra's apartment, and I don't think the cops have them."

"You think the killer took them? Why?"

"No idea. And if that weren't odd enough, Lil didn't seem to care that they were missing."

"What does that mean?"

"Once again, no idea. Which is why I copied the files and absconded with them."

Together they looked at the files quickly, then more slowly.

"Do you see anything?" Tilda finally asked.

"Nothing but female pulchritude, which as you know, is not my favorite flavor of pulchritude. Why don't you try printing them out? It's easier to see details on paper."

"Sure it's okay to use your printer? Nicole won't swoop down and accuse me of misusing valuable resources?"

"She's not that bad."

"Are we talking about the same person? Scrawny, red-haired, pointy nose? Sure she's that bad."

"Seriously."

She turned to look at him. "What brought this on?"

"I've just been thinking that if you're going to work at *Entertain Me!*, you need to come to some sort of understanding with Nicole."

"I guess," she said grudgingly.

"Just think about it, okay? And if you'll print the pictures, I'll get us something to drink. Want a snack?"

"Sure. Anything but pretzels."

He showed up with glasses of Dr Pepper and a bowl of grapes, and they munched while waiting for the pictures to print. Once they had them all, they divided up the stack to look at them under the bright light Cooper used for copyediting.

They saw nothing suspicious.

They switched stacks.

Nothing.

Nearly an hour later, the grapes had disappeared and Tilda was ready to throw something.

"I can't see why anybody in their right mind would care enough to steal these, let alone kill for them!" Seeing Cooper's face, she warned, "I know, I stole them. Don't go there!"

"Not going there."

"Anyway, these aren't that different from the ones the pro photographer took that day, and those pictures have been published and posted and even printed as calendars."

"Do you want me to take another look?"

"Please." She pushed her stack toward him.

He thumbed through all the photos. "Did women have pointier breasts back then or what?"

"It was the way the bras were made," Tilda said.

"They look as if they could take an eye out if you weren't careful."

"Focus."

"I am focusing." Cooper moved to his computer desk. "In fact, I've got an idea."

Tilda pulled up a chair to sit behind him and watch as he went to Sandra's Website and clicked through the list of photos. "Okay, here's the official pirate wench pictures."

"What are you doing?"

"I'm playing 'spot the difference.' " He displayed the first online picture, then thumbed through the stack of printouts until he found the shot that was closest to it. "Same pose, just a different angle. The pro was in front, but our guy was off to one side."

"That makes sense. The pro would pick the best vantage point."

"On the plus side, the pictures from the side show a clearer view of the threatened maiden's heaving bosom. I think the pro photographer was more of an ass man—the amateur was a breast man."

"Do I want to know what kind of man you are?"

"No. On the minus side, the amateur ended up with other guys with cameras in the frame."

"Those must be the other camera club members."

"Having them there definitely destroys the illusion of a pirate at sea."

"As if that set could fool anybody!"

"Special effects were more primitive then." Cooper made the same comparison with several more shots, each time spending a few minutes looking for differences, but as far as Tilda could tell, all it did was to verify the facts that the amateur wasn't as good a photographer as the pro and that he had an inordinate fondness for breasts.

"Is this showing us anything?" she finally asked.

"Not me, anyway." He made another pass through the pictures, but Tilda could tell his heart wasn't in it. Then he started reordering the photos.

"What are you doing?"

"Putting them into chronological order, as best I can."

"Why?"

"Because I have an orderly mind."

"How can you tell which comes first?"

"The clock on the wall, the movement of the models, the level of liquid in that glass. Plus comparing them to the pro shots."

"You're good."

"Of course." He fiddled with the stack a little longer. "Okay, I think I've got it."

"Now what?"

He riffled the pages. "You know, I could make a pinup flip book."

"There's probably a market for it."

"Definitely. But now I do see something. Is this all of the pictures that camera club member took?"

"That's all that Lil had on the hard drive. Why?"

"I just noticed that the amateur was a lot slower than the pro. Look, they both took a shot of the pirate with the maiden over her knee."

"Right."

"Then the pro has shots of the hand midway down and then with her hand firmly on rump. The amateur missed the spanking action, which I would think was a big deal."

"This is a very strange conversation," Tilda pointed out.

But now that Cooper had mentioned it, there were other places where the amateur had missed good shots. "Maybe the amateur had a slower camera or had to reload. Maybe he took too long to focus. Maybe he culled the shots that didn't come out right. Maybe he went to the bathroom—"

"Or maybe you didn't print all the photos."

She gave him a look, but said, "If it will make you feel better, I'll check my thumb drive." She reached over him to call up the list of files. "How many photos do you have?"

He counted them. "Twenty-four."

"And I have twenty-four stolen files, so everything has been printed. Now we know why the amateur was an amateur—he was too slow to go pro."

But Cooper said, "Wait a minute. Look at the file names."

All the files had the prefix *bhawks* followed by a three-digit number: bhawks001, bhawks002, and so on. Except that there were gaps—there was no bhawks003 or bhawks007. All in all, there were eight gaps in the numbers.

"That's odd," Tilda said. "From what I saw on that hard drive, Lil is meticulous about how she stores and names files." She looked at the file list again. "See the time stamps for when the files were created? She scanned them methodically, too, one after the other."

"Except that some of them aren't here."

"Now why would that be?"

"Maybe Sandra deleted them."

"Are you kidding? Even if her hands weren't bothering her, she told me that she barely knew how to turn the computer on."

"She also said she taught Bettie Page everything she knew about posing."

"Good point. Plus she could have asked Lil to do it for her—she could have made up some excuse. Or Lil could have done it for some reason of her own."

"What about the killer?"

"Maybe." She drummed her fingers on the desk until Cooper slapped her hand. "I wish I could get back to that hard drive and rummage around the deleted files, but Lil took the computer home with her, and I'm not sure where she lives."

"Otherwise, you could do a spot of breaking and entering. Except, of course, that it's both illegal and dangerous."

"Another good point. So the photos are missing, and the scanned copies of those photos are gone, or at least somewhere where I can't get to them. Which leaves the source."

"Except you don't know where they came from." He paused. "Don't I get a 'good point'?"

"Not this time. I know where they came from. Sandra said the photographer lives in Medford."

"She did? I don't remember that."

"Not everybody in that room was slavering over pirate photos—I was listening."

"So all you have to do is find a guy in Medford who was in a New York camera club in the 1950s. Good point?"

"Nope. I know his name or at least part of it. His last name is Hawks, and his first initial is B."

"The file names! Smart!"

"Good point," she said, then ducked when he slapped at her head. A quick look at an online phone book found only one B. Hawks in Medford, a Bill Hawks on Fulton Street. Unfortunately, there was no answer when she called his number, which left them out of ideas.

They were not, however, out of Westerns on DVD, so after scrounging for yet more food, they spent the evening trying to decide which of *The Magnificent Seven* was more studly. Eventually Tilda took her pinup photos and headed home.

She slept soundly that night, maybe because she was making progress of some kind. She just wished she knew where it was leading.

Chapter 22

There's a side of my personality that goes completely against the East Coast educated person and wants to be a pinup girl in garages across America . . . there's a side that wants to wear the pink angora bikini!

—MIRA SORVINO

TILDA tried to call Bill Hawks a couple of times the next day, though she wasn't supposed to be working on Sunday. It was hard enough for a work-at-home freelancer to keep her life separate from her work, so Tilda usually tried to protect her weekends. But given that the conversation with Hawks was only semi-work-related, she gave herself dispensation, and since she never reached him, it was moot anyway.

Instead she did boring weekend stuff: laundry, housework, duty calls to her mother and stepfather and to her father and stepmother. Plus she e-mailed Lil the stuff she'd promised. Later on, she tried to make peace with Colleen by taking her out to dinner at the Malden branch of Applebee's restaurant. It might have done the trick had Tilda not had another noisy nightmare.

That was the night that Colleen moved past concerned, past annoyed, and on to downright resentful, and she made no bones about it. Tilda was really apologetic and had remorse to burn, but Colleen was not appeased.

Despite interrupted sleep, Tilda got up early on Monday and spent the first part of the morning doing *Cowtown*-related research, but as soon as it was late enough she called Bill Hawks once again, pumping her fist in the air in celebration when somebody answered.

"May I speak to Mr. Hawks please?"

"This is Bill Hawks."

"Mr. Hawks, my name is Tilda Harper. I work for the magazine *Entertain Me!*, and I'm researching Sandra Sechrest. You may know her as Sandy Sea Chest." Tilda was tweaking her ethics, since it sounded as if she was working on an article for *Entertain Me!*, but she hadn't exactly lied.

Hawks said, "I read in the paper that she'd been murdered. What an awful thing! Have they caught the killer yet?"

"Not as far as I know. I was hoping we could meet so I could ask you some questions about her."

"Me?"

"I understand you were one of the photographers who was there for one of her most well-known shoots, and I thought you could tell me what it was like, seeing it live."

"Sure, why not?"

They arranged to meet at his house in Medford at one, which gave Tilda enough time to finish what she was doing and eat a sandwich before heading over. But first she wrote a note about where she was going and e-mailed copies to Cooper and June. Being pushed onto a busy street had made her a little more cautious, and if she went missing, she wanted to make sure there was a neon-lit trail to follow.

Mr. Hawks lived in a solid, well-established neighborhood not all that different from Tilda's, and only ten minutes away, though since it was in Medford the houses probably cost ten to twenty thousand dollars more for the same floor plan. She'd long since given up trying to decipher what made one town higher up the economic totem pole than another, especially when the towns shared a border the way Malden and Medford did.

Tilda parked her car on the street, hoping the person who'd shoveled the spot clear of snow wouldn't return before she left and get mad at her for usurping it. Mr. Hawks must have been watching for her, because he opened the front door before she could ring the bell. "Ms. Harper? Come on in. I'm Bill Hawks."

She stepped inside, and followed him into the living room, which screamed that it was an older person's house. Tilda wasn't sure how it was she could usually spot that. The furniture tended to be dated, but no more so than in many Cambridge apartments devoted to retro styles. Often there were more pictures, maybe more knickknacks, too, but not all the time, and not so much in Hawks's house. It was something else. Maybe it was just that the furniture looked relaxed, as if it knew it wasn't going anywhere.

Mr. Hawks offered her a drink, which she refused, and a seat on the couch, which she accepted. He settled into a La-Z-Boy as she pulled out her notepad and pen and sized him up. He was in his seventies, at least, and moved slowly and deliberately. His hair was down to just a fringe around the edges, and his eyes were a clear, almost luminous blue.

"Thanks for seeing me so soon. As I told you on the phone, I'm writing a story about Sandra—Sandy Sea Chest."

"You know, I should have told you before that I really didn't know her that well. I'd only recently found out she was living in the area, and before that I hadn't seen her in fifty years or more."

"I understand that you were in one of the camera clubs that used Sandra as a model."

"That's right. That's how I met her. In fact, if it hadn't been for that, I wouldn't have minded asking her out."

"You lost me."

"Our club had strict rules. We weren't supposed to contact the models outside of our shoots. I guess there had been problems with other clubs, and our club decided we had to keep things on the up-and-up. We wanted to make sure everybody knew we were serious photographers, even artists, not just men ogling pretty girls."

"Is that right?" Tilda said, raising one eyebrow.

He let loose with a laugh. "Of course we were ogling pretty girls—otherwise we could have taken pictures of landscapes and puppies! But we really were serious about the photography, and having that rule protected the girls. We could look, but we couldn't touch. Roy—he was our president—he used to bring his older sister to the sessions, and she'd watch out for the models. One guy forgot one day. All he wanted was to get the model to move her chin a little to the left, but as soon as he touched her, Roy's sister let out a screech and slapped his hand away. Scared the crap out of him!" He laughed again. "Oh, hell, who am I fooling? It was me, but I really did just want her to move her chin!"

Even though Tilda already knew a lot about how the camera clubs worked through her previous research, she asked a few more questions, just to make sure Hawks was relaxed. Finally, she said, "I spoke to Sandra the day she died, and she showed me that batch of pictures you'd sent her, the ones from the pirate session. You do good work."

"Not bad for an amateur, anyway. I hated to let those pictures go, too, but the wife insisted. Crazy, isn't it? Jealous of a woman I hadn't laid eyes on in fifty years!"

"Well, they are pretty provocative pictures."

"Oh yeah, I took some great shots that day, and Sandy was one hell of a poser. No Bettie Page, but the camera loved her. The other gal, Virginia, was good, too. Those pictures were works of art, you know what I mean." He threw up his hands. "But Jazz—she's my wife—Jazz said they had to go. She said that if I wanted to keep cheesecake pictures around, they damned well better be of her."

Tilda blinked. "I beg your pardon?"

"Jazz can't stand the idea that I ever used another model. I keep telling her that once I met her, I didn't have any interest in taking pictures of anybody else."

"Your wife was a pinup model, too?"

"Was? Is! She's still got it—we've got our own Website and it's doing great, thank you very much. Plenty of guys want women with a little mileage on 'em. Here, let me show you some." Hawks levered himself out of the recliner and went to a well-filled bookcase to pull out a large photo album. "We've gone digital, of course, but there's nothing like having prints to look at," he said as he handed her the album.

Tilda was prepared to freeze her face into an expression of polite interest so as not to offend the man with any distaste, or a worse reaction, but she needn't have bothered. After the initial shock of seeing an older woman in sensual poses—No, she wasn't older. Jazz Hawks was old—nothing had been airbrushed or Photoshopped out—but she was still as sexy as hell. She was also quite well endowed, proving that Hawks was still a breast man.

"These are amazing," Tilda said as she flipped through the pages.

Hawks beamed with pride. "Now those are the glamour shots—some of the other stuff we do is a little bit kinkier. Jazz doesn't have any hang-ups. Except about me having other models, of course."

Tilda decided that she didn't need to see those pictures, and closed the album. "So she didn't like you having photos of other women?"

"She made me promise to get rid of any pictures I had

of other women when we got married, and I did get rid of most of 'em. She thought they were all gone until she found a cache I had in the basement. I told her I'd forgotten they were there, but I'll be honest with you—I kept those pictures on purpose. That session with Sandy was some of the best work I ever did until I started working with Jazz, and I couldn't just throw that stuff out. I thought I had the perfect hiding place, but she found them, and they had to go. I'd heard about Sandra's Website, so I decided to send 'em to her for old times' sake. Do you know if anybody is going to be posting them on her Website now that she's gone?"

"Unfortunately, the pictures you sent are missing," she said. She was skirting the truth again, since she knew Lil had file copies.

"No!" Hawks said. "What happened?"

Tilda wasn't willing to launch into her suspicions, so she settled for, "Nobody knows for sure. Actually, I was hoping you might have copies, but if your wife objected that strongly, I suppose not."

But Hawks was wriggling in his seat. "To tell you the truth . . . Look, you won't tell Jazz, will you?"

"Absolutely not. I deal with confidential sources all the time."

"Well, I was going through the negatives, just for one last look, you know, and I just couldn't resist."

"You made more prints, didn't you?"

"Nah, prints are too hard to hide. I put 'em on disk. I've got this gadget that takes slides and converts them to .jpeg files. Then I put the files on a thumb drive, and hid the thumb drive."

"Mr. Hawks, you are a sneaky man."

He grinned proudly.

Half an hour later, Tilda had the files copied onto her own thumb drive and was on her way back home. Another hour, and she'd downloaded all the photos onto her hard disk, identified which weren't included in the files stolen from Sandra's hard drive, and printed them.

All she had to do was figure out why they were worth killing for.

Chapter 23

It is easier to get an actor to be a cowboy than to get a cowboy
to be an actor.

—JOHN FORD

TILDA eagerly grabbed each of the formerly missing pictures as the printer spat them out, but though she really couldn't have said what she was expecting, the reality was depressingly anticlimactic. The photos looked pretty much like Bill Hawks's other photos—they showed lots of bosom and had other photographers in the frame.

Okay, she had to be missing something. She picked up each picture and looked more closely. The first shot: pirate, maiden, and the profile of a dark-haired photographer whose face was mostly hidden by his own camera. The second: pirate, maiden, and two photographers. Hmm . . . One of them was the same guy, now with the camera held below his chin as he decided on his next shot. The third: pirate, maiden, and the dark-haired photographer again, this time holding the camera in one hand as he leaned against a table or sideboard. Fourth: pirate, maiden, dark-haired photographer. Tilda flipped through the rest of the newly acquired photos, verifying that each of them included the same photographer. Then she looked through the pictures she'd copied from Sandra's computer. The dark-haired stranger didn't appear in any of them.

That had to be it. The photographer was the missing piece. She grabbed the phone to call Cooper and crow.

"Cooper? It's Tilda."

"What do you need?"

"Nice to hear your voice, too."

"Tilda, it's Monday afternoon. I've got until five o'clock tomorrow to get next week's issue copyedited."

"Shit! I forgot. Call me tonight."

"If I can. No guarantees. Bye." He hung up.

So much for crowing. Tilda pulled out the best shot of the guy, and looked at him closely. He looked as if he were eighteen or nineteen, or a very young twenty or twenty-one. The plaid button-down shirt with gray slacks gave no clues to his identity, and he had no rings or any other identifying marks. His eyes were dark, and he was cute enough if you liked trim guys with 1950s-style crew cuts. So who the hell was he?

Tilda looked up Bill Hawks's number, and called him, hoping she'd get him and not the overly possessive Jazz. Luck was with her.

"Mr. Hawks, this is Tilda Harper again. I've got a question for you."

"Shoot."

"I was looking at some of your photos, and noticed that there's one particular photographer in the frame for several of them." She described him and said, "I was wondering if you could tell me his name for the caption."

"Hang on, let me find the pictures on my computer."

Tilda waited impatiently as he pulled his thumb drive of contraband material out from its hiding place and plugged it into his computer. "Okay, I see the guy you're talking about, but I have no idea who he was. That shoot had guys from three or four different clubs, and that guy wasn't in my club. I don't even know which one he was in."

"Oh well," Tilda said, as if it were of no particular importance. "I might be able to get by without knowing. It just depends on how picky the legal department is getting."

"Lawyers!" Hawks said. "They do complicate matters."

"Sad but true. Maybe I could talk to some of the other photographers from that shoot. Have you kept in touch with any of them?"

"You don't ask for much—that was over fifty years ago!"

"I know, and I'm sorry. The legal department just makes me crazy."

"Take my advice and crop the guy out. It won't hurt anything, and the lawyers will never know."

"I will if I have to, but I really wanted to show the camera club members who were behind the scenes, not just the models."

"I see what you mean," he said, "Tell you what. I'll make a call or two and send some e-mails. If anybody knows anything, I'll get back to you."

"That would be wonderful. I really appreciate it."

"Anytime." She heard a woman's voice. "Hell, Jazz is home. Gotta go!" He hung up before Tilda could respond, and she hoped he'd gotten his thumb drive hidden safely away in time.

Tilda glared at the crew-cut man, with no clue who he was and no idea how to find out. She speculated about using the bulletin boards on Sandra's Website to put out feelers for other photographers who'd been there that day, but she didn't want Lil knowing she'd stolen the pictures.

Of course, there was still the frightened maiden, Virginia Pure. Sandra hadn't known what had become of her, but she might still be alive. She looked younger than Sandra, which made it a little more likely. All Tilda had to do was find a model who nobody had heard from for fifty years, convince her to admit that she'd done work she hated, and hope she remembered one guy out of a host of photographers.

Tilda ran her fingers through her hair. She was losing it, she was totally losing it. Here she was with a fat assignment with a fat paycheck, and the possibility of going full time at a moderately cool magazine, and she was pissing away her day chasing the ghosts of pinups past.

It was way past time to put this stuff aside and get some real work done. Hoping that out of sight would translate to out of mind, she stuffed all of Bill Hawks's photos into a manila folder and put it on the back corner of her desk. Then she went back to her list of *Cowtown* targets to see if there were any other people close enough to Boston that they might consider coming to the Stickler Syndrome Foundation fund-raiser. She came up with three possibilities who lived in cities with frequent plane flights to Boston: one each in Chicago, D.C., and Toronto.

A little background research gave some likely hooks she could use for the interviews. Of course, the big hook would be *Cowtown*, but ten nearly identical articles about "How I Spent My Time in Cowtown" would bore the hell out of Tilda, let alone the readers. She made a few notes, then hit the phones.

First she called Christopher Hale in D.C., who'd switched from acting to writing Western novels. With books to promote, he was happy to give Tilda a phone interview. His memories of working as a stagecoach driver who rescued a group of spunky orphans after the horses ran off were sharp and funny, and spiced with examples of why actors prefer to avoid working with children and animals. He also said he'd be delighted to come to the fund-raiser and help promote the *Cowtown* resort. The only request he made was that he be allowed to sell copies of his books, and perhaps have them stocked in the resort's gift shops. Tilda promised to pass on his name and request to the Ambrose brothers.

Next was Elizabeth Grainger, who'd appeared as a farmer's wife with a secret that threatened to rip Cowtown apart: a child born out of wedlock. She hadn't stayed in show business long before getting married and going back to Chicago to raise a family, which distracted a little from her appeal. This was more than made up for by her rose-colored memories of her brief acting career, and the hook was her discussion of the way times had changed so drastically that a child born out of wedlock in Hollywood today was barely even news. Unfortunately, she wasn't available for the fund-raiser, though she thought a resort appearance might be possible, particularly if she could bring a grandchild or two along.

The next target was one Tilda had been looking forward to. Emmett Ryker, like the Ambrose brothers, had started out life as a real cowboy. He'd been brought up on a ranch, and had spent many years wrangling horses and doing stunt riding for TV. He'd also had a few speaking parts along the way, though his acting was on the wooden side, but that had worked pretty well for his *Cowtown* stint. He'd played a laconic bronco buster come to town in search of the Great White Whale of the West—a stallion who'd never been tamed. Fortunately, Ryker was more talkative than his character had been, and agreed to speak to Tilda at three thirty the next day.

Her cell phone rang as she was halfway through a draft of the Christopher Hale interview, and she answered without looking at the caller ID, assuming it was Cooper.

"Are you still busy?"

"Um. Yeah. Hi. It's Quentin."

Tilda smacked herself in the forehead. "Sorry, I was expecting somebody else. Can we start over?"

He cleared his throat. "Hi, Tilda. It's Quentin."

"Quentin! What a delightful surprise! How are you?"

"Fine, thank you. And you?"

"Other than acting like a complete idiot on the phone, I'm peachy."

He laughed. "How was your weekend?"

Since going into an account of stealing files from a dead pinup's computer didn't seem to be the best way to shake off that reputation of being an idiot, Tilda said. "Not bad. Spent some time with friends, called the folks, did the laundry—life in the big city. How about you?"

"I drove to Pennsylvania for my niece's birthday party. It's amazing how much noise little children can make. It's almost inversely proportional to their size."

Aha! Now she knew why he hadn't called. "I think it's a secret chemical found only in Happy Meals."

"Perhaps I should sneak some chicken nuggets into the lab for analysis."

"I don't know, Quentin. It might fall into the category of things man was not meant to know."

"Aren't men putting the chemical into the Happy Meals?"

"I'm thinking space aliens."

He laughed again. "I was wondering if you're free for dinner some night this week."

Before Tilda could answer, she heard Colleen come in without her usual cheery yet inquisitive greeting—instead she stomped her way into her own room. "How about tonight?" Tilda said. "Or would that blow my studied air of nonchalance?"

"I'll take enthusiasm over nonchalance any day."

This being a second date, Tilda would have been willing to let Quentin pick her up, but since he was currently in Boston without wheels, they decided it made more sense for him to take the T to Malden Center, where she would pick him up in her car. He was about to leave work, so that gave her a chance to perform a quick wash and change.

Colleen spent most of Tilda's prep time shut up in her room, but ventured out as Tilda was pulling on her snazzy new coat and coordinating accessories, presumably making sure that her snit had been noticed.

"Are you going somewhere?" she asked Tilda.

"Just on my way out. See you later."

"Look, about last night . . ."

"Colleen, I do not blame you for being pissed about my waking you up. I'm not happy about it, either. If I knew a way to stop it, I would."

"I know it's not your fault." She really did look apologetic, but she blew it with, "Maybe we should talk it all out tonight when you get back. You know, get it out of your system."

"I won't be back until late," Tilda said, then held up the overnight bag she'd packed, just in case. "In fact, if things go well, I won't be back until tomorrow, so you'll be sure of getting a good night's sleep." She scooted out the door before more questions could emerge, grinning as she hid the bag in her trunk.

Tilda introduced Quentin to the Border Café for dinner, and enjoyed being with him so much that she didn't even notice if the hunky waiter was on duty. First they talked about Quentin's work, which he did a decent job of explaining to a layperson, only occasionally lapsing into overly technical lingo. Then Tilda reciprocated with stories about strange celebrities. Quentin was more in the loop for news about the *Cowtown* fund-raiser than she was, and shared some details she hadn't heard. The topic of costumes for the big night came up, but neither was willing to tell what they'd be wearing. In Quentin's case, it might very well have been his wanting to surprise Tilda. In Tilda's case, it was because she'd forgotten she needed a costume.

They took their time over dinner, and when Tilda drove Quentin home to Woburn, he invited her into his condo for an unspecified "little while." She was pleased to observe that he was neat without being obsessive, and believed in comfortable furniture. He had plenty of books, DVDs, and CDs, with enough convergences and divergences from her own tastes to provide conversational fodder, and if the pictures on his walls were bland, at least they weren't pinups.

She was even happier to discover that he was a much better kisser than he'd had time to demonstrate at the end of their last date. He was skilled at other things, too, and it turned out to be a good thing that she'd packed the overnight bag.

It would have been almost perfect if she hadn't woken him up in the middle of the night, screaming yet again.

Chapter 24

The interpretation of dreams is the royal road to knowledge of
the unconscious activities of the mind.
　　　—*THE INTERPRETATION OF DREAMS* BY SIGMUND FREUD

TILDA managed to get up when Quentin needed to, and
played her role as guest as needed: helping him fix breakfast, kissing him good-bye with sincerity and enthusiasm,
and wishing him a day as wonderful as their night together
had been. But as soon she got back to her apartment, she
admitted to herself that she couldn't let the bad dream situation go on any longer. As a mature, independent woman,
she needed to tackle the problem head-on. So she called
her big sister.

By a few minutes after noon, Tilda and June were working their way through a basket of fresh-baked rolls at Ber-
tucci's. As she'd hoped, June had been happy to get away
for Italian food with her, despite the frigid temperatures,
and was equally happy to have Tilda pick her up so she
could wait a little longer to dig her own car out from under
the inch of snow that had fallen while Quentin and Tilda
were distracted.

It didn't take long for them to talk their way through the
usual warm-up topics: June's kids, Tilda's work, and the
ritual cursing of Massachusetts winters.

Then Tilda said, "I've got a question for you."

"It's about time you got down to business."

"How do you do that?"

"I'm your sister, a psychologist, and a mother. It's what I do."

"I see your point."

"Besides, you look like shit."

"Thanks so much."

"I call 'em like I see 'em. What's wrong?"

Tilda ran her fingers through her hair, figuring it couldn't hurt her styling anyway, since she already looked like shit. "I'm having problems sleeping."

"For how long?"

"A couple of weeks."

"Since you found that woman dead, right?"

Tilda nodded. "No surprises there, I suppose."

"Not to me. Do you want to talk about it?"

"Would it help?"

"How should I know?"

"I was hoping that Ph.D. after your name would give you a hint."

"Research, not clinical, remember?"

"Then I was hoping you had researched it."

"Sorry."

"What about motherly knowledge? Ross's night terrors?"

June shuddered at the memory. "God, don't remind me. He'd wake up shrieking, without even knowing what it was that had him upset, and the only thing that would calm him down was to watch cartoons until he fell back asleep."

"I tried that."

"Really?"

"Really. At this point, I'm waking up almost every night. I thought the cartoons might work better than guzzling NyQuil."

"But no luck?"

Tilda shook her head. "But I did get an idea for a story about classic voice actors."

"Better that than NyQuil, I guess."

"Tried that, too. It kept me asleep, but it wasn't exactly restful. Instead of waking up from the nightmare when Sandra sat up with blood dripping from her head, I spent the whole night running from her. Longest night of my life."

"Oh, sweetie!"

Their salads arrived, giving Tilda a perfect opportunity to dodge her sister's sympathy. It wasn't that she didn't appreciate it—she was just lousy at accepting sympathy.

Once they'd had time for a taste or two each, Tilda said, "Anyway, I was hoping you'd have an idea."

"Sleeping with a familiar object?"

"June, I haven't slept with a stuffed animal since I was in junior high school."

June took another bite.

"It didn't work."

"How about visualizing a happy outcome when you wake up? That worked for Ross when he had nightmares about monsters. He'd imagine the monsters in tutus."

"Wasn't there a spell in one of the Harry Potter books that worked that way?"

"Yes," June admitted, "but it's still a good idea."

Tilda considered it. "I'm dreaming about a dead woman reaching for me. I don't think a dead woman in a tutu would be much of an improvement."

"I see what you mean. How about relaxation before bed, like a hot bath or soothing music?"

"Tried it."

"What about the other direction? Physical exertion before bedtime to wear yourself out?"

"I tried that last night. My exercise partner was not pleased when I woke him up in the middle of the night."

June choked on her lettuce, and several minutes were required to get her breathing well enough that she could ask, "Who?"

"Trust you to have your eyes on the prize. His name is Quentin, and he's a doctor."

"No, seriously, who was it?"

"Seriously, he's a doctor."

"Where did you meet him?"

"I picked him up via an online ad."

"Tilda!"

She rolled her eyes. "Jeez, you'd believe anything. I met him through work. Did I tell you about the series of articles I'm doing to promote that Western resort? The resort team is sponsoring a charity fund-raiser, and Dr. Quentin Beaudine is a researcher for the charity."

"Is he cute?

"Why would I exercise with a non-cute person?"

"I could provide examples from your past—" June started to say, but fortunately, their orders of ravioli arrived in time to stop her.

Once the waiter was gone, Tilda said, "I will be happy to tell you about sleeping with Quentin, but for now, I'd like to figure out how I can actually *sleep* with him."

June shrugged. "Trauma-induced bad dreams usually fade in time."

"According to my loving and supportive big sister, the only thing that's fading is my looks."

"Maybe we're going about this the wrong way. Let's look at the root cause of the bad dream."

"I'm pretty sure I've got that one. I found an old lady murdered. Simple."

"*Not* simple. Are you upset by her death, or because you'd just been there and it could just as easily have been you?"

"Both, I guess. But I've been around scary, dangerous things before, and had no bad dreams. Or at least not dreams that played over and over again like *Brady Bunch* reruns."

"Then let's look at other causes. Physical problems? New medication? Stress? Unresolved issues?"

"Physically, just lack of sleep," Tilda said, ticking off

the answer on her fingers. "The only medication is that one night of NyQuil. Stress . . . The new assignment is a big deal, but the deadline isn't too bad, and having money coming in is more of a stress-reliever than a stress-causer."

"Unresolved issues?"

"Maybe . . . Did I tell you that Jillian hinted at hiring me full time at *Entertain Me!*?"

"No! That's wonderful." June looked at her. "Isn't that wonderful?"

"It's flattering, but the jury is still out on wonderfulness. We haven't talked money yet, and that would make a difference."

"But it's sure to be better than what you make as a freelancer."

"Probably, and even if it's not, there are benefits. Vacation, sick time, and insurance so I can pay a psychologist to help me deal with bad dreams instead of bugging my sister."

"But?"

"There's no but. I just don't want to count on anything until I get a formal offer."

"That sounds reasonable," June said, eyeing Tilda suspiciously. "Anyway, we've got emotional trauma, an important deadline, a possible job offer, and a new relationship. Sounds like a perfect recipe for bad dreams to me."

"Great. I'm the Emeril of nightmares."

"On the good side, knowing what the problems are is half the battle, and all of these issues are going to reach some sort of closure. The deadline will pass, you'll either get the job or not, and the relationship won't be new for long. As for the emotional trauma, it really should fade."

"If the cops would find Sandra's killer, that would help considerably."

"Has there been any progress?"

"Not really. Of course, the cops aren't telling me anything."

"You aren't a suspect, are you? I read that the police always look at the person who finds a body."

"I don't think so. They haven't questioned me since that night. Cooper gave me an alibi, and the waiter at the California Pizza Kitchen probably remembered us because it was so quiet that night. I couldn't have done it, even if I'd had a motive."

"That's a relief."

"Anyway, I called the detective who questioned me, but got nothing."

"Don't you have a source in the department?"

"Why would an entertainment reporter have a source in the department?"

"I thought all reporters had a source in the department."

"I'll see about getting one, but in the meantime, all I know is what I read in the papers. They don't know why anybody would have killed Sandra, and the MO doesn't match any known serial killers. The last time I spoke to Lil, they were still looking at her, probably because she was Sandra's heir and was in business with her. I bet they're thinking embezzling or something like that."

June eyed her. "You aren't thinking about taking a more active role in this investigation, are you?"

Tilda turned her attention to her ravioli.

"You've already taken a more active role, haven't you?"

"I've been moderately active," Tilda admitted.

June sighed. "Let's hear it."

Tilda told her how she'd copied the files from Sandra's computer, realized some were missing, and visited Bill Hawks to get the full set. Unfortunately, June was sharp enough to figure out that Tilda must have had some reason for thinking pictures were involved, so Tilda had to describe the incident with her being pushed into the street.

"Did you tell the police?"

"Tell them what? 'I think somebody pushed me down,

and somebody stole something from my purse. Only I wasn't hurt, and I didn't see anybody, and the pictures weren't worth anything anyway.'"

"Yes, you could have told them that."

"Well, I didn't. I didn't decide I was pushed on purpose until I noticed the pictures were missing, and by then, all the witnesses were long gone."

"Still."

"Besides, I'd feel funny bringing myself to the attention of the cops again. It was disconcerting as hell when Detective Salvatore looked at me at Sandra's funeral. You know how Mom could make us feel guilty whether or not we'd done anything? It was like that, only I'm worried about jail time instead of getting grounded."

"Did I mention that paranoia is a classic symptom of lack of sleep?"

"So am I paranoid for thinking the cops suspect me, or paranoid for thinking somebody tried to kill me?"

June opened her mouth, closed it, opened it again, and filled it with her last forkful of ravioli. Only when she'd thoroughly chewed and swallowed did she say, "I'm not sure."

"Me, either," Tilda said. "So, going back to the bad dreams, do you think it really would help if I did more snooping?"

"I do not remember saying that. In fact, I'm almost sure I didn't say that."

"But you did say I need closure, and knowing who killed Sandra would provide closure, right?"

"I remember you trying your twisted logic on Mom, too."

"If you can't win 'em over with logic, baffle 'em with bullshit."

"Okay, here's my considered advice. If you can investigate cautiously, without drawing attention to yourself from either the killer or the police—"

"I think I already have attention from both."

"Then if you can do so without drawing *further* attention to yourself, it might help with the bad dreams. Of course, now I'll be having bad dreams worrying about you."

"I suggest physical exertion before you go to sleep. I'll call your husband and let him know."

Chapter 25

"Sure he's a real cowboy," Lu squeaked indignantly. "It's them cowboys out West that ain't real. Why, last winter we was playin' in a museum in New York—that's a dime museum, you know—and they had a big rodeo at Madison Square Garden. Some of them cowboys came to see Bronko's act and was they surprised! He showed 'em lots about rope-spinnin' and whip-crackin' they never knowed about. Why, they couldn't hardly understand a lot of the real cowboy talk he uses."
—MEMOIRS OF A SWORD SWALLOWER BY DANIEL P. MANNIX

LUNCH took a decidedly nonserious tone after that, and after giving June a detailed report about her evening with Quentin, Tilda barely got her sister back to her house in time to greet the kids and herself back to Malden in time to call Emmett Ryker, the real-life cowboy.

Ryker was both charming and hilarious as he told about handling not just the horses, but the people involved: a starlet's first face-to-face encounter with a horse; one poor soul who was so allergic to horses that they had to use a stunt double every time a horse came on-screen; and a guest star who swore up and down that he knew how to ride when he was nothing but a river sand cowboy. Tilda had to ask for an explanation of that last phrase—it meant somebody who'd rented a horse once or twice and then pretended to be an expert rider.

It was great stuff, but every time Tilda nudged Ryker

toward his shared background with the Ambrose brothers, he shied away like a mustang spotting a rattler.

Finally she asked, "Emmett, am I missing something? Did you have a problem with Tucker and Hoyt Ambrose?"

He sighed heavily. "No, I don't have anything against them, but . . . Tilda, can we keep this off the record? I really want a shot at some of that promotional money if they've a mind to spend it, but if this gets out, I'll be out of luck."

"Sure. Off the record."

"Those boys weren't cowboys any more than you are."

"Are you serious?"

"I can't tell you exactly where they were from, but I guarantee it was from the eastern side of the Mississippi."

"But what about the stories of their being raised on a ranch? Up at dawn, herding cattle, busting broncos, dodging tumbleweeds, square dancing on Saturday night?"

"They'd spent some time on a ranch somewhere, I'll give 'em that, but I'm guessing it was the kind you paid to stay at."

"You've lost me."

"A dude ranch, darlin'."

"The Cowboy Kings are dudes?" Tilda couldn't decide if she was appalled or amused. "Those stories were phony?"

"Like a wooden nickel."

She finally came down on the side of amused, and burst out laughing. After a few seconds, Ryker joined in.

When she got her breath, she said, "I can't believe they pulled that off. Didn't anybody notice?"

"Not that I know of, but you've got to remember, they weren't scissorbills," Ryker said.

"They weren't what?"

"A scissorbill is somebody who doesn't know the front end of a horse from the back. The Ambrose boys could both really ride, and Hoyt was damned good, but when it came to working with cattle, or in a barn, or anything like that, they were useless. Besides, their accents wouldn't have fooled anybody except a bunch of Hollywood yahoos who didn't know any better."

"They fooled me," Tilda admitted, "but then again, I'm a Massachusetts yahoo."

"Oh, they've improved considerably, just by listening to people who had authentic accents."

Tilda still couldn't get over it. "Here I thought I was as cynical as they come, and it never occurred to me that they weren't real cowboys." Then, thinking of another *Cowtown* icon who wasn't quite what she seemed, she added, "Next you'll be telling me Cynthia Barth wasn't a virgin."

"Now don't you go bad-mouthing Miss Barth," Everett warned, with a bit of an edge in his voice. "She's a fine lady—you didn't often see anybody like that in Hollywood."

Obviously he didn't know about Morning Glory, and Tilda saw no reason to enlighten him. Instead she asked a few more questions, and he gave her more great stories.

Afterward, Tilda wished she hadn't let Ryker go off the record before he told the truth about Tucker and Hoyt. It would make one hell of a story. Admittedly, now that she knew, it wouldn't be too hard for her to find evidence elsewhere of where they were really from, but if they wanted to remain the Cowboy Kings, who was she to depose them?

Her next job was to get back to work on the Christopher Hale article she'd interrupted in order to go to dinner with Quentin. At five on the dot, Cooper called.

"Did you get the issue put to bed?"

"Just barely," he said with a groan. "We had a last-minute addition which caused a last-minute meltdown."

"Did somebody have a baby, file for divorce, or get caught doing something they shouldn't have?"

"All three, and I don't want to talk about it. I'm going to switch to your side of the industry, Tilda—your people never cause last-minute changes. They're stable."

She wished she could have told him about the Cowboy Kings just to prove him wrong, but her lips were sealed.

"Anyway, I'm sorry to have blown you off yesterday and I was too wiped to call you back last night."

"That's okay. I was out getting laid anyway."

"Seriously, what did you call about?"

"You remember the mysterious missing pictures?"

"Yeah?"

"I got copies from the amateur photographer in Medford."

"And?"

"And each one of these pictures shows a particular guy, apparently one of the other photographers?"

"And?"

"And I haven't got a clue who he is, or why Lil deleted these pictures from the file."

"Damn, girl, you got me worked up for nothing."

"It's not nothing," she said, irked. "I haven't given up. I've just been busy."

"Doing what?"

"Working, for one. Getting laid, for another."

"You *really* got laid?"

"It does happen now and then."

"Then what are you wasting my time for? Who, what, when, where, and why?"

"Who: Quentin. What: I think that's obvious. When: I already told you—last night. Where: His condo. And if you have to ask why . . ."

"What about how?"

"Again, if you have to ask—"

"I mean how was it?"

"Nice."

"Just nice?"

"I'd go so far as to say 'very nice.' Playing doctor is every bit as much fun as it's rumored to be." She decided not to mention her bad dreams—it would only lessen the value of the gloat.

"My little Matilda, boinking a doctor," Cooper sighed.

"I believe we agreed that you would not use that form of my name. Ever."

"Sorry. It just slipped out."

"Sure it did. Other than the last-minute meltdown, how's tricks at the office?"

"Why don't we just change the name to *Cowtown* central and be done with it?" Cooper groused. "Shannon and Nicole are spending more time on that fund-raiser than they are on their jobs, which is part of the reason for the meltdown. Plus Nicole made Shannon cry."

"What for?"

"Shannon is arranging swag bags for the VIPs—and no, you do not get one."

"Did I ask?"

"Anyway, Shannon ordered engraved iPod shuffles, and by the time Nicole found out, it was too late to cancel them."

"What's wrong with iPods?"

"According to Nicole, they're trés passé. Everybody gives them out now, even regular businesses. I've got three or four myself."

Obviously Tilda hadn't been getting the right swag bags—the only iPod she owned had been a Christmas gift from June. "Tell Shannon to check into getting the iPods preloaded: the theme from *Cowtown*, cowboy songs, and so on. That would make them different."

"That's brilliant! Hang on." Cooper covered the phone, but Tilda could still hear him. "Shannon, Tilda has an idea. Get the iPods downloaded with the theme for *Cowtown* and cowboy songs!"

Even at a distance, Tilda winced at the resulting squeal, which was followed up by Shannon saying, "Tell Tilda I love her."

Cooper returned to the phone. "Shannon loves you."

"My life is complete."

"Seriously, original thinking is just what we need around here."

"It's not that original. My niece won an iPod from the Disney Channel that was filled with soundtracks and Hannah Montana."

"Whatever. We hadn't thought of it."

Tilda heard Shannon calling Cooper's name.

"I've got to go. Shannon wants me to help pick out songs. Let me know what you find out about the mysterious man."

"Will do."

"And if you get laid again."

"You'll be the third to know. Unless it's a threesome—then you'll be fourth."

"You wish!" He rang off.

Tilda continued working on the article, but at the back of her mind she was speculating about how she could identify the mystery photographer. Searching for Virginia Pure was still ridiculous, of course, but there had to be another way.

After all, she knew two people who'd been around New York camera clubs back then. First there was Louise Silberblatt. Though she hadn't been present at this particular shoot, maybe she'd known the photographer from a different one. Second was Cynthia Barth, aka Morning Glory, but Tilda didn't think she was going to suddenly open up to her. She hadn't even been in touch to set up an interview about *Cowtown*, let alone her pinup past. Louise was the better choice, but she was skittish, too, so it wasn't a question Tilda could ask out of the blue. She'd have to devise an approach.

In the meantime, she finished the Hale article, and after a break for dinner, wrapped up the Grainger piece. Deciding that she'd done enough for one day, she spent what was left of the evening watching TV companionably with Colleen. She even answered her roomie's nosy questions about her date the previous night, as long as she asked them during commercials.

After that, she slept the whole night through, without a single bad dream to disturb her sleep. She knew it was probably because of her talk with June, but she had to wonder if continuing to nose around Sandra's murder was part of the reason, too.

Chapter 26

I never minded the bondage stuff. At every other shoot, it was all "Look this way," or "Put your leg up on the chair" or "Lean over and touch your toes." But once I was tied up, all I had to do was look scared. It was kind of restful.
—SANDRA SECHREST, QUOTED IN "QUEEN OF THE PINUPS" BY TILDA HARPER, *NOT DEAD YET* MAGAZINE

TILDA was up early, at least by a freelancer's standards, meaning that she was working away on the article about Emmett Ryker by nine o'clock, and had it finished by lunchtime. She e-mailed it and the previous day's pieces to Jillian, along with suitable artwork, and was in the living room with a ham sandwich waiting to be eaten and an episode of *30 Rock* on DVD ready to be watched when her cell phone rang.

"Jillian wants to know how much longer she's going to have to wait for the *Cowtown* stuff," Nicole said, wasting no time on the needless demands of etiquette.

"I just sent in three pieces. That makes—"

"She means the Cynthia Barth article. That's the cornerstone of the series."

"Miss Barth was supposed to be in touch with me about scheduling."

"Is that how you find people? By waiting for them to call you?"

Tilda took a bite of sandwich, and swallowed it along with the reply she wanted to make. "You're right."

"Don't argue with me—What?"

"I'll call that Barth woman right away and demand that she see me. So what if she's a major investor for the resort project?"

There was a pause. "Look, if she's being hesitant . . ."

"No, no, I realize now that I've got the power of *Entertain Me!* behind me, and I'll use that power to force her to talk. Thanks, Nicole, this has been the inspiration I needed to get the job done."

Tilda hung up, counted the seconds until Nicole called again, and let it go straight to voice mail. Then she finished her sandwich and laughed at *30 Rock*.

Once she was finished with both lunch and the show, she admitted to herself that Nicole did have a point, even if it had been presented badly. She needed face time with Miss Barth, whether or not Miss Barth wanted to face her.

She looked up the actress's contact information, but just in case she was dodging Tilda's calls, used her landline, which had blocked caller ID because of complex issues with a former roommate. Miss Barth picked up on the third ring.

"Hello?"

"Miss Barth. This is Tilda Harper calling."

"Oh, I didn't realize it was you. I'm afraid I'm on my way out and—"

"This won't take a minute. I just want to schedule a time when we can get together for me to interview you about your experiences on *Cowtown* and since." That should make it plain that she wasn't going to ask about the pinup stuff.

"Oh yes, but I'm so dreadfully busy—"

"I know the resort work must be eating up time, and I'll keep our talk as brief as possible. We could even do it by phone, if you can supply pictures."

"Pictures?!"

Tilda could have kicked herself. "If you've got something

recent, that is. I've already got some wonderful shots of you from your *Cowtown* days."

The woman was still hesitating, and Tilda wracked her brain to come up with something convincing. Damn it, she had to stop thinking of Miss Barth as Cowtown's official virgin. The woman was an actress with her best days long behind her, and Tilda had never found a bait more appealing to the formerly famous than flattery.

So she said, "Of course, I'd really rather sit down with you personally. I can get a lot of the facts from other sources, but that's no substitute for personal contact with the woman who was the heart and soul of *Cowtown*."

"You're sweet," Miss Barth said, starting to warm, "but it really was an ensemble."

"Oh, absolutely. The whole cast was strong. But when it came to expressing the show's meaning, it was always Arabella Newman. You personified the Cowtown Code!" Tilda faked an embarrassed laugh. "I mean, Arabella did. That's how I see the show, anyway."

"That's very perceptive of you, dear. I've never quite thought of it that way before."

"I'd love to get your perspective, if you can squeeze me in."

"Of course I will," Miss Barth said, as if she'd never considered anything different. "What about tomorrow morning? We could meet at my suite at the Park Plaza at ten."

"That would be perfect," Tilda gushed. "Thank you so much."

They hung up, and Tilda sent a quick text message to Cooper.

Tilda: Is Nicole on the phone?

Cooper: Yes. Why?

Tilda: I need to leave her a message.

She called Nicole's number, and when it went to voice mail, said, "Nicole, this is Tilda. I called that Barth woman and told her that if she wants the press, she damned well better make time for me. She folded like knockoff Manolos. I'm meeting her tomorrow."

Then she hung up. She knew she was going to pay for her fun eventually, but she was pretty sure it would be worth it.

There were plenty of working hours left, so she went back to her list of *Cowtown* stars. She'd interviewed six so far, which left four to go, plus Miss Barth.

Frankie Adams was easy enough to find—she'd continued to work in television as she aged from ingénue to young bride to mother to grandmother to feisty old lady. Tilda had seen her enthusiastically chewing scenery as a bag lady on *Law & Order* a month or two earlier. Since she was still working, she had an agent, and since Tilda rarely ran into an agent who wouldn't happily point her toward a client if said client could get a few inches of press, in fifteen minutes she had Frankie's phone number and a selection of head shots e-mailed to her. After Tilda prepared some questions—not a struggle, since she was using the same set for all the *Cowtown* interviews—and researched Frankie's background, she was ready to make the call.

"Ms. Adams, this is Tilda Harper. I'm working on an article about guest stars on the show *Cowtown* for *Entertain Me!* and I was wondering if I could ask you some questions."

"Call me Frankie. And of course you can ask me some questions. My agent would disown me if I didn't let you ask me questions. You'd think an old broad like me never got interviewed." She cackled. "Just because I haven't talked to a reporter in five years! That means you get five years' worth of gossip!"

Tilda liked her already. "I'll have to take a rain check on the recent stuff because this article is just about your experiences on *Cowtown*, but there's room for a plug about what you're doing next."

"You'll be missing out on some juicy stories about Sam Waterston."

"I'd fit it in if I could, but my editor is being pretty strict on this one."

"Her loss. So what do you need?"

Tilda got a couple of mildly amusing anecdotes about Frankie's *Cowtown* appearance. The actress had still been in her ingénue period then, and had played a shy young farmer's daughter who tried to make herself over as a woman of the world to win the eye of a dashing cavalryman. The usual disaster ensued, followed by the usual happy ending. It had not been one of Tilda's favorite episodes, and Frankie sounded bored about it, too.

Since Tilda really didn't want a boring article, she cast around for something to liven it up. "How was the regular cast to work with?"

"They were fine, but they knew I was just passing through, so they didn't waste much time with me. Tucker Ambrose hinted about taking me on as a regular, maybe killing off the husband so I could be a young widow, which would have been great because I looked terrific in black. But that might have just been pillow talk."

Tilda blinked. "So you and Tucker had a relationship?"

"Just a one-night stand. Well, technically a one-night-and-two-afternoon-quickies stand. It was one of the quickies that kept me from getting the regular job. Cynthia Barth walked in on us, and that put paid to the whole idea. Jealous bitch!"

"You mean that she and Tucker were—"

"God, no. She just didn't want anybody having any fun, and when it's done right, sex is a whole lot of fun. Barth went running to Hoyt, talking about how I wasn't right for the show because I was such a tramp, and how the sponsors would leave in droves and people wouldn't let their kids watch. Keeping me would probably have caused cancer, too! Anyway, Hoyt caved and Tucker never argued with him, so I was out. At least Tucker felt guilty about it—he bought me a nice diamond necklace, and made sure I got some work on one of their other shows later on."

"Miss Barth must really have disliked you."

"I never figured out why, either. I was no threat. She was as good an actress as I was, she was prettier, and she was the show's female lead. She even got to spout the voice-over every week. But she sure wanted me gone. She even dragged in stuff about my modeling, and she must have done some digging to find out about that."

"Modeling?" Tilda said, wondering what was coming next. Usually she guided an interview—this time it was all she could do to keep up.

"Pinup stuff. I know you've heard of Bettie Page. Well, I worked with her. Taught her everything she knew about modeling, too."

Clearly Bettie had had many teachers. "Did you work with the camera clubs?"

"You know about that stuff? Yeah, I did camera club work, and a few magazines. That was when I was still trying to make it on Broadway. Eventually I figured out that wasn't going to happen. I had the right look for musicals, but couldn't sing or dance, and I was too wholesome for the serious stuff. So I switched coasts and went into television."

"And you don't know how Miss Barth found out about the modeling?" Of course, Tilda had a hunch that it had had something to do with Barth having been Morning Glory.

"I sure as hell didn't tell her. She never spoke more than half a dozen words to me—the first day I showed up on set, she stuck her nose up so far in the air I'm surprised she didn't trip over something. All I can figure is that she saw my pictures somewhere. For all I know she had a stack of back issues of *Titter* sitting under her bed to whack off to every night, though I didn't really see her as a dyke."

"She doesn't seem that way to me, either," Tilda said, "just very proper." *Other than her pinup pictures, of course.* She was starting to think that every actress in Hollywood back then had pinup pictures in her past. "You know, Frankie, I've recently run into several actresses of your generation who did pinups. Was it that common?"

"Hard to say. Nobody talked about it—once you were out of it, you kept your mouth shut if you wanted to get acting work. Look at what happened to Bettie. What was that movie they made about her?"

"*The Notorious Bettie Page.*"

"That's the one. It was hard enough getting work—being notorious would destroy your career."

"But there have always been vamps."

"Yeah, but they only allowed a few at a time, and you had to look like a bad girl—sultry, dark-eyed, that whole style. I had big brown eyes and freckles—I looked like a good girl, so I had to be a good girl, whether I liked it or not. These days, nobody cares what you do. Hell, the more of a mess you get into, the better the press coverage."

"It must be frustrating."

"Yeah, it is. Then again, I didn't have to starve myself to a size zero either. I had some hips on me, baby. Still do!"

Tilda looked down at her notes, not sure what else to ask. She had plenty of material, and while a lot of it would never make it into the *Cowtown* series, she'd find a place for it somewhere, and would have to wrangle some sort of assignment to find out the dirt about Sam Waterston.

One last question occurred to her, since Frankie had been part of the camera club scene. "This has nothing to do with the *Cowtown* article, but I've got a photo of a guy I'm trying to identify. He was a member of one of the old New York camera clubs. He shows up in the pictures taken by another amateur, but that guy never knew his name, and I'm having a hard time finding anybody who was around back then."

"You mean anybody who's still alive."

"Something like that," Tilda said, not wanting to mention how recently at least one of the people had died. "If I e-mail you some photos, could you look and see if you know who the guy was?"

"Tilda, I'd be happy to help you, but I wouldn't be able to recognize anybody. You see, my eyesight never was much good, and this was long before contacts were sold in every shopping mall. I wore glasses, and I'm talking ugly horn-rims with Coke-bottle-bottom lenses. Me being as vain as the next gal, and of course not wanting to blow the pinup image, I always took them off before I went to a photo shoot. That meant I was going by voices and shapes, not faces, and I don't think I could identify any of the photographers then, let alone now."

"It was a long shot, anyway," Tilda said philosophically. She asked a few questions about Frankie's next project, which turned out to be another bag lady, this time on *CSI*, then thanked her for her time.

After a break to get a glass of Dr Pepper, she called Aaron Stemfel, the character actor who'd been on *Star Trek*. There was no answer, but since he lived in California, there was a chance she could get him later in her evening, which wouldn't be late for him, so she left a message and started writing the article about Frankie. The timing gods must have been pleased with her, because just as she finished the first draft, Aaron Stemfel called back.

They exchanged greetings and the requisite amount of small talk for a previous interviewer and interviewee, and then Tilda started in on her *Cowtown* questions.

"That's a show I don't get asked about very often," Aaron said. "I've probably been interviewed at least once for every second of airtime on *Star Trek*, but there's not much interest in the old TV Westerns."

"The new resort might change that."

"Could be, but I've been around this business far too long to count on anything."

Stemfel had appeared on four episodes, each time playing the unimaginatively named Cookie, who drove a chuck wagon during cattle drives. It hadn't been much of a part at first, just a bit of comic relief, but he'd been colorful enough that they kept bringing him back, with more and more of a story each time, until he finally died in a truly heart-wrenching scene where he bravely placed himself and his chuck wagon in the middle of a pass to block a stampede that would have destroyed Cowtown.

He had plenty of tales to tell about the show, enough for Tilda to write an article two or three times longer than she'd been asked for. She almost didn't bother to ask about working with the Ambrose brothers and Miss Barth, but threw it in on the off chance that she'd get an even better batch of quotes.

"I always liked working with Hoyt and Tucker," Stemfel said. "A lot of producers spent most of their time in the office, but those two were hands-on. Tucker was good with people, keeping everybody happy, and Hoyt had a real eye for camera angles, what would look good on film. Not something I'd have expected from a couple of cowboys."

Tilda bit her tongue for what seemed like the millionth time since she'd found out the truth about the Ambrose brothers. "What about Miss Barth?"

He hesitated long enough to get Tilda interested, but all he said was, "Cynthia wasn't always an easy person to work with."

"I've heard she could be standoffish," Tilda prompted.

"I don't think she meant to be. She was always focused on the show, and the message we were presenting. Now, my character was just there for laughs, which was fine. Even Shakespeare put in characters to keep the groundlings happy. But Miss Barth wasn't satisfied with that. She wanted him to mean something, to set some kind of example. That's where the idea for Cookie turning hero came from. I shouldn't complain—it gave me a hell of an exit. On the other hand, I didn't get any more work on the show."

"Do you think she was trying to get rid of you?"

"No, Cynthia just thought it set a better moral tone for

the show. She was wound tight as a drum, which is probably why she had her problems later on."

"What problems do you mean?"

"The drinking." He hesitated again. "You hadn't heard about that before, had you?"

"No, I hadn't," she admitted.

"I shouldn't have said anything. Tilda, can we keep that part off the record?"

"Of course, if that's what you want," Tilda said, stifling a sigh at having yet another juicy bit of information that she couldn't use. "But if you wouldn't mind telling me a bit more just for my own curiosity . . ."

"It would be cruel to leave you hanging. Here's the thing. Cynthia was typecast as Arabella, which happens a lot. Sometimes I regret I never got a series lead, or even a good supporting role, but all in all I think I've had a better life for being a nomad. I've worked more than a lot of people—I could be working now, if I wanted to. Cynthia didn't have that option. And it wasn't just the typecasting. Her having been so formal didn't help her when it came to getting more work—she hadn't made many friends. The Ambrose brothers had gone on to other things, and I think they tried to use her, but they had to answer to studio bosses who wanted fresh faces, so all they could do was give her the occasional guest shot. After a while, Cynthia's own agent wouldn't return her calls, and well, she dove into a bottle and stayed there a long time."

"How long?"

"Years," he said sadly. "It's not like now, when everybody and his brother goes into rehab and there's an AA meeting in every church basement. Cynthia had to pull herself out, and it took her a lot of hard nights, but she did it. Word is that she's been sober ten years or more now, and I respect that, which is why I don't want you bringing it up now."

"I'll be interviewing her tomorrow," Tilda said, "but if

she doesn't mention it, neither will I." She asked him about attending the fund-raiser, purely out of habit, since she didn't think the Ambrose brothers would spring for a trip from California, but it turned out that Stemfel was going to be at a collectibles fair in New Hampshire the day after the event, and since he was planning to fly into Boston anyway, they could have him for the cost of a hotel room for the night.

They wound up the call, and Tilda had to laugh when before hanging up, Stemfel said, "You live long and prosper now."

After getting a refill on her Dr Pepper, Tilda put together an e-mail with contact information for all the guest stars who were willing to attend the fund-raiser, and shot it off to Jillian. With less than a week to go, there wouldn't be time to arrange any more, so she hoped the trio she had would pass muster.

Then she flipped through her notes, picking out the tidbits about Cynthia Barth. The woman was a mass of contradictions, and it seemed incredible that she'd kept her secrets for so many years.

On one hand, there was Miss Barth's past as a pinup model. Tilda had no idea how she'd ended up in that line of work, and if she'd liked it or hated it. She thought about asking Louise Silberblatt or Frankie, but didn't want to rouse suspicions, especially when Louise had seen Glory herself. Come to think of it, wasn't it odd that neither woman had recognized Barth when working with her on *Cowtown*?

Tilda opened the notebook with her notes on the interview with Louise to check something. The episodes she'd worked on were flashbacks, and she said she'd never been on set with the main cast. Then Tilda checked the episode list in her copy of *Cowtown Companion*, and saw that the only work Miss Barth did on those shows was the voice-over of the Cowtown Code. Louise might never have seen Miss Barth.

But wouldn't Louise have recognized Miss Barth from watching the show? Tilda called up more files on her computer, one of the pictures of Morning Glory and one of the publicity stills from *Cowtown*. Even knowing that they were the same woman, she could just barely see it. Glory was thinner than Arabella, which showed in her face, and of course, the women were dressed very differently. Arabella wore a high-necked dress, which only hinted at the bosom that Glory displayed in all its, well, glory. Then there was the body language. Though she felt sexist even thinking such a thing, to her, Morning Glory looked like a tart, and Arabella looked like a virgin, or at least chaste.

But the most obvious difference was the hair. At some point, Miss Barth had either dyed hers or she'd worn a wig like Louise. Whichever it was, Arabella Newman had had jet black hair while Glory's was glossy blond. In retrospect, Tilda realized that if it weren't for the hair, she wouldn't have made the connection. Blond Glory didn't resemble brunette Arabella, but she did look like silver-haired Miss Barth.

So it wasn't completely bizarre that Louise had recognized Miss Barth, but not Arabella. As for Frankie, with her eyesight, it was no wonder she hadn't recognized Miss Barth as a fellow pinup.

So that gave her a successful actress who was hiding her past no matter what it took, and clinging to the values that she'd spouted each week in the Cowtown Code voice-over. Wound tight didn't begin to cover it, and it was no wonder that she'd turned to drink once the show went to that big roundup in the sky. All these years later, she still wouldn't admit that she'd been Morning Glory—somebody had gone to the trouble of telling Joe's Lost Pinups site that Glory was dead, and Tilda wouldn't have been a bit surprised to find out that it was Miss Barth herself who spread that rumor, just to keep her secret.

It still seemed odd that *nobody* knew. Unless . . .

Why had Miss Barth gone to Sandra's funeral? How had she known about her death? They must have known one another back in the day, and presumably since then as well. Sandra had told Tilda that she knew where some of her former colleagues were, but that she was keeping their names to herself. Could Miss Barth have been one of the models Sandra knew about? Could Sandra have been the only one who knew about Morning Glory?

Except that now Sandra was dead, and Miss Barth was safe. At least she had been until she spotted Tilda looking at pictures of Morning Glory. Less than an hour later, somebody had pushed Tilda into the middle of traffic, where she could easily have been killed.

Could Miss Barth have killed Sandra, and tried to kill Tilda?

Physically? Without a doubt. She seemed to be in good health, and neither act had required much strength. Emotionally? Anybody who'd held herself that much in check for so many years was probably capable of just about anything.

Miss Barth had motive, means, and opportunity. And tomorrow, Tilda was going to be alone with her in a hotel room.

This time she wouldn't have to wait until bedtime to start having nightmares.

Chapter 27

You can't have a Western without pretty gals. Hell, look at *Brokeback Mountain*! Those cowboys didn't even like women, and they gave 'em Michelle Williams and Anne Hathaway. My brother and me always hired the prettiest gals we could find for *Cowtown*, and Cynthia Barth was the prettiest one of all.

— TUCKER AMBROSE, QUOTED IN *COWTOWN COMPANION* BY RUBEN TIMMONS

TILDA'S first celebrity interview had been with James Doohan, the man who'd played Scotty on *Star Trek*, and she still remembered how nervous she'd been. He'd been in town to speak, and she was ecstatic about the assignment to interview him for her college newspaper, right up until the morning they were supposed to meet. Then her stomach had shriveled to a lump, making breakfast unthinkable, and she seemed to forget how to speak, leaving her wondering if it would be okay to give him pieces of paper with the questions and write down his responses.

Tilda couldn't help thinking fondly about that first interview as she walked down the corridor toward Miss Barth's hotel suite. Not just because it had ended well. Doohan had proven to be warm, funny, and patient with an inexperienced interviewer. No, as she looked back she realized that as nervous as she'd been before that first interview, it was nothing compared to how she currently felt. She hadn't been nearly as worried that Doohan wanted to kill her.

Miss Barth was waiting for her at the door to her suite. "Hello, Tilda. Please come in."

Tilda thanked her and preceded her into the room, hating the feeling of vulnerability from having her back exposed. She turned around as soon as she could, but didn't sit down on the couch until Miss Barth sat in the armchair.

Though the suite was a little smaller than the one where the Ambrose brothers had had their meeting, it was still plenty plush by Tilda's standards, with a full-sized living room and a large picture window with a view only partially veiled by the sheer drapes.

She said, "Miss Barth, I really appreciate your taking time to talk to me. When I was talking to Cooper today— You remember Cooper, the *Entertain Me!* copyeditor?"

Miss Barth nodded.

"I told him I was coming to see you this morning, and he said that he knew you must be awfully busy. In fact I talked to him again as I was on the way up in the elevator, and he said several of the people at the office know I'm here talking to you, and they all realize how busy you are."

"Isn't that nice?" she said, looking bemused by Tilda's technique.

Maybe Tilda hadn't needed to emphasize that people knew where she was and who she was with quite so much. She took a good look at Miss Barth, with her hair carefully styled to disguise the fact that it was getting thinner, dressed in a perfectly tailored rose-colored suit. She was in her seventies, for God's sake, and Tilda had never seen anybody who looked less threatening in her whole life, and that included her first glimpses of June's newborn babies. She was being ridiculous.

"Would you like something to drink?" Miss Barth asked.

"No, thank you," she said quickly. After all, you didn't have to look threatening to slip something into a drink. She got out her notepad and pen. "Are you ready to start?"

"Of course," Miss Barth said, though she was sitting so stiffly that she couldn't have looked less ready. In fact, Tilda had to admit that the actress looked as uncomfortable as she felt herself.

An hour later, Tilda was starting to think Miss Barth was sneakier than she thought—maybe the woman was planning to bore her to death. It was her worst interview ever.

When Tilda asked about Miss Barth's upbringing, all she got were vague references to a happy childhood in Iowa. Schooling? Fond memories, but nothing specific. Parents? Gone. Brothers and sisters? None. Other family? None. The woman wouldn't even admit to having had a pet.

The first honest emotion Miss Barth showed was when Tilda asked her why she went into acting. Unfortunately, it was the all-too-familiar story of going to the theater and becoming completely lost in a fantasy world. Almost every actor told that story, with the only difference being which play or movie it had been. Miss Barth's inspiration was a local production of *As You Like It*—Tilda would be able to get a sentence out of that, or with padding, a short paragraph.

Then it was back to generalities, with Miss Barth's inevitable realization that Small Town, Iowa, wasn't big enough for her to grow as an artist, so she packed up to head to the Big Apple. Acting classes, bit parts in forgotten plays, and so on. Tilda wasn't sure if she should bring up the modeling or not—on one hand, she was curious to see how Miss Barth would react, but on the other hand, she didn't want that reaction to involve attempted murder. She compromised by asking about any day jobs the actress had held to keep body and soul together as she learned her craft, and when all Miss Barth would admit to was selling dishes at Macy's, she let it go.

Next it was on to California, and the dream of a film career. Tilda managed to squeeze a little human interest out of Miss Barth's train ride across the country. She'd had no money for the dining car, so she'd carried a loaf of bread and a jar of peanut butter, and to this day, couldn't eat a peanut butter sandwich.

Once in Hollywood, things moved quickly. She met the Ambrose brothers at a party during her first week, and when they started casting *Cowtown* a month later, she was their first choice for Arabella. She'd spent eight years in the role, and her eyes seemed to glow when she talked about it. Unfortunately, her stories did not. Miss Barth remembered every plot and every character from every episode and, for all Tilda knew, she had every script memorized, but knew nothing of the actors' and backstage workers' real lives or personalities. Even when Tilda tried to prompt her with stories she'd heard from *Cowtown* guest stars, she got nothing out of her.

Tilda pressed on, trying to find out about Miss Barth's personal life. Marriage? No. Children? A shocked look— the idea of children without marriage was unthinkable. Boyfriends? Only short-term. Partying? Casual dating with dear friends. Still no pets. No hobbies, no causes, and very little work outside *Cowtown*. The woman seemed to exist only on screen.

Tilda hinted around at the drinking issue as subtly as she could, but either Miss Barth didn't get the hints or didn't care to address the subject. Tilda was just as glad. She didn't really think the world needed another tale of a celebrity succumbing to addiction, only to regain sobriety after heroic efforts. Not that such stories weren't genuinely heroic, but they were only important to those involved. The rest of the world was pretty jaded—or maybe it was only Tilda herself who didn't want to hear about it.

Finally Tilda was down to her last question, the one that she'd asked several of the guest stars without getting any interest at all. If that didn't work, she was going to have to go with asking Miss Barth what kind of tree she'd be if she were a tree. "How did you see the Cowtown Code?"

For the first time, Miss Barth had something to say. "I think the Cowtown Code was the most important thing about *Cowtown*—it's what gave us our moral underpinnings. Without it, we would have been just another TV Western."

Tilda was afraid to say anything that might stem the sudden flow of words, so she just nodded.

Miss Barth went on. "You probably don't realize it, but the voice-overs I did were the hardest part of the scripts to write—sometimes they'd come first, and sometimes not until after the show was shot. One time we realized we didn't have an appropriate Code for a show, and had to reshoot pieces to make sure we were making a statement." She looked down modestly. "I'm no writer, but I can honestly say I wrote or rewrote almost every section of the Code. They had to be just right. Some of the outside script writers and directors didn't understand how important that was. But Tucker and Hoyt understood. Without the Code, a cowboy is nothing more than a colorful character, but with the Code he becomes something noble. Every single episode of *Cowtown* somehow demonstrated the Code."

Tilda said, "I always thought that the best episodes were the ones where the Code didn't agree with the law. Like when the woman ran away from an abusive husband, and the preacher said she ought to go back to him, but Arabella hid her and helped her escape."

" 'No true man hits a woman, and no woman should ever be forced to endure the violence of lesser men. That's the Cowtown Code,' " Miss Barth quoted. "The Code always prevailed."

"What about murder?" Tilda asked, watching carefully for the woman's reaction. "Weren't there a couple of episodes where murder was condoned by the Code?"

"They weren't murder, not if the killing was done by the Code," Miss Barth insisted. " 'There are sins that the law cannot punish, but which a true man cannot abide. Some men need killing. That's the Cowtown Code.' "

"You don't think that's a moral problem?"

"Well, *Cowtown* was set in a different time, in a very different place."

Tilda nodded, but she did notice that Miss Barth hadn't exactly refuted the idea of justifiable homicide. "One last question. Which tenet of the Cowtown Code did you find the most meaningful?"

She didn't hesitate. "It was the one from the very first episode, when Arabella opens the saloon. At the end, you hear her voice saying, 'When you come to Cowtown, it's as if you never existed before. All your sins are forgotten, and all your virtues as well. The only things that matter are what you do in this time and place. That's the Cowtown Code.'"

Chapter 28

There's more ways to skin a cat than stickin' his head in a boot jack and jerkin' on his tail.
— *DON'T SQUAT WITH YER SPURS ON* BY TEXAS BIX BENDER

IT was nearly noon by the time they finished the interview, and though Miss Barth invited her to lunch, Tilda lied about having another appointment. Though she was no longer as worried that Miss Barth was going to try to kill her, she didn't think her nerves would stand a meal of guarding her food from poison, let alone the possibility of somebody giving the woman a steak knife.

As soon as she got to the lobby, Tilda gave Cooper a call to let him know she'd survived the interview. She really had called him on her way up to see Miss Barth, just in case.

"You don't really believe that nice old lady would try to kill you, do you?" Cooper scoffed.

"Cooper, I don't know what to believe. Sandra was a nice old lady, too, and *somebody* killed her. Besides, Miss Barth had a motive. Sandra knew who she was."

"So what? Sandra must have known for years. Why would Miss Barth suddenly need to get rid of her?"

"That's a good question. The timing must mean something. You want to have lunch and talk it out?"

"Not today. I'm off to get some accessories for my costume."

"What costume?"

"My cowboy costume for the Stickler fund-raiser Saturday night. Don't tell me you've forgotten that you'll need a costume."

"Oh, that costume. Of course I haven't forgotten—I took care of mine ages ago. I thought you were talking about something kinky for you and Jean-Paul."

"You forgot, didn't you?"

She didn't want to lie to him, so she said, "Cooper, are you there? Cooper? Cooper, if you can hear me, I'm losing the connection." She tapped the mouthpiece a few times, then hung up. Hanging up was, after all, a way to lose a connection.

Well, at least she had a plan for the afternoon that didn't involve brooding over Sandra's death. Instead she was going to have to find a cowboy costume in Boston in January. How hard could that be?

Twenty-four hours later, she had her answer: extremely hard. Apparently Western wear wasn't a big seller in Boston, and apparently whatever outfits would normally be available had been grabbed up by people coming to the fund-raiser. This was encouraging news for the Stickler Syndrome Foundation, but a royal pain for Tilda.

She called costume shops, theatrical costumers, and even adult novelty companies, trying to find something that she liked, could afford, and that would fit. Normally she would have asked Cooper for help, but since she'd fudged the facts and didn't want to admit it, she had to look elsewhere. So she called June, who went through her connections: local theater groups, companies that supplied costumes for school plays, and even Kidstock, where Tilda's niece and nephew took movie-making classes during the summer. Finally June tracked down an old buddy who'd starred in their college production of *Annie Get Your Gun* and who still had her costume in her attic. It wasn't precisely what Tilda had had in mind, but by the time she got it, she was in no mood to be picky and she took it with thanks.

Not that costume hunting was the only thing she did during that interval, of course. She still had time to finish writing up the interviews she'd completed, including the one with Miss Barth, and sent them off to Jillian for her approval. Plus she managed to track down her last two *Cowtown* guest stars and interview them. One was a Mexican man who'd played a Comanche brave, and the other was a Japanese woman who'd played a Chinese mail-order bride. *Cowtown*'s casting had been as ethnically accurate as any other show from that era, which is to say not very accurate at all.

After that, she took a break to straighten up the clutter that always accumulated on her desk during a project, trying to organize her notes. Under one pile she found the folder of the pictures she'd gotten from Bill Hawks, including the shots of the mysterious nameless photographer. She was staring at the best shot of him when Colleen came home from work and stopped by Tilda's room for her nightly interrogation.

"How's it going?" Colleen asked, but before Tilda could answer, she followed up with, "What are you doing? Who's that in the picture?"

"The women are pinup models, but it's the guy I'm interested in."

"Why?"

"Because somebody tried to hide this picture."

"Why?"

"I don't know."

"Who is he?"

"I don't know. I'm trying to figure it out."

"Why don't you ask somebody? That's what I'd do."

Tilda resisted the impulse to comment that Colleen's reaction was always to ask questions, and instead said, "I've got nobody to ask. The man who took the picture didn't know, the woman dressed as a pirate is dead, and I don't know where the other woman is."

"Can't you Google her or something?"

"Yeah, I could, but—" Tilda stopped.

"But what?"

"But—" Damned if Colleen wasn't actually making sense. Tilda was caught up with her work, she had her costume, and if she wanted to piss away some of her own time hunting down an elderly former pinup, why shouldn't she? She was still a freelancer, and what was the use of being a freelancer if she didn't do exactly what she wanted to. "But nothing. I'm going to hit the Web and see what I can find. Thanks, Colleen."

"You're welcome," she said doubtfully, not quite sure what she'd said. "Do you want to get some dinner?"

"Why don't you call for pizza? My treat." To stave off the inevitable she added, "Pepperoni, and I don't care which place you call."

Tilda found the pad with her notes from that last interview with Sandra, which gave her the distressed damsel's real name: Esther Marie Martin. She paired that with "Virginia Pure," and "pinup" and Googled it, but got nothing.

Next she hunted around various pinup sites for references to Virginia Pure, hoping for some clues about the model's life, but again, there was nothing. No pinup model's career lasted forever—Bettie Page herself had only modeled for six years, and that had been considered a long run. Virginia's tenure had been considerably shorter. Other than pictures of the pirate session with Sandra, Tilda only found two other pictures of her.

She decided to give up on that approach just as the pizza arrived, and she went to pay the delivery man. Under the circumstances, she thought it would only be polite to join Colleen for dinner, and even answered a few more of her roommate's questions before running out of patience. Then she asked Colleen about her day, and zoned out while

Colleen answered in painful detail, paying just enough attention to nod and make appropriate noises of ersatz interest. As soon as the pizza was gone, she went back to the computer.

Tilda decided that if she couldn't find Virginia Pure, she'd focus on Esther Marie Martin. Entering the name into Google gave her over three hundred thousand hits, which was far too much to wade through, but putting it in quotes only gave her about a hundred and fifty, and she started visiting links. Unfortunately, none of them got her further along.

Another look at her notepad got her the tidbit that Esther had been from Virginia. So she plugged that into her search string—one hundred and fifty thousand links. If she could have limited by the town, that might have helped, but Sandra hadn't mentioned it by name.

What next? There were sites that had phone listings by year, but poring through a New York phone book for any year did not appeal. Besides, what if Esther hadn't had a phone?

She needed a new approach. Sandra had told her that Esther had gone to New York to be an actress. Maybe Esther had managed to get a part or two, and if so, she might be listed on IMDb. A quick visit there gave her one makeup artist, four actresses, and a director, but none of them were in the right age range. Of course, Esther could have gone in for the theater instead of either the big or small screen, so Tilda repeated the process on the IMDb analog for Broadway. More Esther Marie Martins, but not the right one. For good measure, she searched various actor's organizations and unions, but got nowhere.

She drummed her fingers on the desk, wishing Esther Marie's parents had given the poor child an easier name to search for. There were just too many women named Esther Marie Martin, Esther Martin, and Esther M. Martin, and if Esther had gotten married, she could be Esther Rabinowitz for all Tilda knew. She almost searched for that name before being overcome by common sense.

Of course, the Martins hadn't been thinking about the Web when they named their little girl, since it hadn't even been a gleam in Al Gore's eye back then. Maybe they thought it was unique—she could well have been the only Esther Marie Martin in her hometown. If she just knew which town she'd been from!

Tilda stomped to the kitchen for a glass of Dr Pepper. Colleen must have heard her—she zoomed in.

"How's it going? Did you figure out who the guy is?"

"No."

"What about the woman? Did you find her?"

"Nope, I can't find her either."

"What are you going to do now?"

What she wanted to do was pour the Dr Pepper over Colleen's head, but that was against their signed and notarized roommate agreement. So she just shrugged.

"You can't give up now!"

"Why not?"

"Because you'll never know the answer. If you can't find that woman, ask somebody else. Isn't there anybody else you can ask?"

"I told you. The photographer doesn't know who he is, and the other woman is dead."

"Did the dead woman have any friends who might know?"

"It's not that simple. You try finding—" Tilda was once again stopped by the realization that her roommate was right about something. "Actually, I do know of someone. Maybe two or three." She'd already speculated that Louise Silberblatt and Miss Barth could have known the photographer. Then there was Lil—Sandra could have told her about the man. In fact, maybe his identity had something to do with why his pictures had been deleted.

Then she looked at the clock. It was almost ten o'clock,

way too late to try to call anybody. "Colleen, I'm tired of working. Do you want to play a game?"

"What game?"

"How about Trivial Pursuit?" Just this once, she'd encourage her roommate to ask questions.

Chapter 29

There's no place 'round the campfire for a quitter's blanket.
—*DON'T SQUAT WITH YER SPURS ON!* BY TEXAS BIX BENDER

MAYBE because she was at least asking the right questions, Tilda slept like a log that night, even sleeping through her alarm. The phone woke her at nine.

She must have sounded bleary when she answered, because the response to her mumbled "Hello" was Nicole snapping, "Are you still in bed?"

"Yes, I am."

"Are you even planning to get up today?"

"I'm not sure." She yawned loudly. "I'm still kind of snoozy."

"Well you better get un-snoozy! Jillian wants you at a meeting to iron out the last-minute details for the fund-raiser."

"Where and when?"

"The Ambrose brothers' suite at one."

"I think I can manage that."

Nicole hung up without answering.

Tilda lounged for about five more minutes before remembering she had phone calls to make, then got out of bed to get showered, fed, and dressed before calling Lil.

"Lil? This is Tilda."

"Hi, Tilda."

"How are you doing?"

"Getting by. It's hard, but I think I'm coming to terms with it all."

"Good for you. I'm actually calling because I've got a question." The next bit was tricky, since she didn't want to admit that she'd stolen pictures from Sandra's hard drive, let alone going behind Lil's back to Bill Hawks. "You know those photos that went missing from your aunt's apartment?"

"I told you, I've got them on the hard drive—I posted them on the Website last night."

"Oh, good. I was wondering if you knew who any of the men in the pictures are?"

"What men?"

"The camera club members shown on the edges of the photos. Did Sandra know any of their names?"

"How should I know? I never asked her about them, if that's what you mean."

"Okay, it's no biggie. I was wondering about that stocky guy in one picture." She forced a chuckle. "He kind of looks like one of my grandfathers, and Gramps used to live in New York. It would be funny if it was him."

"Don't you think you should ask your grandfather if you're so curious?" Lil said stiffly.

"I probably should," she said. "Did you get a chance to call any of my programmer friends?"

"I did," she said, sounding more relaxed. "Vincent was really nice, too. I'm going to send him my resume and he said he'd see if his company is hiring."

"That's great. Vincent is a good guy. He'll do what he can for you. I hope something comes up."

"Thanks again for the help, Tilda, but I've got to get going."

Tilda hung up the phone, only a little disappointed. Lil had been a long shot anyway, since Tilda didn't know if she'd even seen the pictures of the mystery man.

Next up: Louise Silberblatt. "Louise? This is Tilda Harper."

"Tilda, how goes the *Cowtown* roundup?"

"Keeping me busy," she said, "but the reason I'm calling is to ask you a favor."

"Oh?"

"First off, I want you to know that I have every intention of maintaining confidentiality about what we talked about before."

"Yes?" Louise said, sounding apprehensive.

"But there is someone you might have known back then that I'm trying to identify."

"If any of the models prefer to stay anonymous, I'm certainly not going to expose them."

"It's not a model," Tilda said. "It's a photographer. I've got some photos that were taken by a different amateur photographer, a man named Bill Hawks. I don't know if you remember him."

There was no response.

"One of the other camera club members shows up in several of the shots. Mr. Hawks didn't know him, and I'm trying to find out who he is."

"Why do you want to know?"

"It's kind of complicated, but it's very important."

"Important enough that I should betray a man who I may have been friends with? I'm sorry, but I need to know why you want this information. The photographers have just as much right to their privacy as the models."

"Fair enough. I'll explain, but since I'm keeping your secret, I want your word in return that this stays off the record."

"All right."

"You know that I interviewed Sandra Sechrest the day she was murdered. During that interview, she showed me the pictures that Bill Hawks took. Those photos disappeared."

"The killer took them?"

"I don't know for sure," Tilda admitted, "but it's possible.

At any rate, most of those photos were still on Sandra's computer, but some had been deleted. Bill Hawks supplied the missing ones, and when I looked at them, I noticed that every one of the deleted photos included this one man. I want to find out who he is."

"Why?"

"Because maybe this guy is involved in Sandra's murder. And before you ask, no, I have not gone to the cops because I know it sounds insane. Sandra's niece Lil told them about the missing pictures, but even she thinks I'm nuts for worrying about them. But the fact is I've been having nightmares ever since I found Sandra dead, and the only thing that's going to make them stop is finding out what happened to her. I can't do what the cops do, but I can do what I do, and what I do is find people. So I'm trying to track this guy down."

There was a long pause. Then Louise said, "What do you want me to do?"

"Just look at the photos and tell me if you recognize him. I can e-mail them to you right now."

"All right."

Tilda could hardly make her fingers work correctly to send the photos, and then she couldn't sit still while waiting for Louise to look at them.

"I'm sorry," Louise finally said. "I don't know who he is. If it helps any, I'm fairly certain I remember seeing him at some of the camera club shoots, but I never knew his name."

"I appreciate you trusting me enough to try," Tilda replied, which sounded better than what she was actually thinking. "Can I ask you another favor? Sandra told me she'd been in touch with some other pinups who were staying in the closet, as it were. If you are in touch with any of them, could you show those pictures to them and ask if they know who he is? I don't want their names and I'm not interested in outing them—all I need is his name."

"I can do that." Then Louise wished her good luck, and hung up.

Tilda wanted to kick something. All that gut-wrenching for nothing! She didn't know if Louise was going to follow through or not, and now all she had for a source was the enigmatic Miss Barth. She could only imagine how well it would go over if she waved the pirate session photos around at the fund-raiser planning meeting and asked if she could ID the guy. Maybe she could hold her hand over the parts with the nearly naked women.

Now Tilda was ready to kick herself for being an idiot! The solution was obvious. It only required a little work at the computer, and a small amount of self-deprecating lying on Tilda's part—nothing she couldn't handle. She checked the clock. There was still plenty of time before the meeting.

She was at the Ambrose brothers' suite at the Park Plaza several minutes early, wearing her Cooper-approved coat, with her preparations made. She'd been hoping to steal a few moments with Quentin before things got going, but he zoomed in the door at the last minute, so there was only time for a quick kiss on the cheek. Nicole noticed it, of course, and scowled.

Once again, the Ambrose brothers, Miss Barth, Jillian, Shannon, Nicole, Tilda, and Quentin gathered around the ridiculously sized table and once again the meeting was enough to put Tilda into a coma. Her part, at least, was brief. She reported on the articles written, and the two others she needed to finish. Christopher Hale, Lucas McCain, and Aaron Stemfel had been confirmed as celebrity guests for the fund-raiser, and since Shannon would be acting as liaison to make sure they had everything they needed, Tilda gave her a little background on each plus a description of their personalities. Once that was done, she zoned out.

Not that she wasn't impressed by the sheer amount of work that had been done to pull the fund-raiser together in such a short time, but hearing a debate about stocking cocktail napkins versus dinner napkins on the bar was more boring that watching paint dry. Still, mindful of Jillian's wish for her to be an *Entertain Me!* team player, Tilda kept a look of interested concern on her face, and when that wore thin, switched to concerned interest.

Finally it was over, and Tilda was ready to put her plan into action. Miss Barth was still sitting down, so she headed for her.

"Miss Barth, can I speak to you for a moment?"

"Of course. What can I do for you?"

"Well, this is kind of embarrassing, but I've had a mix-up, and I was hoping you could help me out. I had several folders of photos on my desk, and when my roommate came into my room to borrow something, she knocked the folders onto the floor. Now the photos are all scrambled, and I'm not sure who is who. Could you take a peek at them for me?"

"You really should label your photos, then this wouldn't happen," Miss Barth chided, but she was smiling to take the sting out. "Let's see what you've got."

Tilda pulled out the folder she had ready, put it on the table, and opened it. "I think this is Christopher Hale."

"No, I believe that's Emmett Ryker."

"Is it? I'm so glad I checked." Tilda flipped the photo over to mark the name on it, then turned to the next one. "But this is William Sonnett, right?"

"That's right."

Again, Tilda marked the name.

They went through a couple more before Tilda turned to a photo of the mystery photographer that didn't include the pirate captain or buxom captive. Tilda had used Photoshop to crop the women out of the original photo, center it around the photographer to make it appear as if he were the subject, and enlarge it. She'd lost some resolution, of course, but the man was still recognizable.

"How about this one?" she said, hoping that she sounded nonchalant.

Miss Barth hesitated, then picked the photo up to look at it more closely. "Was he on *Cowtown*?"

"I'm not sure. Do you know who he is?"

"No, I don't believe I do."

Tilda bit her tongue to keep from saying what she really wanted to say. Then, hoping it might shake something loose, she said, "That one must be from a different project. I interviewed a pinup model named Sandra Sechrest, and I had some photos she'd printed mixed up with everything else."

"Perhaps . . ."

"Yes?"

"Perhaps if you used different-colored folders for your different projects, you wouldn't get them mixed up."

That time Tilda had to bite her tongue twice. "I'll have to try that next time."

After that, she had to continue the charade of having Miss Barth identify three more pictures when Tilda knew exactly who they were, even enduring jokes about flighty females when Tucker wandered over and wanted to know what they were doing.

Once the painful exercise was over, she found Quentin, hoping he'd be available for lunch or maybe a quick make-out session, but he had to run back to his office for another meeting and only had time to give her a slightly more thorough kiss than before. She was so glum that even Nicole looking daggers at her didn't cheer her up, and she stayed gloomy all the way back to Malden.

It was just as well Colleen was at work instead of waiting to ask more questions—Tilda would have said all the words she'd swallowed while talking to Miss Barth, putting up with Tucker's jokes, and not getting a consolation lunch with Quentin.

The worst part was that Tilda didn't know who else she

could ask. Frankie was the only other pinup she knew, and without her glasses, wouldn't have noticed if Hugh Hefner himself had been at one of her photo shoots.

Then again . . . Maybe Frankie couldn't identify the mystery man, but she might know something about Virginia. It was worth a phone call, anyway.

"Hello? Frankie Adams," she answered, sounding out of breath.

"Hi, Frankie, this is Tilda Harper. I'm sorry—did I interrupt something?"

"No, it's fine," Frankie panted. "God, I hate Pilates. Isn't it awful?"

"Terrible," Tilda agreed, though her knowledge was purely theoretical. "I've got another couple of questions for you, if you've got time."

"I knew you couldn't resist hearing about Sam Waterston."

"You're right, I can't, but this is about your pinup modeling."

"My ta-tas were so much bigger then," Frankie said with a sigh. "Of course they could be that big again if I'd go under the knife, but what's the use of having those look young when the rest of me looks old?"

Since that was a question Tilda wasn't prepared to address, she said, "There's another model I want to find. She used the name Virginia Pure."

"Esther! I remember her. Whatever happened to her anyway?"

"That's what I'm trying to find out."

"Hell, I don't know. She left modeling before I did, and I heard she went back to ole Virginny."

"I don't suppose you know what town she was from, do you?"

"She told me once, and I felt bad because I laughed, but it was a funny name. Dumb-bunny, dim-bulb, dinsdale . . . Dinwiddie!"

"Dinwiddie? Seriously?"

"Dinwiddie, Virginia, which just happens to be the county seat of—wait for it—Dinwiddie County."

"I guess Dinwiddie is no worse than some of the town names around here."

"Hyannis always struck me as a good one," Frankie observed.

"Do you know anything else about Esther that might help me find her? Family members, anything like that?"

"Nope, sorry. I only spoke to her a couple of times, and after I laughed about Dinwiddie I wasn't her favorite person."

"One other thing. Have you got contact information for any of the other models or the photographers from back then?"

"You mean somebody who might have known Esther?"

"Not necessarily. You remember I told you about that guy I've got the picture of? I'm hoping there's somebody who might know his name."

"You're a persistent cuss, aren't you? I wish I could help, but I only modeled for a few months, and after I stopped, I lost touch with every one of the other girls before a year had gone by. Most of them felt funny about having done that kind of work, so we didn't exactly form an alumni group. And like I said, I didn't know any of the photographers then, let alone now. This guy you're looking for? Was he good-looking?"

"Not bad."

"Damn. I wish I'd worn my glasses more often. Anything else?"

"Not today, but I'll be talking to you about Waterston someday soon."

"Any time!"

Not that she didn't trust Frankie, but she was a little doubtful about finding a town named Dinwiddie—Frankie could have heard it wrong all those years ago. But when she hit the Web, it took only a few seconds to verify that Dinwiddie, Virginia, was an honest-to-God place. It was named for Robert Dinwiddie, and it really was the county seat of Dinwiddie County. With fewer than twenty-five thousand people living in the whole county, she might just have a shot at tracking down Esther after all.

Two hours later, she was back in the dumps. She'd spent most of that time on the phone with a remarkably helpful librarian at the Dinwiddie Library who was amazed that a national magazine like *Entertain Me!* was interested in somebody from Dinwiddie. She would probably have been less amazed if Tilda hadn't fudged the facts a bit.

The librarian told Tilda to call her Smiley and, from the cheerful way she talked, she'd earned the name fairly. Smiley had searched through archived newspapers to find reviews of Esther Marie Martin's triumphant performances in several high school plays and an article about the bon voyage gala her parents threw before Esther headed to New York to become a star. Unfortunately, there was no companion piece about Esther returning, or any other references to her. She wasn't even mentioned in the obituaries for Esther's parents, an item that shocked the smile right out of Smiley's voice.

Tilda was about to thank her for her efforts when Smiley asked her to call back in about half an hour, which would give Smiley a chance to check one last source. Thinking that she meant another database or archive, Tilda agreed and spent thirty minutes tending to e-mail and playing games. But when she called back, it turned out that Smiley had been talking to her mother, one of a long line of Dinwiddie natives, who knew where all the bodies were buried. Or in this case, weren't buried. Smiley's mother was certain that Esther had never returned to Dinwiddie.

Though she'd written faithfully for the first few months after she got to New York, at some point, the letters had stopped coming. Eventually the Martin family had talked to the New York police to try to find their daughter, but had had no luck. There had been no money for a private investigator or a trip up to New York, so the Martins had just waited, patiently, for the rest of their lives. Esther had been an only child, and the parents were long gone, so there was no home for Esther to come to anymore.

Tilda calmly thanked Smiley for all her efforts, and promised a complimentary yearlong subscription to *Entertain Me!* for the library. But as soon as she was off the phone, she started stomping through the house, suggesting profane and geometrically impossible uses for household furnishings and looking for something to kick. Though she found a couple of possibilities, she was afraid Colleen would squawk if she noticed boot prints on her favorite chair or that really ugly chest of drawers. Then she considered breaking out the rum, the frozen strawberries, and the blender to see how many daiquiris she could guzzle.

Finally Tilda remembered she was supposed to be an adult, and that she still had two interviews to write up. She finished before Colleen got home, and was reasonably satisfied with the result. She had definitely surpassed "decent," and while she may not have made it to "damned fine," she was sure that she'd achieved "wicked good."

However, professional satisfaction was not enough to inure her to an evening with Colleen and the never-ending rounds of twenty questions, so she thanked all the gods in all the pantheons when Colleen announced she had a dinner date, even managing to look interested as her roomie told her more about the man than Tilda had ever learned about any interviewee. By the time Colleen left, Tilda was wondering if she should let her take the job at *Entertain Me!*.

Being alone for the evening could have led to brooding, but before Tilda had a chance to begin the process, Quentin called, full of apologies for not having had time to spend with her earlier in the day. He offered to make it up to her by bringing over takeout, and Tilda happily accepted. While waiting for him, she hid her fund-raiser costume in the back of her closet, just in case he went in the bedroom to snoop. She also changed her sheets, just in case he went into the bedroom for a different reason.

Quentin soon arrived, bearing cheesesteak subs and fries. He was so excited about the next night's fund-raiser that it was all he could talk about, but since Tilda was delighted to have something to think about that didn't include murder, she was more than willing to let him babble.

He also tried his best to find out what she was going to be wearing, but she wouldn't give him so much as a hint, even when he tried to bribe her with his favors. Then he expressed his willingness to demonstrate those favors to see if he could change her mind, and she agreed that it couldn't hurt to try. Afterward, she noted that she could have saved the clean sheets—they never made it out of the living room.

Quentin couldn't stay the night, which was an odd kind of relief. She could kiss him good night and not be worried that she was going to wake him with bad dreams again. Unfortunately, Colleen wasn't so lucky—Tilda woke her up at two thirty. But she didn't complain too much, either because she knew she'd be able to sleep in the next day or because her own date had gone so well.

Tilda woke about midmorning, ran a few errands, and then putzed around until time to get ready for the fund-raiser. Getting all the components of the costume on in the right order took a little bit of doing, because—as Colleen said with uncharacteristic understatement—it wasn't Tilda's usual style.

Chapter 30

Wear a hat with a brim wide enough to shed sun and rain, fan
a campfire, and whip a fightin' cow in the face.
— *DON'T SQUAT WITH YER SPURS ON!* BY TEXAS BIX BENDER

SINCE Tilda was covering the Stickler Syndrome fund-
raiser for *Entertain Me!*, she arrived at the Hillside Steakhouse early. It had been a while since she'd been there,
but she still remembered the way to the section known as
Dodge City. At least it was normally Dodge City. Now a
banner hung over the doorway proclaiming it the Cowtown
Saloon.

Shannon was on duty at the door, dressed in a bright red
satin saloon girl ensemble, complete with fishnet stockings
and a plastic derringer in her garter.

"Hi, Tilda," Shannon said, crossing her name off a list.

"You look great," Tilda said, "but aren't you cold?"

"A little," Shannon admitted, "but how often do we get a
chance to dress up? Didn't you wear a costume?" Shannon
asked, since Tilda's coat wasn't particularly appropriate for
the Wild West.

"Absolutely. Just need to put a few finishing touches on.
See you later."

The function room was just as Tilda remembered from a
family wedding she'd once attended there. It was modeled
on a Western saloon writ exceedingly large. There was a
stage at the back end of the room, with a good-sized dance

floor in front of it. To the left was the bar, lovingly paneled in wood, with spittoons that she hoped were for decoration only. To the right was a wide staircase that led to rooms that would have been for encounters with saloon gals in a real saloon, but these doors led to storage closets and private areas currently being used as green rooms for the *Cowtown* celebrities. A balcony deep enough for a row of tables ran the length of that wall and about halfway across both sides of the front and back walls. At the family wedding, Tilda had found a corner up there to hide in when the groom called for the chicken dance, and had stayed hidden when the bride stood at the top of the stairs to toss her bouquet.

Tilda stopped at the coatroom to leave her outerwear, then stepped into a nearby ladies' room to put on her hat and make sure everything was straight before stepping proudly into Cowtown.

She hadn't gone ten feet before Cooper appeared in front of her. He was dressed head to toe in doe-colored suede, or a reasonable facsimile thereof. His open-neck shirt was held together with thongs, and he was wearing a star-shaped badge.

"Howdy, Sheriff," Tilda said. "*Blazing Saddles*?"

"Got it in one. Sheriff Bart, at your service." He politely tipped his hat.

"Very nice."

"But you . . . That outfit is amazing."

"Thank you, Sheriff." She twirled, and the fringe on the hem of her aqua blue skirt twirled, too. So did the fringe on the white leatherette vest, the white boots, the matching bag where she'd stowed her camera and pad, and the ends of the string tie worn around the collar of her aqua satin Western-style blouse. The cowgirl hat, blue with white trim, was fringe-free, but the beaded band brightened it.

"Truly you are the Queen of Kitsch, the Empress of Irony." He paused. "You are being ironic, aren't you?"

"Well, I started out that way, but I think it's growing on me. I have an inexplicable urge to square dance."

"Stop that. You're scaring me."

"Where's Jean-Paul?"

"Setting up."

"Does he even have any cowboy music?"

"Jean-Paul is a professional. He has access to all kinds of music."

"iTunes?"

"You bet. Want a drink?"

"A sarsaparilla would go down mighty good right now."

"Stop it!"

The ersatz sheriff offered his arm, and they made their way through the thickening crowd to the bar. Though not everybody was in costume, enough were to make it a people-watcher's delight. Tilda was impressed by the elaborate getups people had found in the wilds of Massachusetts. She spotted flirty dance-hall girls and hardy pioneer women, honest cowpunchers and black-hatted cattle rustlers, shifty-eyed gamblers and steely-eyed sheriffs. There were Clint Eastwood clones, at least two Lone Rangers, plus a hefty *Bonanza* buff wearing a ten-gallon hat Hoss Cartwright would have been proud to own. One impressive specimen wore an Indian costume that was apparently inspired by the Village People.

Tilda said, "He's brave to wear that. Get it? Brave?"

"Har! But if you think he's brave, wait until you see Nicole."

They spotted her by the bar, and Tilda blinked. Twice. She'd thought Shannon was dressed inappropriately for winter, but Nicole's saloon girl ensemble was cut two inches lower in front than Shannon's, and the pitiful excuse for a skirt was six inches shorter. Perhaps she thought she'd made up for the loss of inches with the heels on her boots.

"That's our girl. Putting the 'ho in hoedown," Tilda said.

Cooper snickered.

Nicole saw them, and frowned. "Tilda, if you're going to be representing *Entertain Me!*, you're going to have to start choosing your outfit with more care."

"I know, I know," she said. "I forgot I was supposed to wear a costume."

Nicole ignored her. "Cooper, you've got the right idea, but I'm surprised you didn't go for something more butch. Surely you have a pair of leather chaps in your closet?"

"Honey, all of the leather chaps I know are *way* out of the closet."

Now it was Tilda's turn to snicker.

"Might I remind you both that we are here to work. Cooper, have you—"

"I know my job, Nicole," Cooper said. "Worry about your own, which does not include giving me instructions."

Nicole's eyes narrowed, but she backed down. "Sorry. I just want to make sure that everything runs smoothly. Maybe you two are just here to party, but this fund-raiser is very important—people with Stickler's Syndrome really need support, and the foundation is doing vital work."

Tilda would have been more impressed had she not been looking in the mirror behind Nicole, which showed that Quentin was standing right behind her and Cooper, plenty close enough to have heard the impassioned speech. Though Tilda was willing to believe Nicole was passionate, what she passionately wanted was to share some passion with Quentin.

The good doctor spoke up. "Howdy, ladies, Sheriff."

Tilda checked out his outfit: a black frock coat and hat, and a clearly artificial bushy mustache. She was at a loss until she saw the dental mirror sticking out of his vest pocket.

"Doc Holliday?"

Quentin grinned. "I knew you'd get it."

"It's thematic, but a dentist?"

"It was either that or Doc from *Gunsmoke*, and I thought Holliday was sexier."

"I would have to agree." She leaned forward to give him a quick kiss. "What about Dr. Quinn, Medicine Woman?"

"I thought about her, but I do a terrible British accent. As for you . . ." He looked over her ensemble. "You did say that you wanted to be a cowgirl when you were little."

"All except for that riding the open range alone part—I prefer to ride with a friend."

"Then I'll be your huckleberry."

Another kiss was the only appropriate response, mustache or no mustache.

When they broke it off, Cooper was smiling and Nicole was fuming, so all was right with the world. Tilda was tempted to continue smooching, just to see how riled she could get Nicole, but that wouldn't have been fair to Quentin. Besides, his mustache tickled.

Jillian joined them, wearing a divided riding skirt and a flat-brimmed hat, a picture of Western elegance that reminded Tilda of Barbara Stanwyck in *The Big Valley*. "Quentin, glad you're here. You know the schedule, right? We'll give people a chance to mingle and eat, then Miss Barth is going to give an introduction. Next you give your slide show, and the other celebrities will do their speeches. After that, Jean-Paul will get the dancing started, and the celebrities will go to their stations for meeting, greeting, and autograph signing. The silent auction and the photo booth are already getting business, so it's looking good. Why don't you get your dinner now, while you've got a chance?"

Quentin nodded, which was about all there was time for before Jillian continued.

"Tilda, I want you to get atmosphere and quotes. I've got a couple of photographers wandering around, so you don't have to worry about pics—if you see something worthwhile, point one of the photographers in the right direction. Good outfit, by the way."

"Got it. And thank you."

"Cooper, you know what to do?"

"Keep Jean-Paul happy, get people dancing, keep an eye out for trouble."

"Nicole—"

"I'll be supervising the silent auction and liaising with the catering staff," she said importantly.

"Good. But first find something to put on over your outfit. Miss Barth says you're not in keeping with the Cowtown Code, whatever the hell that is. And everybody, smile. This is a party, so look as if you're having fun."

Knowing that she'd be working the crowd, Tilda had assumed she wouldn't have a chance to get to the buffet until later, if ever, and she'd grabbed a bite at home. So she told Quentin she'd be there for his speech, and went looking for people to talk to.

She was happy to see that the place was filling up nicely. There hadn't been much time for the advance ticket sales, so they'd been hoping for plenty of walk-ins, and it looked as if they'd gotten them. She made a note to herself to check later to see how many tickets had sold. If it was a big number, Jillian would want her to include it in her article, and if not, it would be easy enough to keep it vague.

Though there were plenty of attendees in costume, many of those who weren't had gotten into the spirit with straw cowboy hats, *Cowtown* T-shirts, and Red Sox jerseys that said, "Cowboy up."

Up on the stage, Jean-Paul produced an actual triangle to strike and announced, "Chow time!" to let people know that the buffet was open for business. A reasonably polite stampede in that direction ensued, followed by people taking seats at the tables scattered all through the room. Having folks sitting down made it easier for Tilda—it was harder for a seated subject to blow her off.

Her first target was a family group dressed in Western wear, and Tilda got enthusiastic quotes from both of the parents and all three kids. Next she tracked down the barely dressed Indian she'd spotted earlier, purely for journalistic integrity. He had a nice take on the portrayal of Native Americans in *Cowtown*. Then she talked to a trio of women in T-shirts that said, "We're Sticklers!" They were all mothers of children with Stickler's Syndrome—or Sticky children, as they called them—and were delighted by the attention the foundation was getting, not to mention the money.

After them, she took a break long enough to get a Coke from the bar and a cookie from the dessert table, and checked her watch. The program was supposed to start in a few minutes, so once she finished her snack, she took the opportunity to visit the ladies' room. She did her business, and was checking hair and makeup in the mirror when Miss Barth emerged from a stall and started doing the same.

Tilda had a particular distaste for paparazzi who staked out bathrooms in order to get face time with celebrities, so she just smiled and said hello, meaning to leave the woman in peace. But Miss Barth said, "Hello, Tilda. You look lovely."

"Just trying to get into the proper spirit, though I think the getup is more Dale Evans than Arabella Newman."

"It suits you."

"Thank you," Tilda said, reasonably sure it had been meant as a compliment. "You look wonderful."

All the outfits Tilda had seen Miss Barth wear had had some sort of Western flavor, like a modern cowgirl, but this time, Miss Barth had adopted the bustle, lace, and ruffles of the formal wear of the *Cowtown* era, complete with gloves and a fan. The full-length dress was a dusty pink, and her pure white hair was pinned up with just the right number of tendrils hanging loose.

"I never got to wear a dress like this on *Cowtown*. It's what a society woman back East would have worn, not the kind of thing Arabella would have worn to the saloon."

"If the Ambrose brothers had realized how gorgeous

you'd have looked, I bet they'd have written a special script just to give you an excuse to dress this way."

Miss Barth smiled with obvious pride.

Tilda turned to go, but Miss Barth stopped her again. "Tilda, I meant to ask if you ever identified that photo, the one you thought was of a *Cowtown* guest star." The woman was ostensibly looking in the mirror, but Tilda could see she was actually watching her.

Deliberately keeping her voice casual, Tilda said, "Oh, the guy with the camera? No, but at least I figured out where the picture came from. I think I mentioned that I'd interviewed a former pinup model last week, and that was one of the pictures she was going to put up on her Website. But I can't ask her who he is because . . . well, she was murdered that same day."

"How terrible," Miss Barth said, with a completely convincing portrayal of someone hearing about a tragedy for the first time. "Was it something to do with her previous life?"

"Nobody knows. The police have no suspects. Though . . ." She let her voice trail off.

"Yes?"

"Well, I have a source who says that some pictures disappeared from Sandra's apartment. They may not be connected of course, but I wonder if I should give them that one I found, now that I think about it."

"What good would that do if you can't identify the man?"

"They might be able to track him down—if he's involved, that is."

"I suppose so. Well, I need to get out to the stage. The show will be starting in a moment."

"I'll be right there. I just want to fix my hair." She pulled out a brush but put it back in her bag once Miss Barth was gone. What Tilda really wanted was a moment to think. Though she'd known Miss Barth was a good actress, she'd never realized just how good. The woman had maintained her mask of polite interest perfectly, with just a touch of morbid curiosity for the human touch. Had Tilda not seen her at Sandra's funeral, it never would have occurred to her that Miss Barth had even heard of Sandra, let alone shared a career with her.

Why had she asked about the mystery man's photo? If she could hide her emotions that well, she could certainly have hidden knowledge of that man's identity. But Tilda didn't know how she'd ever be able to pry that knowledge out of her.

Chapter 31

When a neighbor is in need, no real cowboy can turn his back.
That's the Cowtown Code.

—"THE COWTOWN CODE," *COWTOWN COMPANION*
BY RUBEN TIMMONS

SINCE she couldn't very well brood in the bathroom all night, Tilda took a deep breath, straightened her hat, and went back to the party. It was nearly time for the program, so she edged close enough to the stage that she could see clearly.

The people due to speak were milling in the confusion that precedes even the most rehearsed performances, which this was anything but. She suspected from the way Quentin was mouthing words as he focused on a stack of index cards that he was suffering from a major case of stage fright. When he looked in her direction, she gave him a reassuring smile and a thumbs-up, but though he returned the smile, it didn't look as if the comforting sank in.

Just then, Jean-Paul, resplendent in his black cowboy duds and scarlet vest, started up the theme song from *Cowtown*, and as it faded, announced "Cowboys and cowgirls, put your hands together for the one and only, Cynthia Barth, Arabella Newman of *Cowtown*!" Applause was thunderous, and Miss Barth beamed as she stepped front and center.

Her speech was short and simple. She thanked everybody for coming, picked out a few costumes in the audience for special attention, and spoke about how much it meant to her that people were so willing to help with such a worthy cause. Then she introduced Quentin to tell them more about the fine work the Foundation was doing.

He stumbled a little at first, but the audience was both forgiving and approving of his message, not to mention admiring of how cute he looked in his costume. He explained Stickler Syndrome and how it affected people, then cued Shannon to show a ten-minute video about the condition.

Tilda kept an eye on the audience, and was glad to see that most people were actually listening, and not just eating or waiting for the music to start up again.

Once the video ended, Quentin asked everyone to do what they could to help—meaning to open their wallets—and finished up. The applause wasn't as loud as it had been for Miss Barth, but it was respectable, and Tilda saw him wiping his forehead in relief once he was out of the spotlight.

Miss Barth returned and introduced the three guest stars, each of whom gave a short speech about the cause. Next she introduced the Cowboy Kings themselves. Hoyt just waved and smiled, but Tucker called up a bunch of Sticky kids and taught them one of the hokiest rules from the Cowtown Code.

> *A true cowboy never breaks his word. When you're out on the plains with nobody but your horse to keep you company at night, you've got to be able to respect yourself. That's the Cowtown Code.*

Then he distributed *Cowtown* badges and hats to each, and the hug he got from one of the cutest of the little girls could even have been unscripted. Tilda saw more than one kerchief being used to wipe a cowboy's manly tear.

Miss Barth came back just long enough to announce that the silent auction would be going on for two more hours,

and that she and the rest of the *Cowtown* actors would be
signing autographs and posing for pictures and hoped that
people wouldn't mind making a small donation in return.

As applause faded, Jean-Paul started country music
playing, and on cue Hoyt offered his arm to Miss Barth
and they started up a spirited polka. They were soon joined
by other members of the *Entertain Me!* staff who'd been
tasked to get people moving. Tilda hadn't been given a
dance assignment, and was not pleased to see that Nicole
had laid claim to Quentin. Then Cooper came over and
said, "Might I have this dance, ma'am?"

"I'd be plumb pleased."

Tilda knew she wasn't very good, but she was probably
no worse than most of the other dancers on the floor, so
enjoyed it just the same. She noticed that Cooper was dancing her over toward Nicole and Quentin, and a second later,
Jean-Paul announced, "Now everybody switch partners."

Cooper, who must have known what was coming,
released Tilda toward Quentin, grabbed Nicole, and
promptly got her dancing in the other direction.

"Ma'am?" Quentin said to Tilda.

"Please."

They danced to the end of that song and one more before
Tilda begged off. "Thank you kindly, Doc, but I'm afraid
this cowgirl has to round up more doggies or something."

"Then I'll go check in with Jillian. I'll catch you later!"

Tilda grabbed a few more people, in costume and out,
even though she knew she was getting more material than
she needed. Most stories were like that—she got all the
info she could, and then used the most interesting or enter-
taining bits.

Over by the silent auction, she chatted with a longtime
collector of TV and movie Western memorabilia—he had
signed photos from people even Tilda had never heard
of, as well as cowboy hats from James Arness on *Gunsmoke*, Dan Blocker on *Bonanza*, and Robert Conrad on

The Wild, Wild West. His prize was one of Lash Larue's actual whips, with a recording of the actor using it for his famous whip crack. Tilda took the man's name and number, speculating about a series on nostalgia collectors.

At the signing tables, she saw an equal number of autograph hounds, Western fans, and folks who were being carried along by the excitement to donate a few bucks for the privilege of taking home an eight-by-ten signed by an obscure actor. Unlike the prospectors who passed through Cowtown in Season Five, the Stickler Foundation had struck gold.

As time went on, family groups started to circle up the wagons to head home and the party got a little rowdier, though not unduly so. The celebrities, having apparently signed everything offered to them, had closed their stations and retreated to the green room to gossip. Tilda would have loved to have been a fly on the wall, but decided they deserved a little privacy.

She was looking to see if Quentin was available for a drink when she saw Miss Barth standing at the very top of the stairs, looking down at the room. The rest of the upstairs was dimly lit, but of course the stairs were designed for brides to make their entrances, and that meant good lighting for photos. So Miss Barth seemed almost to glow. It was more than the light. The smile on her face was so proud, almost maternal. The Ambrose brothers had never staged a moment as breathtaking as that one.

Tilda looked around for one of the roving photographers, but neither was in sight, so she reached into her bag for her camera to take a picture herself. It wouldn't be a great shot, of course, but she wanted it anyway. She looked away long enough to rummage in the bag, which is why she didn't see Miss Barth fall. It was only when she heard the scream that Tilda looked up and saw the woman tumbling down the wooden stairs, her arms flailing as she tried to catch herself. Afterward Tilda wasn't even sure if it had been Miss Barth or one of the bystanders who'd screamed, but it had stopped by the time the actress hit bottom with a sickening thud.

Tilda ran for her, yelling, "Call 911!" as she went, but once she got there she realized she didn't know what she was supposed to do. "We need a doctor!"

She heard rather than saw Quentin pounding down the stairs to take over, and scrambled back to give him room. One of the women with the Stickler's Syndrome T-shirts appeared, and said, "ER nurse—what do you want me to do?"

Quentin barked incomprehensible orders at the woman, who complied while Tilda watched. Realizing that she didn't know if anybody had called 911 or not, Tilda used her own phone to do so and was relieved when the dispatcher said an ambulance was on the way.

The Ambrose brothers showed up. "Is she all right?" Hoyt wanted to know, while Tucker asked, "What happened?"

Quentin and the nurse were too busy to answer, so Tilda said, "She fell. There's an ambulance coming."

"Dear lord in heaven!" Hoyt breathed. Then he surveyed the crowd around them, some people looking on in shock while others jockeyed for better positions. Tilda realized more than one camera was aimed in their direction, and snapped, "Put those things away before I—"

Hoyt patted her shoulder, then stood straight, incidentally blocking most of the cameras. "Folks, you can see Miss Barth has had an accident, and she needs your prayers. Please step back and give the doctor room to work, and if somebody could go to the door and make sure the ambulance knows where to come . . ." Half a dozen people rushed off to take care of that, including Cooper.

In the meantime, Tucker had gone over to where the photo backdrops were temporarily forgotten, and started

dragging one over. Realizing what he was doing, Tilda
went to help him, and together they put a partition of sorts
around the area where Quentin was working on Miss
Barth.

Deciding she wasn't needed, Tilda started to step
out, but suddenly Miss Barth gasped and opened her
eyes. "I fell," she said wonderingly. "It hurts." She looked
around in alarm, and actually reached down to pull on
her skirt to make sure no unseemly amount of leg was
showing. Quentin whipped his black duster off and laid it
across her.

Tilda couldn't help thinking of her own fall, just a few
days before, and how she'd been hyperaware of every stage
of her progress to the ground. Had Miss Barth been that
conscious as she tumbled down the stairs?

Quentin murmured for her to lie still, and said something comforting, but when Tilda caught his eye, she knew
exactly what he was thinking. Miss Barth was dying.

Then Miss Barth saw her. "Tilda!"

Tilda knelt beside her, and the older woman reached out
and grasped her hand far more strongly than Tilda would
have thought possible.

"I'm here," she said.

"Promise me."

"Promise you? Promise you what?"

"Don't tell. Please don't tell!"

Quentin and the nurse were looking at Tilda in confusion, but she knew what Miss Barth was talking about. She
didn't want anybody to know about her pinup past.

"I won't tell. I promise."

Miss Barth nodded, and Tilda thought she was done,
but she started to say, "I–I—"

"Don't talk," Tilda said. "It's okay."

But Miss Barth wouldn't be stopped. "I–I wasn't
drunk."

"What?"

"I only had one glass of wine. I wasn't drunk. Tell them I wasn't drunk!"

"You weren't drunk," Tilda repeated. "Only one glass of wine."

Miss Barth nodded, then closed her eyes and seemed to relax. Tilda had never thought of dying as relaxing before.

Chapter 32

[T]hat nothing's so sacred as honour, and nothing's so loyal as love.

—EPITAPH FOR WYATT AND JOSEPHINE EARP

TILDA was still holding Miss Barth's hand when the ambulance arrived, and Cooper had to take her by the shoulders to move her out of the way. Not that there was anything the EMTs could do, of course. The actress was gone. The police arrived even before they took her body away, and started rounding up party attendees.

Later on Tilda realized that she could have made a comment about the irony of rounding up cowboys, rather than cows, but at the time, she was oddly numb, other than somehow still feeling the pressure of that last squeeze Miss Barth had given her hand.

A uniformed Saugus police officer got to her fairly early in the process. "Officer Frank Tallman," he said. "And you are?"

"Tilda Harper." She gave him her contact information automatically, thinking that it was terribly wrong that she was so familiar with the procedure for talking to the police at the scene of sudden death.

"Can you tell me what you saw?"

"I was standing there," she said pointing, "and I saw Miss Barth at the head of the stairs. She was looking at everybody dancing and she had this indescribable look of joy on her face. You know she was on *Cowtown*, right?"

He nodded.

"I think that role was really pivotal to her life, and for a long time, she was forgotten. Then this whole resort idea came up, and she got a chance to see all the people who still remembered the show. She was so happy. I looked away to get my camera, and that's when she started to fall." Tilda blinked several times, trying to keep from crying. "I'm sorry—I know you just need to know what happened and not that other stuff."

"No, it's fine. I understand you were the first one to get to her."

Tilda nodded. "Most people froze, of course, the way people do. I got to her, and then Quentin—Dr. Beaudine showed up, and right after that, a nurse. I don't know her name."

"Did Miss Barth say anything?"

"She asked me not to tell anybody."

"Tell anybody what?"

"She didn't say. I didn't ask because I didn't want her to waste her energy talking." Both of those statements were technically true, and as much as Tilda could tell without breaking her promise. "Then she said that she wasn't drunk."

"Did she have a drinking problem?"

"I'd heard rumors, but only from years back." Since others knew about Miss Barth's drinking, probably including the Ambrose brothers, it didn't bother Tilda's conscience to admit that much.

"Was there anything else?"

"No, she just died. But—"

"Yes?"

Tilda hesitated, thinking about that horrible tumble down the stairs. "I think there was something odd about how she fell. When I slip on the stairs, usually my feet go out from under me first, and I land on my bum. Miss Barth seemed to fall headfirst." Much as she herself had fallen on Boylston Street, Tilda thought. "Could somebody have pushed her?"

Tallman regarded her curiously. "Did you see anybody push her, or anybody near her?"

"No, but like I said, I wasn't watching every second."

"So you don't know how it looked when she first fell?"

"No," she admitted.

"Do you have reason to believe that she was in fear for her life? Had anybody threatened her?"

"Not that I know of. I didn't really know her that well." Tilda explained how she'd come into contact with Miss Barth. "So I met with her a couple of times, and I interviewed her about her work on *Cowtown*. That's about it." She was uncomfortable about leaving out the encounter at Sandra's funeral, but she hadn't spoken to her there anyway. If she brought it up, it could lead to subjects Tilda wanted to avoid.

Tallman closed his notebook. "Well, we'll certainly look into all possibilities, but I have to tell you that I've seen a lot of people who've fallen down stairs, and they don't always fall neatly."

He gave her his card, and asked her to call if she thought of anything else he should know, but it was pretty clear that he'd put her into the category of civilians shocked into irrationality when encountering sudden death. Maybe he was right. Had it not been for her own recent encounter with a shoving hand, she wouldn't have even considered the idea that Miss Barth's fall was anything but an accident.

Tallman moved on to the next person, and Tilda went to find the *Entertain Me!* crew. Jillian and managing editor Bryce were bitching at one another about insurance coverage, Shannon was red-eyed and sniffing, and Nicole looked peevish.

"I told the bartender to cut people off if they'd had too much to drink," Nicole said to Shannon.

"She wasn't drunk!" Tilda snapped.

"How do you know?" Nicole snapped back.

"She said she wasn't, and I didn't smell alcohol on her breath. Her dying breath, by the way, and I would appreciate it if you'd show a little respect."

"Hear, hear," Quentin said, coming up from behind Tilda. He put his arms around her, and she leaned into him gratefully. Nicole glared at them, but had enough sense to keep her thoughts to herself.

"How are you holding up?" Quentin asked her softly.

"Not great," she answered. "How about you? Does it ever get easier for you?"

"God, no!" he said. "Why do you think I'm a researcher, and working with a nonfatal disease at that?"

The Ambrose brothers joined them, and Tucker said, "The police are asking some mighty strange questions, like who might have wanted to hurt Miss Barth, and I don't understand why. It was a terrible accident, but it *was* an accident. Did any of 'em say anything to any of y'all?"

Tilda shifted uncomfortably. "The cop I talked to said they were investigating all the possibilities. I guess it never hurts to be sure."

"It could hurt a whole lot if something like this gets out to the press." Then, as if realizing he was talking to members of the press, Tucker said, "I mean, nobody wants a bunch of crazy rumors to hurt Miss Barth's reputation."

"Or the resort," Tilda said.

"This project meant the world to Miss Barth—I know she'd want us to carry on," Tucker said solemnly, and Tilda had to admit that he was probably right.

Jillian and Bryce looked at one another, and for once, seemed in agreement. "Unless the police tell us differently, we're all calling this an accident," Jillian said. "Right?"

Everybody nodded, including Tilda, but she didn't like it.

"Tilda," Jillian went on, "I want an obit by noon Monday to get into the next issue. Are you up to it?"

"Sure," Tilda said.

After that, the Ambrose brothers went into a huddle and the regular *Entertain Me!* staff went to work clearing up and packing up.

"I suppose I should get going," Tilda said to Quentin, who also seemed at loose ends.

"Me, too. I don't know about you, but I really don't want to be alone right now. Would you like to come over to my place?"

"If that invitation includes getting something to eat, you've got a deal. I'm starving, and I'm not eating here."

"I have eggs and I know how to scramble."

"You may be the perfect man."

After stopping to say good night to Cooper and Jean-Paul, and to let Jillian know they were leaving, they took off for Quentin's condo. After the eggs were duly scrambled and enjoyed, they moved to the couch and talked about nothing in particular. Then they moved to the bedroom, and didn't talk at all.

It was no particular surprise to Tilda that the bad dreams came again, but now with two grotesque pinups instead of just one. Quentin tried to be understanding when she woke him, but she could tell it was a strain, so when he fell back asleep, she kept herself awake for the rest of the night, watching for the dawn to sneak in beneath the window blinds.

Chapter 33

Episode 32: Repent in Leisure
When farmer's daughter Samantha Crawford is swept off her feet by a visiting gambler, she thinks all her dreams have come true. But then some of her husband's gambling victims come after him, and she learns he isn't the paragon she thought he was.

—*COWTOWN COMPANION* BY RUBEN TIMMONS

WHEN Quentin began to stir, Tilda pretended that she'd just woken up, too. He showered, then went off to fix breakfast while she hit the bathroom. She hadn't been prepared for a sleepover this time, and felt more than a little ridiculous putting her cowgirl finery back on, but it was all she had. At least she kept the hat off as she followed the encouraging scents into Quentin's kitchen.

"You cooked breakfast," she said. "I'm impressed."

"Don't be. It's eggs again. That's all I can cook well."

"Maybe someday you can branch out to boiling water."

"You'll have to teach me."

They settled companionably around the kitchen table to eat, and at first, neither of them wanted to bring up the previous night's events. Finally Tilda could restrain herself no longer. "Quentin, where were you when Miss Barth fell?"

"In the green room. Why?"

"I was just wondering if you saw her fall."

"You did, didn't you?"

"How did you know?"

"Something you said during your bad dream last night."

"Sorry about that."

"Don't be. It's no wonder you have nightmares, between that other body you found and now seeing Miss Barth. In your dream you were telling somebody not to push her."

"It doesn't take a genius to figure out why, I guess."

"What do you mean?"

"I mean I think somebody pushed her."

"Are you serious?"

She nodded.

"Why would somebody do that?"

"I don't know, but it's just too much of a coincidence. First Sandra, and now Miss Barth."

"Sandra?"

"The woman I found murdered."

"What's she got to do with Miss Barth?"

"Well—" Tilda stopped herself. It wasn't that she didn't trust Quentin, but she'd made a promise to a dying woman. How could she violate that before Miss Barth was even buried? "I can't explain it," she said, "but I do think that the deaths are connected."

Quentin reached over and took her hand. "Tilda, I think you need to get your mind off of death. You've had the extreme bad luck to be around two untimely deaths, which has you fixated on murder."

"Sandra's death *was* murder."

"But Miss Barth fell by accident."

"Unless somebody pushed her."

"Did you see someone push her? Did *anybody* see someone push her? Do the police think someone pushed her?"

"No to all three."

"Then?"

"I still think somebody pushed her."

He sighed and pulled his hand back. "I'm sure the police will investigate thoroughly."

"I hope so," Tilda said, but she knew she didn't sound convincing because she wasn't convinced, and she couldn't explain her reasoning to Quentin. In fact, she was a little resentful that he didn't seem to trust her instincts. Sure, they hadn't known each other that long, and it was true that he didn't know all the facts because she couldn't tell him. And of course, neither of them had had a full night's sleep. And yes, she had woken him up with bad dreams both of the nights they'd slept together. But shouldn't he have been able to see that she wasn't a nut job, despite all that? Maybe it was the cowgirl outfit.

They ate in silence after that, and Tilda turned down Quentin's halfhearted invitation for her to stick around for the day. Instead she manufactured a lunch date with her sister, and left after helping him with the breakfast dishes. To his credit, he did give her a thorough good-bye kiss, and they made tentative plans to get together later that week.

As fuzzy as she was from lack of sleep, Tilda welcomed the cold air that smacked her in the face as she left Quentin's condo and kept her reasonably aware of her surroundings during the drive to Malden. She tiptoed into the apartment in order to dodge Colleen the question queen, but fortunately for both of them, she wasn't there. Tilda's immediate target was her bed, but she stopped by the phone first to set up lunch with June. During her ride home, she'd decided that her impromptu excuse was a good idea. June hadn't heard about Miss Barth's death until Tilda told her, but she was smart enough not to press for further details and agreed to come to Malden for lunch.

With that settled, Tilda managed to get in three solid hours of nightmare-free sleep before the alarm woke her. After seeing a possibly terminal case of bedhead in the mirror, she jumped in the shower for the second time that day, and this time had clean clothes to pull on. At some point during her nap or ablutions, she'd missed both the return of Colleen and June's arrival, because when she went into the living room, she found them deep in conversation. She didn't know if she should be alarmed or not.

June hopped up to give her a rare sisterly hug, and for once Colleen didn't ask a single question. She didn't even hint about accompanying the sisters as they got ready to go to lunch.

"What drug did you put on the dart you shot Colleen with?" Tilda asked as June was driving them to Applebee's.

June laughed. "She is kind of nosy, isn't she?"

"Yeah, like a wolverine is kind of cranky. What did you do to her?"

"I just answered her questions."

"Why? What business is it of hers?"

"None whatsoever, but it didn't hurt me to talk to her. Some day, she'll figure out that most people's lives are at least as tedious as hers, and stop asking about them. Having to hear the details of the PTA battle over whether or not to include Bratz books at the school book fair might cure her for a little while. The meeting about that was so boring that I nearly nodded off while telling her about it."

"You mean I could have stopped her at any time by giving her too much information?"

"Immersion therapy," June said smugly.

"Damn. I never thought of that."

"I supposed you never considered the irony of a professional asker of questions being besieged by questions in her own home, either."

"I did so."

"Did not."

"Did so."

"Did not."

That continued until they pulled into the parking place at Applebee's, and Tilda got in the last triumphant "Did so!" as they got out of the car.

That ended learned discourse until they'd gotten inside, been seated, and had ordered.

"So what are we discussing today?" June asked. "Bad dreams again? Because you're still not looking your best."

"Last night was pretty much designed to bring on nightmares," Tilda pointed out.

"Fair enough."

"But actually, what I'd like to discuss is patient confidentiality."

"Excuse me?"

"I know you aren't a clinician, but didn't you do some sessions with people during college? And when you were researching, you interviewed subjects, and that's covered by patient confidentiality, isn't it? How seriously do you take that?"

June cocked her head. "Extremely. I'm not saying I'd *never* break it. If somebody threatened Glen or the kids, I'd tell everything I knew, but otherwise my subjects' secrets are safe."

"What about me?"

"Maybe you, too, depending on how threatened you were. Is there some reason for the ethics lesson?"

"Hypothetically, yes."

"Oh, goodie, I love hypothetical conversations. Like the time you wanted to know what could happen if you'd hypothetically dented my new car."

"Your reaction wasn't exactly hypothetical."

"Neither was the dent."

"Okay, forget the hypothetical stuff. I'll go for vague instead. As you know, sometimes I'm given information that is off the record."

"Right."

"And I take that pretty seriously."

"Of course."

"Lately, I've been trusted with more secrets than a hairdresser, and I've figured out even more. One secret in particular was one I figured out, so technically it wasn't off the record. But the woman involved knew I'd figured it out and asked me not to tell anybody. I promised I wouldn't. Then she died."

"Did that secret cause her death?"

"I don't know. Her death could have been an accident."

"But you don't think it was."

"It would have been a hell of a coincidence. You remember the woman I found dead before? The two women had a connection."

"What kind of connection?"

"The kind that I promised not to tell about."

"Did this connection have anything to do with the first woman's death?"

"I think so, but I don't have proof."

"Are the police involved?"

"Two sets of police. Two different cities."

"And they have no reason to compare notes unless you make this connection known. Correct?"

"Correct."

June considered the matter. "Let's look at possible scenarios. Scenario One: The second death was an accident, so the connection is meaningless."

"That would simplify matters."

"Scenario Two: The second death was also a murder, but for totally different reasons. The connection is a coincidence."

"That would be my second choice."

"Scenario Three: The second death was a murder, and the connection has something to do with it."

"That's the one that gave me nightmares last night."

"No wonder you look tired. Anyway, that third scenario is the only one we have to worry about." Then June snapped her fingers. "No, wait! I've got a fourth. Do you suspect the second dead woman of having killed the first?"

"I did. Not now, obviously."

"What if she did, and then killed herself out of remorse?"

"That would make all kinds of sense," Tilda said, almost happy at the idea.

The waiter brought their burgers, and Tilda let him and June arrange the table while she thought it through. By the time he left, she was shaking her head. "Suicide isn't going to fly."

"Why not?"

"It comes down to psychology, if you don't mind my poaching in your patch. Pardon me if I start using names now. The vague thing was getting on my nerves."

"Fair enough. I take sister confidentiality seriously, too."

"Anyway, last night Miss Barth was in her element. The fans were treating her like a star again, probably for the first time in years, and I just can't imagine her cutting that short."

"People have been known to kill themselves at the top of their game, before it can end."

"If she'd wanted to do that, she wouldn't have used such an undignified method. This was one carefully controlled woman. I can picture her slitting her wrists like a Roman senator, or with some fast-acting, non-nausea-inducing poison. Maybe drowning, if it was somewhere that she could be sure no fish or crabs would snack on her body. But she wouldn't have thrown herself down a flight of stairs, not when she was wearing a dress."

"What does her dress have to do with it?"

"It was flapping all over while she fell, and one of the first things she did when she came to was push her skirt down. She would not have worn a dress and then killed herself that way."

"Okay, I see your point. That gets us back to Scenario Three. The connection between the two women had something to do with their deaths."

"Right," Tilda said unhappily.

"Will the cops find the connection on their own?"

"I doubt it. It's pretty deeply buried. Besides, the Saugus cops are leaning toward accident on Miss Barth's death, so they've got no reason to dig."

"Would knowing the connection help them find the murderer?"

"I don't know." Tilda ran her fingers through her hair. "Suppose I tell the cops there's a connection, but not what the connection is?"

"And of course, they'd take you at your word."

"You don't think they would?"

"More likely they'd give you the third degree until you cracked."

"As if!"

"It took me three minutes to get the story of the dented car out of you."

"That was a totally different situation." Before June could argue the point, Tilda said, "What if I send an anonymous tip to both departments? Even if the police didn't find the connection, they'd look at the deaths differently, and I'd be in the clear, ethics-wise." But June was giving her the eye. "What?"

"Let's assume that this link is so deeply hidden that the police never find it. Might they find some other link?"

"There's only one link."

"Really?"

"Really." Then it hit her. "Shit! Me. I'm a link."

"Which would make you a suspect."

"So what?" Then she remembered the uneasy guilt she'd felt when Detective Salvatore still had her on his list. "Okay, I wouldn't enjoy it, but since I didn't kill either of them, it's not like I'd be in real trouble."

"No? Your being taken in for questioning wouldn't affect your life or your work? Not to mention your pocketbook, from hiring a lawyer? Eventually you'd have to spill the beans."

"At which point, my reputation would be mud forever.

I'd never get another story assignment, and would have to go to work at Dunkin' Donuts and live in your attic."

"You may be exaggerating a bit," June allowed, "but being a murder suspect would not be pleasant."

"Been there, done that, hated the T-shirt," Tilda said. "Plus investigating me could distract the police long enough for the real killer to get away."

"That, too."

"So what do I do?"

June shrugged. "I don't know."

"That's a big help."

"I mean, I don't know why you're asking. You knew before you got me to come to lunch that you were going to continue snooping around, didn't you? So do you want me to try to talk you out of it, or encourage you to do what you intended to do all along?"

"I had not made up my mind."

"Yeah, right."

"Okay, I did think about it, but I figured you'd talk me out of it."

"The way I talked you out of taking my car the day it got dented?"

"Oh, right. You really suck at this, don't you?"

The waiter's visit to check on them prevented June from answering in kind, but once he was gone, she said, "Listen, Tilda, I know you've been snooping."

Tilda opened her eyes as widely as possible, trying to look innocent.

June snorted. "Note my lack of surprise. I also know that you're going to continue, and since I have no chance of stopping you, I am going to insist on two things. First, as I said before, be careful. If this person has already killed two women, I don't think he or she will hesitate to take you on."

"I'm not a seventy-year-old."

"And your age made such a difference when you got pushed into Boylston Street."

"Granted," Tilda said. "I'll be careful. What else?"

"Call me if I can do anything to help."

"You've already helped. You listened, you helped me think things through, and you took me seriously." Something Quentin had not been able to do, she thought wistfully. "Not to mention buying my lunch."

"When did I say I was paying for lunch?"

Chapter 34

A photograph can be an instant of life captured for eternity
that will never cease looking back at you.
—BRIGITTE BARDOT

AFTER June paid for lunch, she dropped Tilda off at her
apartment, where Tilda found Colleen folding laundry in
the living room.

"How was lunch?" she wanted to know. "Where did you
two go? What did you have? Did June go back home?"

If June's diagnosis was correct, all Tilda had to do was
answer every question with a flood of extraneous detail,
and eventually Colleen would stop. She opened her mouth
to do just that, but somehow, all that came out was, "Very
nice. Applebee's. Cheeseburgers. Yes." Giving in to Colleen's nosiness just didn't come naturally.

Tilda headed for her bedroom, shut the door firmly
behind her, got a pad of paper and a felt-tip pen, and sat
cross-legged on her bed. Though she'd never had writer's
block, there were times when she just couldn't figure out
what to do about an article, when she had plenty of facts but
no narrative to tie them together. One method that helped
her get past that was to doodle. Why she could think better
while she was doodling was a mystery she'd never tried to
solve. She was just hoping it would work with murder.

So she started doodling.

Why would anybody want to kill two ex-pinup queens?

If she went back to Joe's Lost Pinups site and reported that a second pinup had died under mysterious circumstances, the conspiracy theorists would duke it out with those convinced that a serial killer was lurking. But both of those solutions implied that somebody knew both women had been pinups, and while it had been no secret that Sandra was Sandy Sea Chest, as far as Tilda knew she was the only one who'd known that Miss Barth was Morning Glory. Then again, why was she assuming that she was the only one? Tilda had a good eye, but so did other people, and there were some devout pinup fans out there.

She abandoned the doodle and went to her computer to search for references connecting Cynthia Barth to Morning Glory. Forty-five minutes later, she'd found absolutely nothing. It wasn't proof positive, but Tilda was reasonably convinced that Miss Barth's past had been known only to a few.

She resumed doodling.

What about Louise Silberblatt? She'd recognized Glory at Sandra's funeral, and it wouldn't have been too remarkable for her to realize that the woman she'd known as Glory was also Cynthia Barth. Though she couldn't have been in Boston to kill Sandra, she could have hired somebody to kill her, and while she'd claimed to be unavailable for the fund-raiser, she could have come in disguise. Tilda just couldn't imagine a motive for her to want her former colleagues dead, or why she wanted them dead now particularly.

Timing . . . The timing of the murders must mean something. What had happened recently to inspire murder? There was Sandra's Website, but it had debuted back before Christmas, and then there was the *Cowtown* project, but that didn't concern Sandra at all. Her only connection with *Cowtown* had been Miss Barth.

Tilda ran her fingers through her hair in frustration. Her brain was overstuffed with contradictory facts, secrets that she couldn't share with anybody, and questions she couldn't ask without betraying confidences.

Secrets . . . Was it too outlandish to assume that a secret had led to the murders? If so, which one?

First, there was the fact that Louise had been Fanny Divine. Sandra had known that, and presumably Miss Barth had, too, since Louise had identified herself to Miss Barth. But why would Louise have admitted it just to turn around and kill Miss Barth for knowing? That made no sense.

Then there was the fact that Miss Barth had been Morning Glory. Louise could have known that, but she still had no motive.

What else? Miss Barth used to drink, and presumably a few people knew that, but unless she'd killed somebody in a drunken rampage, Tilda didn't see how that could lead to murder so many years down the road.

The Ambrose brothers weren't real cowboys. What if Miss Barth had known that and had been blackmailing them with the threat of exposure? The only thing was, it would have been a pretty toothless threat. Who cared? Sure it would embarrass Tucker and Hoyt if the truth came out, but otherwise the only potential damage was the *Cowtown* resort tanking, and that would have hurt Miss Barth, too.

Then there was Bill Hawks hiding photos of nearly naked women other than his wife. He'd described his wife Jazz as jealous, but was she crazy enough to hunt down Sandra and beat her to death? It seemed unlikely. Besides, before Sandra died, she'd said she was going to make herself beautiful for somebody, which Tilda thought meant that the expected guest was a man. Sandra could have been a lesbian of course, but Tilda had spent a fair amount of time with her, and she'd been pretty open about her sex life. She liked men—in fact, she'd liked a lot of men.

What about Hawks himself? Maybe he'd kept the pictures of Sandra because they'd been having a torrid affair all those years. When Jazz found the pictures and realized the truth, she demanded that he break if off. So he went to give Sandra the news in person and when she wouldn't accept it, he got physical. The problem with that was it gave him no motive for killing Miss Barth. Tilda didn't think she could stomach the idea about him having an affair with her, too.

None of her theories could adequately explain both murders and, come to think of it, none of them explained the pictures that had been stolen from Sandra's apartment.

Pictures . . . Two days ago, she'd shown the best picture of the mystery photographer to Miss Barth, who'd disavowed knowledge of them. The next day, Miss Barth had asked about it for no reason, and then proved that she was a really good liar. A few hours after that, Miss Barth was dead.

The pictures had to mean something. Tilda abandoned her doodling again, found the pictures on her desk, and flipped through them, stopping at the cropped photo of the phantom photographer.

Even without further doodling, she reached a conclusion. She could either stare at the photos until her eyes bled, or she could enlist a fresh set of eyes to tell her what it was she was missing.

She reached for the phone. "Cooper? This is Tilda. Are you free tonight? I need somebody to bounce ideas off of."

"Sounds painful. Your place or mine?"

"Yours." In her current mood, she was afraid that she would resort to violence if she had to endure more of Colleen's curiosity.

Two hours later, she and Cooper were back in his office. Jean-Paul had been warned she was coming for dinner, and had had salad and pasta waiting, but once the three of them were finished eating it and killing half a bottle of wine, he'd shooed Cooper and her off while he cleaned the kitchen. Tilda decided that if she ever got a sex-change operation, she was going to get rid of Cooper so she could marry Jean-Paul herself.

Once they were settled, Tilda explained to Cooper as much of what she'd been doing and thinking as she could without revealing the "off the record" and "please don't tell" conversations. Once she was done, she handed Cooper two stacks of photos.

"These are the pictures that I got from Sandra's hard drive, and these are the ones from Bill Hawks that fill in the gaps. See if you can figure out what was so important about the ones that somebody deleted."

He looked at them. "All of the formerly deleted photos have this one guy in them."

"I know that. I was hoping you'd see something else."

"That seems to be the big difference."

"Do you see anything that might identify him?"

"Like what?"

"A mole, a tattoo, a nametag that says, 'Hi, my name is Butch.' Anything!"

He obligingly pulled out a magnifying glass to examine the photos. "Late teens or early twenties. Dark brown hair. Brown eyes. I'm thinking around six feet tall. Nice build. Fair skinned. Recently shaved or very light beard. Good complexion. No visible moles or birthmarks. Clothes are horrible, but probably stylin' for the day. Hands look clean. Nails trimmed. No rings. I'd date him." He put down the magnifying glass. "That's all I've got."

"Damn it!" Tilda ran her fingers through her hair for what seemed like the millionth time that day.

"Is little Matilda having a bad day?"

She glared at him. "You know better than to call me that."

"Poor little Matilda," he cooed.

"Cooper, I'm warning you . . ."

"Oh dear, little Matilda is getting cranky!"

"Did you know that I called your mother after you called me that last year?"

"You tattled on me?"

"No, but I did ask her if you had any childhood nicknames."

Cooper's smile dissipated. "She didn't tell you—"

"Oh yes she did, *Pookie*. The story behind it is awfully sweet. Does Jean-Paul know?"

"He does, but nobody else. Oh God, please don't tell the people at the office."

"This is your last warning, Pookie. If you ever call me Matilda again, I will tell Nicole and Shannon, and I may even put it on Facebook."

"Damn, girl, you play dirty!"

"I play to win."

"So, *Tilda*, what do you want to do now?"

"I don't know. There's got to be something in those pictures to help us identify that guy, something worth killing for."

"I'll look again," Cooper said. After a few minutes, he said, "Hmm . . ."

"What?"

"Nothing really, I was just thinking that it's a shame that Virginia Pure didn't do more of this kind of work. She was quite shapely, if you like that kind of thing."

"Obviously Bill Hawks did, but according to Sandra, she didn't like modeling. Modesty exacerbated by being uncomfortable with her figure."

"Why would anybody be unhappy with that figure?"

"Sandra said Virginia was shy about her bosom size."

"Are you kidding?" Cooper said. "Look at her dress! If she'd taken a deep breath, she'd have ripped it in two!"

"Most women dislike their looks," Tilda said thoughtfully, "but for her to be unsatisfied with that bustline seems excessive." Tilda went to Cooper's computer, Googled photos of Virginia, and displayed one. "That's odd."

"What?"

"Cooper, look at her bosom."

"Never have I looked at so many bosoms," he grumbled. "If Jean-Paul catches me, he'll think I've gone straight."

"Just look!"

He did so, then checked the photos in his hand. "She looks bigger in her captive maiden costume."

"A lot bigger."

"Did she get work done?"

"Did they do that kind of work back then?"

"I'm not sure, but they did stuff bras."

"I don't think she's wearing a bra."

"Her bodice, then."

"Possibly, but why? Sandra told me that Virginia was embarrassed that she wasn't better endowed, but she was getting plenty of work. So why start padding?"

"How do you explain it?"

Tilda went through reasons for a woman's bust size to increase. "Okay, probably not plastic surgery or stuffing. It was way too late for her to hit puberty, and I don't think she put on weight—the rest of her looks the same. Shit! Cooper, June told me that she went up two cup sizes when she got pregnant the first time."

"Seriously?"

"She was quite pleased about it, too."

He went back to the photos. "You think Virginia was pregnant? But her stomach is flat."

"One, that skirt could hide a little bump. And two, the breasts start to swell before the stomach. June explained every step of the process in excruciating detail. You don't want to hear about mucus plugs."

"No, I most definitely do not."

"Anyway, a pregnancy would explain a lot, like why she never did another shoot with Sandra. Sandra said it was a shame because the pirate shoot went so well that the photographer wanted to use the two of them together again. What is it about two girls together, anyway?"

"You're asking the wrong man."

"Sorry. Anyway, Virginia quit modeling and everybody thought she'd gone back home to Virginia, but she didn't." Tilda explained the efforts she'd made to track Esther down.

"So you're guessing she didn't go home because she was pregnant?"

"When a girl 'got in trouble' in the 1950s, she usually disappeared for a while. Or, in this case, for good. She could have moved somewhere else and started over."

"Meaning that our pure virgin was neither. But what does that have to do with anything else?"

Tilda shrugged her shoulders. "Hell if I know. Maybe nothing." She thought about Esther Martin's family, waiting all those years for their daughter to return, never knowing they had a grandchild. It seemed so sad.

While she was getting maudlin, Cooper had started combining the two stacks of photos.

"What are you doing?" she asked.

"Now that we've got them all, I want them in chronological order."

"Has anybody ever told you what *anal retentive* means?"

"Hello? I'm a copyeditor? Do you want a 'big picture' guy going over your stories?"

"I bow to your anal retentiveness."

"And well you should." He placed the formerly missing pictures into the stack, flipped through them, pulled a couple out, flipped through again, then rearranged again. "Huh."

"Was that a good grunt or a bad grunt?"

"It's a confused grunt." He went back a few pictures, then forward. "You remember how I originally figured out the order in which the pictures were taken from the models' positions, the clock hands, and the liquid in that glass. I just noticed something funny about that glass, and that's why I've been having a hard time getting the photos in order."

Tilda looked at the top photo and saw a glass on the table behind the mystery photographer. "I think it's iced tea. What about it?"

"Early in the session, it's full." He showed her, then flipped to another picture. "Later, it's a little emptier. Emptier. Nearly empty. Full again."

"She refilled the glass."

"Okay, but keep looking. The glass is full again, then three-quarters full, then half full, then three-quarters full. Since Virginia was lashed to the mast during that time, I don't think she refilled it herself."

"So somebody brought her more."

"Why would anyone bother to bring a quarter of a glass?"

"Are you sure you've got them in the right order?"

"Look at the clock."

"You're right. So where did that extra tea come from? And why?"

Together they looked through the pictures of that part of the photo session, giving special attention to the glass. Then Cooper pointed to the mystery photographer. "Look at that! He's pouring something into the glass!"

Tilda looked closer. "You're right." She'd only been looking at his face, not at what he was doing with his hands.

"So what did he put in?"

"I doubt it was iced tea. What is that in his hand, some kind of bottle? Maybe the 1950s equivalent of roofies?"

"I think it would have been called slipping her a mickey."

"Sandra said Virginia started feeling sick by the end of the shoot."

"You think it was something she drank?"

"Could be. So we've got a pregnant pinup. Somebody puts something into her drink during a photo session, she gets ill, and she's never heard from again."

"That sounds suspicious," Cooper said.

"And potentially very ugly." Tilda thought for a moment. "Can I do some searching on your computer?"

"Sure. What are you looking for?"

"There are a couple of databases I use to find death records."

"You do this for fun?"

"For work, you jerk." She took a seat in his chair, signed in on a death records site in which she maintained a registration, and searched for Esther Marie Martin. Several names came up, but none of the birth or death dates fit. She searched again with an M. instead of Marie, and then without a middle name at all. Still nothing. Just in case a typo had been made, she threw in some wild-card characters to see if anything useful emerged.

As usual, when she was doing database searching, she lost track of time, and didn't realize how long it had been until she noticed that Cooper had put a dish of ice cream next to her and that it was already halfway melted.

"Thanks," she said, taking a spoonful, "but I don't think I've earned it. I haven't found anything."

"That's not necessarily bad news. Maybe she's still alive after all. Or maybe there's no record—they get lost sometimes. Maybe her body wasn't identified, and she was buried as Jane Doe," Cooper said.

"Maybe," Tilda said, taking another bite, "but the police would have checked out all Jane Does when her parents tried to find her."

"I bet they didn't ask after a Virginia Pure."

Tilda nearly choked on her ice cream. "Cooper, you're a genius!" She put the bowl aside and hit the database again. "Shit, nothing. Unless . . ." She threw in wild-card characters again, so she'd find any Virginia whose last name started with P. "I've got a Virginia Pearl, age twenty-two, died Sept. 14, 1952."

"When did that photo shoot take place?"

Tilda flipped to Sandra's site to check. "September 1952."

"That can't be a coincidence."

But Tilda had gone back to the death records. "Cooper, the cause of Virginia's death was recorded as suicide."

"The hell it was!" he said. "It was that bastard in the picture. He poisoned her!"

"According to this, she died from ingesting ethylene glycol." Before Cooper could ask, she was already Googling for more information. "It tastes sweet. That's why she didn't notice it in her iced tea—Sandra said she drank it with tons of sugar. At first Virginia would have felt drunk but within hours, she'd have been vomiting, convulsing, in a stupor, or in a coma. It can take as little as four ounces to kill an average-sized man."

"That looks about what the bastard poured into her glass," said Cooper.

"Get this! It's used in photography for color developing baths, whatever those are."

"And our guy was a photographer. He did it, Tilda. He killed that girl."

"He did, didn't he," she said, staring at his picture. "But who is he? And why did he kill Sandra and Miss Barth?"

"Maybe if we figure out who, we'll be able to get the why."

"The 'who' part is still the sticking point."

"Somebody must know who he is."

"Miss Barth knew," Tilda said. "At least, I think she did, and I think her knowing may have had something to do with her being killed."

"So that means he was at the party last night. That helps, right? I mean, how many men that old were there?"

"What if it wasn't the guy himself who did the killing? I mean, yes, he killed Virginia, but it could be a relative who's killing now."

"So our suspect is either a seventy-plus-year-old man, or somebody related to him. That's a big help."

"Cooper, I've been having bad dreams about this for two weeks now. Did you think it would be easy?"

"You're still having nightmares?"

She nodded wearily. "If I were in my right mind, I might have figured it out by now. Miss Barth might still be alive."

"We did this already, with Sandra. You didn't kill them!"

"I know, but—"

He continued, talking over her. "And you did not cause their deaths. Now cut the crap, and start thinking!"

"Yes, sir," she said mockingly, unwilling to admit that hearing him say that had made her feel better.

"So what do we do next?"

"I don't know. This isn't exactly in my comfort zone."

"Why not?"

"Yes, I did find out about that *Kissing Cousins* curse stuff, but—"

"No, not that—that was a fluke. I know looking for killers isn't in your comfort zone. But pretend you don't know this picture is of a killer. How would you track this guy down if all you knew is that he was connected to a story you were working on?"

She picked up the ice cream, and polished it off while she thought. "First off, I'd ask the person I got the picture from. Which I did, but Bill Hawks couldn't identify him. He did say he'd ask around, but I haven't heard from him."

"So?"

"So I can check in with him."

"Shouldn't you be making a 'to-do' list?"

She stuck her tongue out at him, but took the pad and pen he handed to her. "Fine. Item One: Call Bill Hawks."

"What would you do next?"

"Ask anybody I thought might know. Which would be Sandra, Sandra's niece Lil, Miss Barth, Louise, and Frankie."

"Louise? The lady from the soap opera? And who's Frankie?"

"Don't ask. I can't tell you."

He looked confused, but said, "Okay, not asking."

"Anyway," she said, "I didn't get to ask Sandra because she was already dead. I did ask Miss Barth, who said she didn't know, but now I think she was lying. I also asked Sandra's niece Lil, Louise, and Frankie, but none of them knew."

"Do you need to follow up with any of those last three?"

"I think Frankie was telling the truth, so I don't think a follow-up would help, but I'll call Louise again." She added that to her list. "And Lil . . ." She thought back to her last conversation with her. "Lil seems worth another try. She's an odd duck, and I'm not sure she was telling me everything she knows."

"Well?"

"I'm putting it onto the list."

"Who else?"

"The guest stars at the fund-raiser are around the right age, so I may as well ask them, too. Which would put the Ambrose brothers on the list as well. Miss Barth knew them, and she knew the guy in the picture, so maybe they knew him, too." She added them to her list.

"Anybody else?"

She was about to say that there wasn't, but then she had an idea. "Yes! The fans."

"Poisoners have fans?"

"No—Well, actually, they probably do, but I don't want to know about it. I was talking about pinup fans. I can post the picture on Joe's Lost Pinups site, and ask if anybody can identify him, maybe one of the surviving camera club members. In fact, there are about half a dozen sites I could post to."

"Wouldn't that be tantamount to painting a target on your forehead?"

"I won't use my real name," she said indignantly. "I'll set up a Hotmail account for the responses so nobody will know it's me."

"You're sure?"

"I know a guy who does Web security—he'll help me set it up."

"Okay then, if you're careful."

"Always."

"What first?"

"Can I have some more ice cream?"

Chapter 35

Lying is an indispensable part of making life tolerable.
                                        —DALE EVANS

TILDA was late getting home, which meant that Colleen had already gone to bed, and she followed suit. For whatever reason, she slept just fine, which she desperately needed, and even got up early the next day. She'd intended to get going on the picture hunt as soon as she completed the trifecta of showering, dressing, and eating, but when she checked her e-mail, she found a snarky reminder from Nicole that she'd promised to deliver a memorial piece about Miss Barth to *Entertain Me!* by noon. For once she was grateful to Nicole. With so many other things on her mind, she'd totally forgotten, and it wasn't easy to put everything else aside to write the kind of piece Miss Barth deserved. Assuming, that is, that Miss Barth hadn't had anything to do with any of the murders. Tilda decided that if she did, she'd just have to put that in a later article. For this piece, she stuck with the positive stuff. The time stamp on the delivered story was 11:55 AM, which was considerably closer than she liked to cut it.

With that out of the way, she took a brief break for a ham sandwich and then turned her attention to her to-do list from the previous night. She started by reordering the items so that she could begin with the tasks that she expected to be quick and easy, hoping that she'd find out what she needed with one of those, and not have to move on to the tricky ones. She should have known that wasn't going to happen.

First up was a call to Bill Hawks, but instead of Hawks, she got his wife Jazz, and when Tilda didn't want to leave a message, the woman's reaction hinted that her reputation for jealousy was not unfounded. To keep Hawks out of trouble, she came up with a spur-of-the-moment excuse about wanting to interview him for *Not Dead Yet*, a senior citizen's magazine she'd sold work to before. That reassured Jazz, and she promised to have him return the call. After she got off the phone, Tilda decided it actually wasn't a bad idea, so she wrote a query letter and zapped it off to *Not Dead Yet*. After all, Jillian hadn't given her a job yet.

The next supposedly quick-and-easy item was to talk to Louise Silberblatt. Unfortunately, Louise didn't answer her home phone or her cell. Tilda did get in touch with the publicist of *A Life Worth Living*, only to find out that Louise was going to be in conference with the writing staff for most of the afternoon. Apparently the actress was going to get a new storyline, and Tilda had a hunch she knew what it was going to be about. Though she was pleased for Louise, she'd have been happier if it had happened a week or two later. As it was, all she could do was leave messages for Louise.

Next on the list were Lucas McCain, Christopher Hale, and Aaron Stemfel, the three *Cowtown* guest stars who'd attended the fund-raiser. For them, Tilda's approach required a certain amount of what reporters like to call pre-texting, which was remarkably similar to what most people call lying. Tilda used the same line she'd used with Miss Barth: She had a photo of a *Cowtown* guest star that she couldn't identify, and wondered if they could take a look at it. Fortunately they were all at home and willing to let her fax or e-mail the cropped photo right away. Unfortunately, none of the three recognized the man.

At least that's what they said. Any of them could be lying—it was hard enough for Tilda to detect an actor's lies in person, let alone on the phone. But for the time being, she had to accept it, though she did do a Google search to find pictures of each of them when they were younger, just to confirm that none of them could have been the poisonous photographer himself.

Next were the Ambrose brothers, but she couldn't reach either of them on their cell phones or at the hotel, and was hesitant to leave a message. She'd have to try again later.

That left Lil Sechrest. Tilda dialed her number.

"Lil? Hi, this is Tilda Harper."

"Oh, hi, Tilda."

"How are you doing? Have you managed to get your aunt's condo cleared out?"

"Just finished over the weekend. I had to put some stuff in storage, because I don't have room, but it's empty now and I'll be putting it on the market soon. I thought about moving in myself, but I just can't."

"I don't blame you. By the way, I was wondering if you ever found those missing pictures."

"Pictures?"

"The ones Sandra showed me the day she—That last day."

There was a pause. "Oh, yeah. I found them."

"You did?"

"They were there all along, under the couch. I guess they got shoved there by the EMTs or the cops."

"Lil, I was there, and there weren't—"

"Okay, then by the burglar. He knocked them off or something."

"What burglar?"

"The burglar who killed Aunt Sandra! That must have been what happened."

"I thought nothing was stolen."

"He got scared and ran after—After what happened."

Tilda honestly couldn't tell if Lil was lying to her or to herself, but saw no reason to argue with her about it. "Were all the pictures there?"

"Sure, of course. Why wouldn't they be? Why would a burglar steal photos? I don't know why the police won't leave me alone and go look for the burglar!"

Now Lil was sounding kind of scary, and Tilda remembered what she'd told her about being a rape survivor. She didn't know much about posttraumatic stress, but she was fairly sure it could show up unexpectedly, especially when aggravated by another trauma. Say, for instance, the murder of a beloved aunt.

"Never mind," she said as soothingly as she could. "It's not important. How's the job hunt going? Has Vincent found anything for you?"

"Actually, I decided I'm not ready to think about that right now. Maybe in a few weeks."

Tilda was surprised, since she'd sounded so enthusiastic before, but said, "That's good thinking. You should take some time before rushing into anything."

"That's what I'm doing. Taking some time."

Tilda waited a minute for her to continue, but when she didn't, she said, "Well, let me know how you're doing, or if there's anything else I can help you with."

"I'm fine. Thanks. But I'm fine. I need to go now."

Tilda hung up, then tried to figure out if Lil was lying, in deep denial, or just screwed up. Maybe a combination of all three. But for the first time that day, she felt as if she might be onto something. Unfortunately, she didn't have any idea of how she could get anything else out of Lil without making her freak out even more, and she wasn't willing to do that.

Still, she didn't cross Lil's name off her to-do list.

No messages from the Ambrose brothers had come in, so the only thing left on her list was posting the photo of the poisoner online. In deference to Cooper's concerns, first she called her computer security expert, Javier, and after she bribed him with various bits of swag she'd been saving for just such an occasion, he walked her through creating a secure online identity. After that, it only took a few minutes to post the three best photos of the poisoner to Joe's Lost Pinups site, along with a plea that information about the man be sent to her new e-mail address. Then she spent about an hour surfing the Web, and ended up posting the photos and request on half a dozen other sites.

With that done, and with no responses to any of the messages she'd left, it was time to call it a day. When Colleen got home a little while later, the barrage of questions began—apparently she'd heard about Miss Barth's death at the Hillside and since Tilda had been there, thought she should share every single detail.

Tilda willingly answered the first few dozen questions, not for Colleen's benefit, but for her own. She was hoping that if she thought about the evening's events, she might remember something helpful. But she didn't remember anything except why it was she didn't usually bother to answer Colleen's questions—the woman was never satisfied. Finally she pretended to be overcome by emotion and went to hide in her bedroom, where she sampled viral videos on YouTube for the rest of the evening. And while her dreams were filled with odd images as a result, she didn't think that any dead pinup queens managed to sneak in. Evidently her subconscious was happier with her progress than she was.

Chapter 36

Nowadays it's okay for the woman to ask you out—like it was ever up to you anyway.
—*COWBOY ETIQUETTE* BY TEXAS BIX BENDER

THE phone woke Tilda the next morning, but she didn't mind. It was Bill Hawks, talking in a whisper so that Jazz wouldn't hear him. He said he was sorry not to have been in touch sooner, but while he'd tracked down two of his old camera club buddies, neither of them recognized the man in the picture, and he didn't know anybody else he could ask. She thanked him for his time, promising to be in touch if she got a bite from the magazine editor she'd queried.

Despite her earlier speculations about him, she was willing to scratch Hawks off her list, and it wasn't just because she liked him. One thing she relied on when investigating stories was her instinct, and that instinct said that a man who had to whisper to conceal an innocent phone call from his wife just didn't have what it took to sneak off and kill two women. Besides, it was physically impossible for him to have been the mystery photographer—the nose was all wrong.

Just as she got out of the shower, the phone rang again. This time it was Louise, who was bubbling over with the news of her new storyline, which was indeed going to be about her character's past life as a pinup juxtaposed against a modern story of the problems caused by sexting. Unfortunately, the news about the photo wasn't as good. Louise had shown it to some unnamed friends, but nobody knew the man.

Tilda marked it down as another dead end. Instinct again. Louise might have had some secret reason for killing Sandra and showing up at the funeral to dance on her grave, but she must have known before Saturday night that the writers on *A Life Worth Living* were interested in the new storyline. Tilda didn't think an underused actress would risk losing that opportunity just to commit murder.

There was still no word from the Ambrose brothers, but when she got onto her computer, she was pleased to see that she had a dozen responses to the posting of the poisoner's photo. Unfortunately, four were spam; three were from people who didn't care about the man but who wanted more pictures of Sandy Sea Chest and Virginia Pure; one was a rival reporter who smelled a story; one helpfully identified Sandra for her, though her post had made it plain that she already knew who the women were; two suggested that he was in fact the professional photographer who'd staged the photo shoot; and one gave a name Tilda had never heard.

She ignored the spam, requests for more photos, and rival reporter, but did send polite thank-you notes to the people who'd tried to help. She didn't think the guy could have been Red Connors, the pro photographer, because surely Bill Hawks or Louise Silberblatt would have recognized him, and it only took a few minutes to track down a site with pictures of Connors and verify that. At the time of the pirate/maiden shoot, he'd been forty years old, stout, and naturally, had red hair.

That left her the all-too-brief message with the new name:

I think that man was Arthur Wilson.

It was signed "PhotoFan." Tilda sent a reply asking if PhotoFan could provide any additional information, then hit the Web to see if she could track down Wilson herself. An hour later, she admitted defeat. It was just too common a name—she needed more.

Though she'd requested responses be sent directly to her, she suspected that people would have left answers on the various bulletin boards on which she'd posted the photos, and a visit to Joe's Lost Pinups Site confirmed it. The boards were filled with speculation. But weeding through the posts there and on other sites turned out to be wasted effort—the notes she'd received directly were the cream of the crop.

Tilda knew from past experience that sitting around and waiting on responses would make her crazy, and what she really wanted was somebody to talk to about what was going on. She couldn't use Cooper—it was Tuesday, so he was on deadline. Her next choice was June, but there was no answer at her house, and she remembered something about a school book fair.

That left Quentin, and while he hadn't been particularly supportive on Sunday morning, she was willing to give him a second chance. She got him at work, and though he didn't have time to talk then, he suggested dinner, and they agreed to meet back at Not Your Average Joe's in Burlington.

As soon as she hung up, Tilda checked her watch. Not quite noon. Dinner was at six thirty. Even allowing for primping and travel time, she still had over five hours free. She could either waste time waiting by her computer and phone, hoping for a useful response, or use her time productively by taking care of housekeeping, office chores, or getting her car inspected. She went with Option A but, to her credit, she hated herself for it.

Nothing worth noting happened for the rest of the afternoon.

Quentin was waiting for Tilda at the restaurant with a smile and a kiss, and between the reception and the margarita the waitress delivered with admirable speed, she was soon feeling almost human. After they'd given their orders, she was able to respond politely rather than with a snarl when Quentin asked about her day. "Tedious, frustrating, and mostly unproductive. How about yours?"

"Promising."

"Did you make a breakthrough in the lab?"

"In the boardroom, actually. We hope to be making some changes soon at the foundation. Big changes. We got a preliminary estimate about how much money the fund-raiser brought in, and it was a huge success."

Tilda looked at him.

His face reddened. "That was incredibly callous, wasn't it? Here I am talking about money after that poor woman died."

"It's okay," Tilda said. "Miss Barth wanted to raise money for you guys, after all. I think she'd be glad."

"I hope so. I'd like to think she's watching us now."

"Then I should sit up straighter. She always struck me as a stickler for posture."

"I bet you're right. Of course, I didn't know her as well as you did."

"I don't think anybody knew Miss Barth all that well," Tilda said. "She was pretty self-contained."

"I haven't seen anything more in the paper about an investigation, so I guess the police are satisfied that it was an accident after all. That must be a relief."

She shrugged.

"You don't still think—"

The waitress interrupted by arriving with their mustard-crusted chicken, which was just as well. Tilda wasn't liking his tone of voice.

Once they were alone again, she said, "Can I ask you a medical question?"

"It depends. If you want advice about a spot on your elbow that won't heal, I plead the Fifth, but if you want to play doctor, I'm all for it."

"Neither. Well, playing doctor sounds fun, but I have something else in mind. I want to know about death certificates."

"I beg your pardon?"

"I'm trying to figure out what happened to this woman. The information I found says she committed suicide by drinking ethylene glycol, and I was wondering if there'd be more information about the circumstances of her death in the records of the hospital where she died. Maybe who it was who brought her in, or why they decided it was suicide. Anything really."

"Possibly."

"Cool. I've got the name of the doctor who signed her death certificate, and I'm pretty sure the hospital is still open. It's in New York, and I remember your saying you had family working in a lot of the New York hospitals, so I wondered—"

"Are you seriously asking if I'll get one of my relatives to go snooping through hospital records?"

"I wouldn't have said snooping, but that's what I'm asking. Would that be a violation of medical ethics?"

"Yes," he said flatly.

"Fair enough." She took a bite out of her chicken. "It was like fifty years ago, if that makes a difference."

"It doesn't make any difference to me."

"Okay, I get that. Never mind." She decided that she really had crossed the line when she tried to bring his family in and shouldn't blame him for being offended. So instead of arguing her point further, she concentrated on her chicken while speculating about police records. She was nearly finished eating when Quentin spoke again.

"Why do you want to know more about the circumstances of that woman's death anyway?"

"I don't think it was suicide."

"Don't tell me you think it was murder!"

"Actually, I do."

"Tilda, you're starting to scare me. Have you always had this obsession with murder?"

"Obsession?"

"First there's that woman you found."

"Who was murdered."

"Granted. But Miss Barth's death was an accident, and apparently this other woman killed herself. It happens every day. It's tragic, but it happens."

"People get murdered every day, too, and for a murderer to get away with it is more than tragic."

"Why are you so sure Miss Barth and this suicide victim were murdered?"

"I can't tell you. You've got medical ethics—I've got journalistic ethics."

"What is this, payback for not helping you snoop?"

"Did you get 'snoop' off your word-a-day calendar?"

"Fine. Is this payback for not helping you *investigate*?"

If he'd also held his fingers in mock quotes around the word *investigate*, Tilda would have walked out on him. "It's not payback for anything. I know I shouldn't have asked you to look into private records—I acknowledged that. And I hope you'll acknowledge the fact that I often receive information off the record which I'm honor bound not to reveal. Just like doctors."

"It's hardly the same thing. There's a bond between a doctor and his patients."

"There's a bond between a reporter and her interview subjects, too."

"If you say so."

"I just did!"

Deciding she'd had enough of her food, Tilda pushed her plate aside. Quentin made a go at finishing his, but as the uncomfortable silence continued, he gave up, too. When the waitress came by to ask if they wanted dessert, both refused. After glancing at their faces, she dropped off the check without saying anything else.

When Quentin picked up the check, Tilda said, "I'll pay for mine."

"No, you don't have to do that," he said, sounding abashed. "I asked you out." He ventured a small smile. "With the successful fund-raiser, I'm getting a raise."

Tilda relented enough to say, "Congratulations."

"Not that I expect to get rich this way—I'd make a lot more in private practice—but this is important work."

"I'm sure those Sticky parents and kids I saw at the Hill-side would agree with you."

There was another bout of quiet while the waitress took Quentin's credit card and returned with the receipt for him to sign, but it wasn't nearly as awkward.

Finally Quentin said, "Look, I'm sorry if I was out of line. I'm just worried about you. The bad dreams you've been having aren't just when you're with me, are they?"

"No."

"I'm not surprised. I mean, you've had two traumatic experiences in a short period of time, and either one of them would have knocked most people for a loop. But you're hanging in there, working, starting a new relation-ship. I just want to make sure you're okay." He smiled again, and those adorable dimples made their first appear-ance of the night.

It was the dimples that ensured that Tilda spoke tactfully. "I appreciate that, I really do, but I'm not freaking out. I have reason to believe what I believe. And the only way I can get past the nightmares is to investigate the best way I know how. If I can't find the answers I'm looking for, then I'll let it go."

He smiled, she smiled, and the storm ended. Since the bill had already been paid, they couldn't very well stick around, but they did walk over to the Cold Stone Creamery a few doors down for ice cream, and talked about nothing consequential for a while, which Tilda found reassuring. Still, when Quentin asked if she wanted to come over to his place to end the evening, Tilda begged off. Partially she was uncomfortable with how vehement he'd been about her investigation, but mostly she wasn't willing to risk him witnessing another one of her bad dreams.

Colleen descended on her the second she stepped in the door. "Do you know how many times the phone has rung while you've been gone?"

"Seventy-two?"

"What? No, not that many, but it was enough. Some man is trying to get in touch with you. He called like four times!"

"Did he leave a message?"

"No," she said, and Tilda could tell from her tone of voice that that's what was really bothering her. "He wouldn't tell me who he was, either, but he expected me to tell him when you'd be back. As if it was any of his business!"

"If he wouldn't leave a name or number, he was probably just soliciting for donations. If it's important, he'll call back. Anybody who knows me would have called my cell." As Tilda said that, she was reaching for her phone to check the charge, and realized she had several calls on it, too. "Whoops. I guess he did call my cell. I had it turned off for my date."

"Date? Where did you go? How was it?"

"Very nice," she lied, "but I better check my messages now. Sorry you were bothered. I'll answer the landline myself if it rings again."

She was in her bedroom with the door closed before Colleen could object, but as it turned out there were no messages, just a blocked phone number that had tried repeatedly to call her. That would be awfully persistent for a charity—even her alma mater didn't usually try that hard. Maybe it was somebody else . . .

Great. Now she was afraid of a phone call. Well, if the killer was calling, he could either leave a message or wait until he had a chance to threaten her personally.

After getting ready for bed, Tilda checked e-mail and found twenty messages in the queue for her new address. Most of the responses were wastes of time: spam, answers to the wrong questions, and one guy who swore the picture was of Howard Hughes. Tilda barely skimmed them—her attention was on the note from PhotoFan.

> I think it was Arthur Wilson, but it's been a long time. I don't remember much about him—no address or anything like that. He was in the same camera club as me in Queens for maybe a year, but quit coming not long after this shoot. That's all I know.

Then she went onto the bulletin board for Joe's Lost Pinups, and amidst the junk, found a post from a guy who eschewed clever pinup-related turns of phrase to go by the name of Mark:

> This looks like a guy I ran into a couple of times at New York shoots. He wasn't in my club, though. His name was Art. I can't remember his last name, but I think it started with W.

Arthur Wilson, Art W. Tilda looked at the photo of the guy. "Well, Arthur, I finally know your name. I don't know anything else about you, but I am going to find you."

Despite her concerns about spending the night with Quentin, her night was nightmare-free once again.

Chapter 37

Speak your mind, but ride a fast horse.
                              —OLD COWBOY SAYING

TILDA was up bright and early the next day so she could check e-mail messages and bulletin board posts, but it didn't take long to go through the night's crop. More spam and more dumb answers, but no more mentions of Arthur Wilson, so all she had to go on was the name and camera clubs in Queens. It was not a promising prospect—a quick estimate of links led to the conclusion that she would probably be Louise Silberblatt's age by the time she found the guy.

Sighing, she plotted her attack on the Web, hoping for another e-mail with a link to the GPS tracker on Wilson's car. The phone rang before she could get started.

"Another deadline achieved," Cooper said.

"Truly you are a copyediting deity."

"Don't mock—we were making changes right up to the last minute. Oh, about your piece about Miss Barth . . ."

"What about it?" she asked sharply.

"Well, space was tight . . ."

"Did you cut part of my piece? Why the hell didn't you call me and let me do it?"

"Psych! Didn't touch a word."

"Prick."

"Bitch."

"Wanker."

"Bitch."

"Schmuck."

"Bitch."

"Is 'bitch' all you've got?"

"I could use the *c* word, but if I did, you'd snatch me bald."

"Damn straight."

"Anyway, your piece was good. The Ambrose brothers were moved to manly tears."

"What were they doing there?"

"They were in a kerfuffle about the resort and whether they can keep it going without Miss Barth. Apparently she was providing a big chunk of the operating capital, plus the star power, such as it was. So the investors needed to confer, and Jillian let them use the videoconference stuff here. That meant that the Ambrose brothers were here all damned day, which was just what we needed in the middle of deadline."

"That explains why I haven't been able to get in touch with them," Tilda said. "I wanted to ask them about the photo, but now I might not need to."

"What? Why were you letting me blather if you've figured out who he is?"

"Because I couldn't get a word in edgewise."

"Bitch."

"Don't start that again!"

"Sorry."

She briefly sketched out how she'd gotten the name Arthur Wilson. "I was kind of hoping for a name I'd heard before, or failing that, something a little easier to track down."

"Think of it as a hobby to keep you busy during the evenings once you're working here full time."

"Has Jillian said anything to you?"

"No, but I heard her talking about it with Bryce. Unfortunately, they noticed me eavesdropping and clammed up."

"Then until that comes to pass, I still need to make a living. Has there been any decision about the articles I wrote about the guest stars?"

"Not that I've heard."

"Well, I know Jillian won't totally stiff me. Worst-case scenario, I could rewrite most of the pieces for other markets."

It wasn't a cheery thought, though. *Entertain Me!* paid well and had a higher profile than most of the magazines she sold to. Maybe the full-time job was coming at just the right time. She hung up the phone, and tried not to brood about it, and went back to Arthur Wilson. An hour later, the phone rang again, and having spent that hour searching fruitlessly, she grabbed it gratefully.

"Tilda Harper."

"Honey, did anybody ever tell you you're one tough filly to rope?"

"Not in those words. Mr. Ambrose?"

"Didn't I tell you to call me Tucker?"

"Sorry. Was that you trying to get me last night?"

"That's right. I think that gal you live with was right put out when I didn't leave a message, but I don't like spreading my business around, if you know what I mean."

When it came to Colleen, she knew exactly what he meant. "What can I do for you?"

"We've been talking, Hoyt and me, and we realized there was one interview you hadn't done yet. You haven't talked to the two of us."

"I'm sorry, Jillian didn't mention—"

"Oh, I'm not talking about the magazine necessarily. That's all kind of up in the air right now, what with what happened to poor Miss Barth. In fact, it was losing her that got Hoyt and me to thinking. The Cowboy Kings have had a good run, but now that we're getting toward the end of it, we might better tell our tales while we're still here to tell them. You just don't ever know what's coming, do you?"

"That's true," Tilda said, "but I'm not sure I understand what you want me to do."

He chuckled. "I never was good with getting to the point. The thing is, we don't just want an article. We want us a book. The way all them celebrity books are selling, I bet we could make a pretty penny. Only Hoyt and me don't know nothing about making books. That's where you'd come in."

"You want me to write a book about you?"

"That's right. We've been reading those pieces you've been doing, and they've all been mighty good, but it was that article you wrote about Miss Barth that convinced us that you're the right gal to tell our story. Now I know we'll have to talk money and contracts and suchlike, but we know some people in publishing, and we figure we can work it all out. If you're willing, that is."

"I'd sure be willing to talk about it," she said, "but I have to tell you that I've never written anything that long before."

"Shoot, I figure it's like riding a horse. If you can stay on for half an hour, it ain't that much harder to ride all day long. Tell you what, if you've got some free time today, why don't you come over here to the hotel and we'll start making some plans."

"When do you want to meet?"

"How about four?"

"I'll see you then."

"One other thing," he said. "Do you mind keeping this all under your hat for now? Hoyt says once word gets out we're doing a book, other people might want to try to get one written ahead of us. We don't want anybody rustling our stories."

"Wild horses wouldn't drag it out of me."

He let loose with one of his belly laughs. "Wild horses!

We'll make a cowgirl out of you yet!" He was still laughing when he hung up.

Tilda didn't want to get too excited about something that might not pan out, but she was intrigued. The job of ghostwriting a book was just the right carrot to wave in front of a freelancer whose latest series of articles might be spiked at any moment.

After pouring an extra-large glass of Dr Pepper, she started making calls and hitting the Web. She had a whole lot of research and preparation to do and not much time. As it was, she came close to being late, but managed to be outside the Ambrose brothers' suite at four o'clock on the dot.

The door opened, and Tucker greeted her with a big smile. "Hey there, little lady. Come on in."

She looked around as she stepped into the suite, but saw nobody else. "Is your brother not here?"

He gave an exaggerated sigh. "One of our investors for the resort is fixing to bolt, and Hoyt had to get himself over there to lasso him into place. I thought he'd be back by now, but I expect he'll be along shortly." He waggled his eyebrows. "I'm not fussing. It's been many moons since I've had a pretty thing like you alone in a hotel room."

Tilda laughed dutifully, but made sure to sit on a chair, and not on the sofa where Tucker might be tempted to get too close. Slugging him would not be a good way to start out the meeting.

After offering to take her blazer, which she preferred to keep, and then to get her a drink, which she turned down with thanks, Tucker planted himself on the sofa. "Let's go ahead and get started and not wait on Hoyt. This is how we're picturing the book."

The first part of the spiel wasn't bad, but he got more and more vague as he went on, and it didn't take Tilda long to figure out that he really hadn't given the idea of a book much thought at all. But she nodded in the right places and scribbled down notes while waiting for him to wind down.

"So," he finally said, "what do you think?"

"Well, you've certainly got plenty of material," Tilda said. "Good stuff, too. But I do have a question."

"Shoot."

"Are you two going to keep claiming to be from Texas, or come clean about where you're really from?"

He went for the belly laugh again, though Tilda didn't think it quite rang true. "I should have known a smart gal like you would work that out. I guess it all depends on which would sell more books. Which way do you think we should go?"

"I think it's time for the truth. It'll look a lot better if you confess rather than having to be found out."

"You think?"

"Absolutely. So, Arthur, is there anything else you want to confess to?"

He kept the jovial mask on, but Tilda could tell it was an effort. "Well, now, that's a name I haven't heard in a long time."

"Didn't Miss Barth call you Arthur? Or was it Art? She's the only one who knew, right, other than your brother?"

"That's right."

Tilda nodded, and then, as if it were an afterthought. "Oh, and Sandra Sechrest must have known you by that name, too. Back from when you were in the camera clubs?"

"Who was that again?"

"It's like I said before, Arthur, I think it's time for the truth."

"Yeah, Sandy knew. She'd known all along." He shook his head. "I never would have figured her for a blackmailer, but when I got that letter asking for money or having the whole story told, I knew it had to be her."

"Blackmail?"

"That's right. Why she had to go and do that after all these years is beyond me."

"Why didn't you just pay, instead of killing her?"

"I did pay, but my daddy didn't raise no fools. I knew it was just a matter of time before she came back to the well, and with the resort project, I didn't have it to spare. Besides, there ain't nothing on this earth lower than a blackmailer."

"Not even a man who'd push a woman down a flight of stairs?"

"Hell, you have worked it all out, haven't you. I knew you was going to cause trouble when I saw that you'd figured out Miss Barth used to pose for the camera clubs."

"Did you think I had more photos of you? Is that why you pushed me into Boylston Street?"

"Yep, that's what I thought. I didn't mean for you to get hurt, but I had to get a look at those pictures you had sticking out of your bag."

"Oh, please, you didn't care if I got hurt or not. Besides, the pictures I had were no big deal anyway."

"No, they weren't, so I thought I wouldn't have to worry about you after all. You sure had me buffaloed."

"Not really. I didn't know much then, and what I did know, I wasn't planning to tell anybody. It was you going after the photos that made me wonder about the ones that had gone missing from Sandra's apartment, and that led me to finding pictures of you as a young man. You know, Miss Barth had me convinced that she didn't know who you were. She really was a good actress."

"She was the best I ever worked with, and the finest lady, too, no matter what she had in her past."

"So why did you kill her?"

"You think I wanted to? She'd been with me and Hoyt since the beginning. I'd have done just about anything for that woman. And here she was going to turn me in to the police!"

"She realized that you killed Sandra."

He nodded. "She knew I'd gone out alone for a while that night, and she knew Sandy knew my old name. I guess they'd been in touch, and when you showed her that picture of me and said it came from Sandy's apartment, she put all the pieces together. She could of just gone to the police then, but she came to me instead, there at the fund-raiser. She felt like she owed it to me to give me time to turn myself in, because it said so in the Cowtown Code. Do you know that one? 'Always give a man the chance to do the right thing.' She lived by the Code."

"And died by it. Though I don't remember murdering old ladies being part of the Code."

"Don't you sass me—I loved that woman like a sister. It was all that blackmailing bitch Sandy's fault. She's the one to start all the trouble—I only wish she hadn't died so quick."

Tilda knew she should stay calm, but him saying that about a woman he'd beaten to death infuriated her. "Here's a newsflash, cowboy. Sandra wasn't blackmailing you."

"The hell she wasn't! She had me mail the money here to Boston, and there ain't nobody else living here who'd know who I was."

"What did the blackmail note look like? Was it handwritten?"

"No, printed, like on a computer."

"Then it definitely wasn't Sandra. She couldn't type."

"What are you talking about?"

"Did you bother to look at her hands before you killed her? She had wicked bad arthritis. She could barely dial a phone, let alone use a computer."

"There was a computer in her apartment. I saw it!"

"It was hers, but she didn't use it. Her Webmaster used it for the site. Whoever it was that was blackmailing you, it wasn't Sandra."

"No, it was Sandy I tell you. It had to be her."

Of course Tilda knew the blackmailer must have been Lil. Lil, who'd been out of work for so long. Lil, who took care of the mail and scanned the photos that Bill Hawks had sent in. She'd seen what Cooper had seen, that Wilson had put something in Virginia's drink, and of course, she was the only one Sandra would have told who the mystery photographer was. But Tilda wasn't going to tell Tucker that.

What she said was, "Then explain this. Why would a blackmailer agree to see you alone?"

"She didn't know I'd figured it out."

"Yeah, right. Face it, asshole. You killed an innocent woman."

Tucker just blinked.

"Of course, I suppose killing women comes naturally to you. You got started early, didn't you, with Esther Marie Martin. Or did you call her Virginia Pure when you were banging her?"

"I never touched that girl!"

"I didn't think they had artificial insemination back then."

"It wasn't me. It was Hoyt."

"Hoyt got her pregnant?"

"And he was going to marry her, too, and give up everything to raise that kid of hers! We had plans! Even then, we were aiming for Hollywood, but he was going to tie himself to that slip of a girl for the rest of his life and throw all that away. Not just his future, but mine, too. He needed me, and I needed him. We didn't need no wife and baby. It was her or us."

"Don't you mean that it was her or you? I don't fucking believe you. You murdered three women, not to mention your brother's unborn child. And it wasn't to cure cancer, or save the world. It was so you could make lousy TV Westerns."

In retrospect, Tilda decided she shouldn't have said

"lousy." That's what got him mad, not being accused of the murders.

He stood slowly and deliberately, and pulled a gun out from the back of his Levis. It was so bright and shiny, it looked like a prop, but Tilda had no doubts that it was the real thing. "I think I've heard enough from you."

She didn't move. "Do you really think I came here alone? After two murders—three, if you count Esther. Plus an attempt on my life? In the middle of that, you call me out of the blue and say you want me to write a book, but don't want me to tell anybody where I'm going. You thought I believed it?"

He blinked some more.

"I'm wired, asshole, and the cops are right next door." Hearing noise from the hall, she said, "Correction, I think they're on their way to join us."

"Then I may as well shoot you, just for the satisfaction of watching you die!" he snarled. "They can only hang me once."

"Dude, you watch way too many Westerns. One, we don't have the death penalty in Massachusetts, and two, a jury might let you off with manslaughter for killing some-body you thought was a blackmailer. You could make up something about Miss Barth, too, if you're low enough. But kill me, and you spend the rest of your life in prison. And you won't be the cowboy—you'll be the horse, if you know what I mean."

Tilda counted out the fifteen seconds it took for him to make up his mind. Finally, he carefully handed her the gun and put his hands up in traditional cowboy fashion.

"I've got the gun," she said, to let the cops know what was happening, but kept an eye on Tucker as she went to open the door.

She'd expected Detective Salvatore to be front and center, but instead it was Hoyt who stepped past her and toward his brother. The two men stared at each other for a long moment before Tucker said, "Hoyt—"

Before he could go further, Hoyt slugged him in the jaw, knocking him clean off his feet. "That's for killing the only woman I ever loved." Then he kicked him viciously in the belly. "And that's for killing my baby." He would have kept going if Salvatore hadn't pulled him away.

Chapter 38

We can't all be heroes because somebody has to sit on the curb and clap as they go by.

—WILL ROGERS

"THAT'S incredible, Tilda. I cannot believe you were brave enough to face a murderer."

"All in a day's work," Tilda said, without the slightest trace of modesty, and leaned into Quentin's arms. "Besides, it's not like I didn't have backup."

Quentin had heard a TV news bulletin about Tucker's arrest Wednesday night, before she'd had a chance to call him. She would have, but was too busy dealing with the police and then writing up the story. Jillian and Bryce had gone into what could only be described as a tizzy when the news broke, and were frantically working to distance themselves from the deposed Cowboy Kings. An article implying that they'd known all along that something was fishy would go a long way toward that. Of course, it wasn't really an *Entertain Me!* kind of piece, but the magazine's parent corporation also published a news weekly that would be delighted with the grittier version Tilda had pounded out. Plus she was going to be reworking the whole *Cowtown* series, including the guest star interviews and the interview with Sandra, for a less gruesome version for *Entertain Me!*.

Tilda really hadn't been sure how Quentin would react,

given their previous discussions, but when he showed up at the police station with an enormous bouquet of flowers, she figured that was a good start at an apology. When he drove her back to Malden, she decided it would have been churlish not to invite him in, especially when he mentioned that he'd be calling in sick the next day.

In a surprise twist, Colleen was not brimming with questions. By the time Tilda got back home, she'd seen the TV news and gone online for more details. All she did was stare at Tilda with wide, alarmed eyes. For once, there was something in her roomie's life that she just didn't want to know about. Tilda had a hunch that they'd both be looking for new roommates before their lease was up.

Come late Thursday morning, after a nightmare-free night, Tilda and Quentin were cuddling on the couch of her apartment while she told him everything. The further she'd gone in her story, the closer he'd held her. It made her wish she'd been in more danger, just to see how he'd have reacted.

"A couple of things I don't understand," he said. "How did you know that Tucker was lying about the book project?"

"I didn't, not right away, but I thought something was off, and it wasn't too big a leap to think that a phony cowboy might have a phony name. I mean, the names *Tucker* and *Hoyt* were just too perfect for a couple of cowboys. So I called the guy who'd told me that they weren't real cowpokes, and asked if he'd ever heard them calling each other by any other name. It turns out that one time Tucker got thrown by a horse, and Hoyt yelled out 'Art!' when he was running to see if he was okay."

"And that's all you needed."

"Oh, that was the easy part. The hard part was convincing Detective Salvatore that I wasn't a nut job. Once that was done, we had to get the sting set up in a hurry. My chest is still itchy from the tape they used to hold the mike on."

"I'll be happy to rub something on it later. And you said Sandra's niece was the blackmailer?"

"That's right. She spotted Wilson drugging Virginia's drink in the picture right off—I think it was because she had personal knowledge of men drugging drinks. Given her experience, she assumed it was date rape. She said she would have gone to the police, but she knew it would do no good because of the statute of limitations, plus flimsy evidence and not knowing where the victim was. Besides, she had no particular reason to trust the police after what happened to her. She wanted the money, of course, but part of it was wanting to get back at a rapist, even if she couldn't do anything to her own."

"Except he wasn't a rapist—he was a murderer."

"But she didn't realize that. Of course, when Sandra was murdered, she should have talked to the cops, but for one, she didn't want to be arrested for blackmail and for another, she was in denial that she could have caused her aunt's death. I suspect there was some posttraumatic stress going on, too. Detective Salvatore says he can give her a pass on the blackmail if she testifies and gets some therapy, and I think my sister, June, will be able to find her a therapist who'll work cheap."

"How did you know Hoyt wasn't in on it, too?"

"I didn't until I saw that it was just Tucker in the hotel room," she admitted. "Tucker had sent Hoyt on some errand, expecting to take care of me before he got back. When Hoyt showed up early, the cops grabbed him and had him listening in on Tucker's confession."

"Hoyt really didn't know Tucker had killed Virginia?"

"He didn't have a clue. Tucker, or rather Arthur, was really thorough. He went to that shoot without Hoyt— whose real name is Cecil, by the way—just to take care of Virginia. He was convinced he needed Hoyt to have a career, and if that meant getting rid of Virginia, then so be it. When Virginia came out of the shoot, obviously ill, he offered to get her to a doctor. Since she knew him through his cousin—"

"Cousin?"

"Did I forget that part? The Ambrose brothers not only weren't named Ambrose, they weren't even really brothers. They were first cousins."

"Whole levels of deception."

"Oh, yeah. Anyway, Tucker got Virginia into his car, supposedly to take her to a hospital, but instead drove her around for hours. By the time he finally took her to an emergency room, it was way too late to save her. He told the nurses at the hospital that he'd found her on the street, and when they found the vial of poison he'd planted on her, they assumed it was suicide, especially when they found she was pregnant. Of course, Arthur had already stripped her of all ID, but he thought he better give them a name for the death certificate. He wasn't going to give her real name, of course, and started to say she was Virginia Pure, but knew that sounded phony. So he switched to Virginia Pearl. Then he went to her apartment and packed up all her stuff, making it look as if she'd gone back home."

"What a bastard!"

"The one thing he hadn't counted on was that Hoyt would take it so hard. He went into a deep depression, so Arthur suggested that they get out of town for a while. They'd always liked cowboy movies, so Arthur picked out a dude ranch out west. It was while they were there that they came up with the idea of reinventing themselves to make an impression in Hollywood, and they spent a year or two working at various ranches to get enough local color to fool people. They pretended to be brothers because they thought it sounded better."

"What about Miss Barth?"

"She knew them in New York, when they were still

Arthur and Cecil. Even though she recognized them when she found them in California, she didn't mind keeping their secret—I've gotten hints that she had a secret or two in her own past." Of course, Tilda knew one of those secrets, but she was still keeping it. "When I showed her the picture of Tucker as a young man and tied it to Sandra's death—"

"How did Miss Barth know Sandra?"

"They were friends in New York, too." That was true enough, if not complete. "Miss Barth knew that Sandra knew Tucker, and she'd told Tucker herself that Sandra was living in Boston. She also knew that Sandra had been murdered, so she confronted Tucker at the fund-raiser. He admitted he'd killed Sandra, but Miss Barth wanted to give him a chance to go to the police himself. It never occurred to her that he'd kill her, too."

"Even though he'd already killed two women?"

"She didn't know about Virginia, and Tucker fed her some tale about Sandra's death being an accident. So it wasn't as stupid as it sounds."

"I guess not. But still . . . Wow. And you put it all together."

"I had help."

"But you were the one who wouldn't give up." Quentin kissed her thoroughly, and Tilda was about to suggest they relocate to her bedroom when he pulled back.

"What about the *Cowtown* resort?"

"It's officially in a holding pattern, but unofficially, it's dead."

"And the job at *Entertain Me!*?

"I turned it down."

"Good. I don't want them getting you into trouble again."

"They didn't get me into anything," she said with a trace of irritation. "The investigation was all mine. That's part of why I said 'no.' If I'd been working nine to five, I never would have been able to put in the hours to pull it together, and Tucker would still be free. When I thought about it that way, it was a no-brainer." She'd expected Jillian to at least be disappointed when she told her, or even to threaten to stop using her as a freelancer, but in fact, all she said was, "Whatever. Don't think you're getting higher rates now." She left that part out of her story, as well as the look of joy on Nicole's face when she heard the news, because she didn't want to clutter up Quentin's head with too many details.

Instead she concluded with, "So this cowgirl is going to keep riding the range alone."

"You might feel differently about that when I tell you my good news."

"Did you catch a murderer, too? I'd be happy to reward you the same way you did me."

"Well, I did have a minor success in the lab earlier this week, but that's not what I'm talking about. We had our board meeting yesterday, and after all the press the foundation got because of the event at Hillside—"

"Not to mention the bucks."

"Oh, the bucks were mentioned, I assure you. The upshot of it was that the board is convinced that we need a stronger media presence. They've approved the hiring of a full-time public relations writer."

"That's good," Tilda said, not sure why he was so excited.

"Don't you see?" he asked. "The job is yours for the asking!"

"Excuse me?"

"You can stop living hand to mouth, writing about TV trivia. You can work full time doing something worthwhile. The pay isn't great, but it's steady and you'll have benefits." He displayed the dimples. "Plus, of course, you'll be working with me."

Tilda sat up, inhaled deeply, and let her breath out slowly. "No, thank you."

"What?"

"Number one, I don't live hand to mouth. I'm doing fine, thank you very much."

"But Tilda—"

She ignored him. "Number two, if I wanted a full-time job, I would have taken the one Jillian offered. Weren't you listening just now? I freelance because I like it that way."

"You don't—"

"Number three, I write about classic television because I choose to do so. My work may be trivial to you, but it's important to me.

"But—"

"Number four, I am a reporter, not a PR flack."

He'd given up trying to interrupt.

"And number five, I cannot believe that we're having this conversation. I told you during our very first date why I do what I do, and I thought you understood that."

"I have every respect for what you've done. I only thought you'd be ready to move up."

"Meaning that I'm beneath you? Thanks so much, you pompous son of a—" She stopped herself. "Look, Quentin, you're a nice guy, but this isn't going to work out. I think you should leave."

"But why?"

"Because if you don't get my work, then you don't get me."

When she told Cooper about it over dinner that night, they both agreed that it had been a wonderful exit line. Unfortunately, Quentin hadn't seen it that way, and it had denigrated him into apologizing, then backtracking, and finally whining. Only when he'd worked himself up to a good mad-on did he finally stalk out the door, as if the breakup had been his idea.

If it had been a *Cowtown* episode instead of real life, Quentin's departure would have been a cue for one of Arabella's classic voice-overs:

> *Sometimes the happiest trail is the one a cowboy rides alone. No boss, no pards, just the big blue sky and the knowledge that you're doing exactly what you were born to do. That's the Cowtown Code.*

AVAILABLE IN HARDCOVER

Wolfsbane and Mistletoe

Hair-Raising Holiday Tales

15 All-New Werewolf Tales by

DONNA ANDREWS

KERI ARTHUR

PATRICIA BRIGGS

DANA CAMERON

KAREN CHANCE

ALAN GORDON

SIMON R. GREEN

CHARLAINE HARRIS

TONI L. P. KELNER

J. A. KONRATH

NANCY PICKARD

KAT RICHARDSON

DANA STABENOW

ROB THURMAN

CARRIE VAUGHN

Edited by Charlaine Harris and Toni L. P. Kelner

penguin.com